A Rolling Stone

by

B. M. Croker

A Rolling Stone
by B. M. Croker

ISBN: 978-93-63050-75-4

Published by

DOUBLE 9 BOOKS
2/13-B, Ansari Road
Daryaganj, New Delhi – 110002
info@double9books.com
www.double9books.com
Tel. 011-40042856

ABOUT THE AUTHOR

Bithia Born on November 6, 1849, Mary Croker, sometimes known as B. M. Croker, was a British author who died on October 20, 1920. During the late 19th and early 20th centuries, she was a well-known and prolific writer who was well-known for her captivating novels and short stories. Croker lived a significant portion of her life in India, where her husband was a British Army soldier. Her experiences there had a profound effect on her work. Her paintings frequently portrayed the life of British expatriates in India, providing realistic depictions of the people, customs, and natural surroundings of the area. Croker's writing was distinguished by its intricate character development, captivating narratives, and vivid descriptions.

CONTENTS

CHAPTER I
LADY KESTERS

After a day of strenuous social activities, Lady Kesters was enjoying a well-earned rest, reposing at full length on a luxurious Chesterfield, with cushions of old brocade piled at her back and a new French novel in her hand. Nevertheless, her attention wandered from Anatole France; every few minutes she raised her head to listen intently, then, as a little silver clock chimed five thin strokes, she rose, went over to a window, and, with an impatient jerk, pulled aside the blind. She was looking down into Mount Street, W., and endeavouring to penetrate the gloom of a raw evening towards the end of March.

It was evident that the lady was expecting some one, for there were two cups and saucers on a well-equipped tea-table, placed between the sofa and a cheerful log fire.

As the mistress of the house peers eagerly at passers-by, we may avail ourselves of the opportunity to examine her surroundings. There is an agreeable feeling of ample space, softly shaded lights, and rich but subdued colours. The polished floor is strewn with ancient rugs; bookcases and rare cabinets exhibit costly contents; flowers are in profusion; the air is heavily scented with white lilac; and a multitude of magazines and papers lie scattered about in careless abundance. *The Hibbert Journal*, the *Clarion*, *Le Revue des deux mondes*, and the *Spectator* indicate a Catholic taste; but we look in vain for a piano, a pet dog, or a workbasket.

As Lady Kesters turns from the window, it is seen that she is tall and slim, with dark, expressive eyes, a delicate, tip-tilted nose, and remarkably square chin; her figure, which is faultless, shows to admirable advantage in a simple gown of clinging black material.

And whilst she once more subsides into her sofa and book, we may venture to introduce a little sketch of her personal history.

Leila Wynyard and her brother Owen were the orphan children of a dashing cavalry officer, who was killed at polo, leaving family and creditors to the benevolence of his relations. Sir Richard, his brother, undertook charge of the boy, the girl—some years his senior—fell to the lot of a maiden aunt who lived in Eaton Terrace, and maintained considerable dignity in a small house, on an income to correspond. Leila had lessons and masters, her teeth, complexion, and deportment were objects of anxious solicitude; at eighteen she was brought out and presented, and hopes were entertained that, in her first or second season, she would make a suitable match, and secure a husband and a home. The girl carried herself with grace, had fine dark eyes, and fine fashionable connections; these latter combined to take her into society, and exhibit her at Ascot and Hurlingham, as well as balls and the opera. She visited historical country seats and notable Scottish moors, and was, so to speak, passed along from one house-party to another; and yet, despite her friends' exertions, Leila Wynyard failed to "go off." Perhaps the truth lay in the simple fact that the lady herself was disinclined to move on; and often joked over her social failure with her Aunt Eliza, who had a keen sense of humour and no mind to lose the light of her old age.

On the other hand, Leila Wynyard was known to be penniless! (for what is a hundred a year?—it scarcely keeps some women in hats) had no surpassing accomplishments to lift her out of the ruck; it was also whispered that she had an independent character, and a sharp tongue!

No one could deny that Miss Wynyard's air was distinguished. Some men considered her a brilliant conversationalist, and extraordinarily clever—but these are rarely the attributes of the women they marry!

Time sped along, Miss Wynyard had been out for nine seasons, was spoken of in the family as "poor Leila," and now relegated to the worst spare room, expected to make herself useful, "do the flowers," write notes, and take over the bores. In short, she was about to step into the position of permanent poor relation, when, to the amazement of the whole connection, Leila married herself off with triumphant success! Alone she did it! Her uncle, Sir Richard Wynyard, owner of the family title and estates, was an old bachelor, who lived in a gloomy town house in Queen's Gate, but spent most of his time at his club. At uncertain intervals he repaid hospitalities received, and entertained his friends at dinner under his own roof—he scorned the fashionable craze of assembling one's guests at a restaurant. These banquets were well done—wine, ménu, and attendance being beyond criticism. They would also have been insupportably dull, but for the officiating hostess; and, thanks to Miss Wynyard's admirable supervision, they were usually an enviable success.

The company were of a respectable age—the host's contemporaries— old club friends or City folk, with their sedate and comfortable wives. Miss Wynyard introduced an element of youth and vivacity into the gathering, selected flowers for the table decoration, had a word about the savouries and dessert, and, on the evening itself, radiant and well dressed, enjoyed herself prodigiously—for Leila had the flair of the born hostess—a gift that had no opportunity for expanding in the limited space at home.

On one of these occasions, a certain Martin Kesters sat on Miss Wynyard's right hand—a plain, elderly man, of few words and many thoughts, with rugged features, grizzled whiskers, and a made tie!—a melancholy and reluctant guest who rarely dined abroad, and had martyrised himself to please and appease his old schoolfellow, Dick Wynyard.

The brilliant Leila, who adored playing hostess and giving her talents full scope, drew him out with surprising subtlety, listened to his opinions with flattering deference, put him at his ease and in good humour with himself, and won, so to speak, his heart! She was not aware that Mr. Kesters was a wealthy widower, and mainly responsible for the enormous increase in her uncle's fortunes; but this would not have made an atom of difference. Her attention would have been precisely the same had he been a penniless curate; she could see that he was overpowered by his partner—a magnificent matron who talked exclusively of royalties—his answers were short and gruff;—evidently he was bored to death and longing to be at home; and she instantly made up her mind to capture his interest and rivet his attention.

Leila was on her mettle that night, and achieved a notable success. How she shone! Even Sir Richard was amazed—he was proud of, and not a little afraid of, his clever niece; as for Mr. Kesters, he watched her furtively, noted her upright grace, her animation, her delightful smile, her art of saying the right thing—and saying it well—her insidious dexterity in leading the conversation into interesting channels, yet never obtruding her own personality. It was *not* the excellence of the champagne that made every one at the table feel themselves unusually shining and brilliant. No, poor souls! they were but the pale reflection of this luminous star.

Then the girl's appearance—she was a girl to his fifty-six years—of superb health and vitality. What an inmate for a dull, drab home—what a stimulating companion for a lonely man!

It was a cosy little party of eight, and at a sign from the hostess, three matrons arose and preceded her up to the ghostly drawing-room, there to feel depressingly flat and to sip very superior coffee. After some devastating comments on the British climate and the British domestic, two of the quartette retired, whispering, to a sofa, in order to discuss a cure—leaving Miss Wynyard and Lady Billing *tête-à-tête*.

"This room is rather a dreadful specimen of Early Victorian," said Leila, waving an apologetic spoon. "I fought so hard for these loose chintz covers and lamp-shades; but everything else is as it was in grandmamma's time—there she is, between the windows, in yellow satin and ringlets! The venerable servants who still survive will not hear of a change. Do look at the carpet; it must be fifty years of age. How old things *wear*!"

"I wonder Sir Richard does not live in a flat near his club," suggested her ladyship in diamonds and velvet; "so much more comfortable and up-to-date."

"Yes; but then this is the family town house, and he is never quite sure that he won't marry."

"Marry!" repeated Lady Billing, "what an idea!"

"It is his favourite threat"—and Leila laughed—"if the cooking is bad, the coal indifferent, or the servants too autocratic."

"But isn't your brother his heir?" opening her eyes to their widest extent. "How would he like that?"

"Oh, I really don't think Owen would care a straw; he is rather happy-go-lucky, and never thinks of the future. After all, Uncle Dick is not an old man, and I don't see why he should not please himself. I may dance at his wedding yet!"

"I suppose there is no particular lady in the case?" inquired the other judicially.

Miss Wynyard smiled, and shook her head.

"Do you know, my dear, that you have made an important conquest this evening?" Then, in answer to Miss Wynyard's gaze of amazement, "Mr. Kesters," she added, with impressive solemnity.

"Mr.—*Kesters*?" repeated Leila.

"Your neighbour at dinner, you know. He was simply swept off his feet—any one could see that!" and she flourished a puffy hand.

"Well, I hope he has recovered his equilibrium by now. Why, we never met till eight o'clock."

"He rarely goes anywhere. He is just a money-spinner—enormously rich—he can make money, but he does not know how to spend or enjoy it."

"That's easily learnt," declared the young lady, with a gay laugh; "I'd give him lessons with pleasure."

"Oh, my dear, it is not so easy to spend, when you have the habit of years of economy. His wife was terribly close; they say she counted the potatoes and matches! She was his cousin, and had a nice fortune."

"So, then, he is a widower?"

"Yes, this five years; he lives alone in Eaton Square—such a frowzy house—it has never known a spring cleaning! Mrs. Kesters and I exchanged calls. She would not allow the windows to be opened; loved King Charles dogs (horrid things) and parrots; dressed on thirty pounds a year; and her only extravagance was patent medicines. The premises simply reeked of them! Latterly, she was a helpless invalid, and since her death Mr. Kesters goes nowhere, just occupies a couple of rooms, and devotes himself to business. Business is his pleasure. He is a mighty man in the City—though he is so shy and reserved in society. I declare you quite woke him up to-night; I've known him for years, and I never saw him so animated."

"I suppose I hit on a lucky topic—he told me such interesting things about mining and minerals."

"*Gold* especially; they say everything he touches turns to that! My husband and he are rather friendly, and once or twice he has dined with us, scarcely uttered a word, and looked as if he was going to sleep. Oh, here they are!" as the door opened, and the two ladies on the sofa suddenly concluded a mysterious and confidential conversation, and sat expectant and erect. But the men as one man made straight for Miss Wynyard.

Later, as the guests departed, Mr. Kesters lingered to the last, and his host said fussily—

"I say, look here, Martin, I suppose you have your carriage, and you may as well take my niece home; you are going in her direction."

"My dear uncle, why should you victimise Mr. Kesters?" she protested; "I shall return as I came, in a hansom."

But Mr. Kesters intervened with unexpected gallantry, and declared that to escort Miss Wynyard was an honour that he could not forgo. Subsequently he conducted her down to a shabby, "one-horse" brougham— the coachman's legs were wrapped in a specially odoriferous stable rug— and conveyed her to Eaton Terrace. As he took leave of her at the hall door, he ventured to put a timid question.

He was such a near neighbour—might he come and call?

"Yes, of course," assented the lady; "Aunt Eliza will be delighted to see you—we are always at home on Sundays, four to six."

Subsequently Mr. Kesters became a regular visitor, and met with Aunt Eliza's approval; and, before many Sundays had elapsed, a paragraph concerning the names of Wynyard and Kesters appeared in the *Morning Post*.

And so poor Leila became rich Leila! and, from being an insignificant relation, a person of considerable social importance. Until her marriage few had discovered Mrs. Kesters' beauty—her cleverness had never been disputed. Now, as the result of a visit to Paris, armed with a cheque-book, she glorified her appearance, wore charming frocks and exquisite jewels, and, with her fine air and admirable figure, it was impossible "to pass her unnoticed in a crowd."

Mrs. Kesters organised changes other than personal: the gloomy abode in Eaton Square was sold, its contents dispatched to an auction room—including two old stuffed parrots, and the mangy remains of her predecessor's King Charles; another house was taken and furnished regardless of expense, a motor purchased, and a staff of experienced servants engaged. In a surprisingly short time Mrs. Martin Kesters of 202 Mount Street, Grosvenor Square, had become a popular member of society. Her little dinners and luncheons were famous, not alone for the quality of the menu, but also of the guests. Martin, too, had been transformed as by a wand! His whiskers disappeared, he was persuaded to change his tailor, and given a good conceit of himself. He felt ten years younger, brisk, energetic, prepared to enjoy his money and the Indian summer of his life. Instead of being taciturn, he talked; instead of going to sleep after dinner, he patronised the theatre; he learnt to play bridge and golf. In the society of ladies his manners had become assured, and he no longer was at a helpless loss to know what to say, or stumbled clumsily over their trains. For all these new accomplishments he had to thank Leila; and he was devoted to his brilliant and charming wife. She was more or less in touch with political people, and clever men, and women that mattered. The fascinating Mrs. Kesters was successful in drawing-room diplomacy and the delicate art of pulling strings; and, to her husband's astonishment, he had found himself a K.C.B., and elected to an exclusive club—sitting on important committees, dining in stately houses, and entertaining notable guests.

Lady Kesters' connections held up their hands, cast up their eyes, and declared that "Leila was *too* wonderful!" She had changed a dull, plodding, City man into a well-turned-out, agreeable, bland individual—who was her abject slave—and she had become a leader in her own particular set. Her relatives repeated, "Who would have thought Leila had it *in* her?" But Leila had, so to speak, always "had it in her." "It" represented brains, tact, a passion for affairs and managing, a hidden and ambitious spirit, and an active and impatient longing to taste responsibility and power.

The clock pointed to a quarter past five. Lady Kesters took up the silver caddy and was proceeding to ladle out tea, when the door opened, a servant announced "Mr. Wynyard," and a remarkably good-looking young man entered the room.

Before he could speak, Lady Kesters turned to the butler, and said—

"Payne, if any one should call, I am not at home."

"Very good, my lady," he replied, and softly closed the door.

A maid, who happened to be on the landing, witnessed the recent arrival and overheard the order, now winked at Payne with easy impudence, and gave a significant sniff.

"I don't know what you're sniffing about," he said peevishly. "I suppose you will allow her ladyship to receive her own brother in peace and comfort, seeing as he is just back from South America, and she hasn't laid eyes on him for near a year."

"Oh, so that's her brother, is it?" said the young woman; "and an uncommonly fine young chap—better looking than her ladyship by long chalks!"

"You go down to your tea and leave her ladyship's looks alone. I don't know what you're doing hanging about this landing at such an hour of the day."

Payne was an old servant in the Wynyard family, and he was aware it had been generally said that "Master Owen had the looks and Miss Leila the brains." Master Owen was always a wild, harum-scarum young fellow, and it wasn't at all unlikely that he had got into one of his scrapes. With this conviction implanted in his mind, Payne deliberately descended the stairs, issued an edict to one of the footmen, and retired into his lair and the evening paper.

CHAPTER II
BROTHER AND SISTER

"Well," began Lady Kesters, as the door closed, "I suppose you have seen him?"

"I have very much seen him," replied her brother, who had thrown himself into a chair; "I did a sprint across the park, because I know your ladyship cannot bear to be kept waiting. Everything must be done to the minute in this establishment."

"Yes," she agreed; "and you come from a country where time is no object—everything is for 'To-morrow.' Now, tell me about Uncle Richard. Was he furious?"

"No; I believe I would have got off better if he had been in a rage. He received me in a 'more in sorrow than in anger' frame of mind, spoke as deliberately as if he had written his speech, and learnt it by heart; he meant every word he said."

"I doubt it," said his sister, who had been filling the teapot, and now closed the lid with a decisive snap. "Let me hear all you can remember."

"He said he had done his best for me since I was a kid—his only brother's son and his heir,—that he had sent me to Eton——"

"As if you didn't know that!" she interrupted.

"Engineered me into the Service——"

"Yes, yes, yes!" with a wave of her hand. "Tell me something new."

"He says that he is sick of me and my failures—is that new?"

"What does he propose?" asked Lady Kesters.

"He proposes that, for a change, I should try and get along by myself, and no longer hang on to other people."

"Well, there is some sense in that."

"He says that if I continue as I've begun, I'll develop into the awful loafer who haunts men's clubs, trying to borrow half a sov. from old pals, and worrying them with begging letters."

"A pretty future for *you*, Owen!"

"He swears I must work for my living and earn my daily bread; and that, if, for two years from now, I can maintain myself honourably in this country or the Continent—Asia, Africa, and America are barred—and neither get into debt, prison, or any matrimonial entanglement——" he paused for a moment to laugh.

"Yes, yes," said his sister impatiently; "and if you comply with all these conditions?"

"He will reinstate me, put me into Wynyard to take the place of his agent, and give me a handsome screw. But if I play the fool, he takes his solemn oath he will leave everything he possesses to a hospital, and all I shall come in for will be the bare estate, an empty house, and an empty title—and *that* he hopes to keep me out of for the next thirty years!"

"No doubt he will," agreed his sister; "we are—bar accidents—a long-lived stock."

"He also said that he was only fifty-six; he might marry; a Lady Wynyard——"

"No fear of that," she interposed; "the old servants will never permit it, and never receive her. But how are you to earn your living and your daily bread?"

"That, he declares, is entirely *my* affair. Of course he doesn't expect much from a wooden-headed duffer like me; he knows I've no brains, and no, what he calls 'initiative or push.' He doesn't care a rap if I sweep a crossing or a chimney, as long as I am able to maintain myself, become independent, and learn to walk alone."

"So that is Uncle Richard's programme!" said Lady Kesters reflectively. "Now, let's have some tea," and she proceeded to pour it out. "The little cakes are cold and stodgy, but try these sandwiches. Martin is away to-night—he had to go to a big meeting in Leeds, and won't be home. I shall send for your things. I suppose you are at your old quarters in Ryder Street?"

"Yes; they have been awfully decent to me, and kept my belongings when I was away."

"And you must come here for a week, and we will think out some scheme. I wish you could stay on and make your home here. But you know Martin has the same sort of ideas as Uncle Richard; he began, when he was eighteen, on a pound a week, and made his own way, and thinks every young man should do the same."

"I agree with him there—though it may sound funny to hear me say so, Sis. I hope you don't imagine I've come back to loaf; I shall be only too glad to be on my own."

"I suppose you have no money at all?" she inquired, as she replenished his teacup.

"I have fifteen pounds, if you call that nothing, all my London kit, a pair of guns, and a gold watch."

"But what brought you back so suddenly? You did not half explain to me this morning, when you tumbled from the skies."

"Well, you see," he began, as he rose and put down his cup, "the Estancia I was on was of the wrong sort, as it happened, and a rotten bad one. Uncle Richard was tremendously keen to deport me; and he took hold of the first thing he heard of, some crazy advice from a blithering old club fogey who did not know a blessed thing about the country. The Valencia Estancia, a horse-breeding one, was far away inland—not one of those nearer Buenos Ayres and civilisation,—it belonged to a native. The proprietor, Vincino, was paralysed from a bad fall, and the place was run by a ruffian called Murcia. I did not mind roughing it; it's a splendid climate, and I liked the life itself well enough. I got my fill of riding, and a little shooting—duck, and a sort of partridge—and I appreciated the freedom from the tall hat and visiting card."

"You never used many of those!" she interposed.

"No. From the first I never could stand Murcia; he was such an oily scoundrel, and an awful liar; so mean and treacherous and cruel, both to men and animals. He drank a lot of that frightfully strong spirit that's made out there—fermented cane—and sometimes he was stark mad, knocking the servants and the peons about; and as to the horses, he was a fiend to them. He killed lots of the poor brutes by way of training; lassoed them— and broke their hearts. It made my blood boil, and, as much as I could, I took over the breaking-in business. When I used to jaw him and remonstrate, it made him wild, and he always had his knife into me on the sly."

"How?"

"The stiffest jobs, the longest days, the largest herds, were naturally for the English 'Gringo.'"

"What is that?"

"A dog. He never called it to my face—he was too much of the cur—but we had several shakes up, and the last was *final*. One afternoon I caught him half-killing a wretched woman that he said had been stealing coffee. It was pay-day, all the employés, to a man and child, were assembled in the patio—you know what that is? An enclosed courtyard with the house round it. This was a grand old dilapidated Spanish Estancia, with a fine entrance of great iron gates. It was a warm, still sort of afternoon. As I cantered across the campo I heard harrowing shrieks, and, when I rode in, I soon saw what was up! Murcia, crazy with drink, was holding a wretched creature by her hair and belabouring her with a cattle-whip, whilst the crowd looked on, and no one stirred a finger."

"You did?" leaning forward eagerly.

"Rather! I shouted to him to hold hard, and he only cursed; so I jumped off the horse and went for him straight. He dropped his victim and tried to lay on to me with the whip; but the boot was on the other leg, and I let him have it, I can tell you. It was not a matter of fists, but flogging. My blood was up, and I scourged that blackguard with all my soul and all my strength. He ran round and round the patio yelling, whilst the crowd grinned and approved. I settled some of Murcia's scores on the spot and paid for many blows and outrages! In the end he collapsed in the dust, grovelling at my feet, blubbering and groaning, 'a worm and no man.' I think that's in the Bible. Yes, I gave that hulking, drunken brute a thrashing that he will never forget—and those who saw it won't forget it either. Naturally, after such a performance I had to clear. You may do a lot of things out there; you may even shoot a man, but you must never lay hands on an overseer; so I made tracks at once, without pay, bonus, character, or anything except the adoration of the employés, my clothes, and a few pounds. Murcia would have run me in, only he would have shown up badly about the woman. Well, I came down country in a cattle-train, and found I was just short of coin to pay my way home."

Leila stared into the fire in silence; her warm imagination transported her to the scene her brother had described. She, too, was on the campo, and heard the cries of the woman; she saw the Englishman gallop through the gates, saw the cowardly crowd, the maddened ruffian, the victim, and the punishment!

"But what did you do with your salary?" she asked, after an expressively long pause; "surely you had no way of spending it?"

"That's true. As I was to have a bonus, you know, on the year, my salary was small, and I got rid of it easily enough."

"Cards!" she supplemented; "oh, of course. My dear Owen, I'm afraid you are hopeless!"

"Yes, I suppose it's hereditary! After the day's work there was nothing to do. All the other chaps gambled, and I could not stand with my hands in my pockets looking on; so I learnt the good old native game of 'Truco,' but I had no luck—and lost my dollars."

"And after your arrival at Buenos Ayres in the cattle-train, what happened?"

"Well, naturally, I had no spare cash to spend in that little Paris: the Calle Florida, and the Café Florian, and Palermo Park, saw nothing of *me*, much less the magnificent Jockey Club. I searched about for a cast home! I was determined to get back to the Old Country, for I knew I'd do no good out there—I mean in Buenos Ayres; so I went down to the Digue, where the big liners lie, and cadged for a job. I believe they are pretty sick of chaps asking for a lift home, and I had some difficulty in getting a berth; but, after waiting several days, I got hold of a captain to listen to me. I offered to stoke."

"Owen!"

"Yes; but he said, 'You look like a stoker, don't you? Why, you're a gentleman! You couldn't stand the engine-room for an hour. However, as I see you are not proud and they are short of hands in the stewards' pantry, they might take you on to wash plates.'"

Lady Kesters made no remark; her expression was sufficiently eloquent.

"'All right,' I agreed, 'I'll do my little best.' So I was made over to the head steward. We carried a full number of passengers that trip, and, when one of the saloon waiters fell sick, I was promoted into his place, as I was clean and civil. Needless to say, I was thankful to get away from the horrors of greasy plates and the fag of cleaning knives. I can wait pretty well, the ladies liked me—yes, and I liked them—and when we docked at Southampton yesterday, Owen, as they called me, received nearly six pounds in tips, not to speak of a steamer chair and a white umbrella!"

As he concluded, he walked over to the fire and stood with his back to it. His sister surveyed him reflectively; she was thinking how impossible it was to realise that her well-bred, smart-looking brother, in his admirably cut clothes, and air of easy self-possession, had, within twenty-four hours, been a steward at the beck and call of the passengers on a liner. However, all she said was—

"So at any rate you have made a start, and begun to earn money already."

"Oh, that's nothing new. I was never quite broke;" and, diving into his pocket, he produced a little parcel, which he tossed into her lap.

"For me?"

"For who else?"

He watched her attentively as she untied the narrow bit of red and yellow ribbon, unfolded a flat box, and discovered a beautiful plaque or clasp in old Spanish paste. The design was exquisite, and the ornament flashed like a coruscation of Brazilian diamonds.

"Oh, Owen, how perfect!" she gasped; "but how dare you? It must have cost a fortune—as much as your passage money," and she looked up at him interrogatively.

"Never mind; it was a bargain. I picked it up in a queer, poky little shop, and it's real old, old Spanish—time of Ferdinand and Isabella they said—and I felt I'd like to take something home to you; it will look jolly well on black, eh?"

"Do you know it's just the sort of thing that I have been aching to possess," she said, now holding it against her gown. "If you had searched for a year you couldn't have given me anything I liked so much—so beautiful in itself, so rare and ancient, and so uncommon that not one of my dear friends can copy it. Oh, it's a *treasure*"—standing up to look at her reflection as she held the jewel against her bodice—"but all the same, it was wicked of you to buy it!"

"There are only the two of us, Sis, and why shouldn't I give myself that pleasure?"

"What a pretty speech!" and she patted his arm approvingly.

At this moment Payne entered, salver in hand.

"A telegram for you, my lady."

"Oh," picking it up, and tearing it open, "it's from Martin. He is detained till Saturday—three whole days;" then, turning to the butler, she said, "You can take away the tea-table."

As soon as the tea-things were removed, and Payne and his satellite had departed, Lady Kesters produced a gold case, selected a cigarette, settled herself comfortably in a corner of the sofa, and said—

"Now, Owen, light up, and let us have a pow-wow! Have you any plan in your head?"

"No," he answered, "I'm afraid my head is, as usual, pretty empty, and of course this ultimatum of Uncle Richard's has been a bit of a facer; I was in hopes he'd give me another chance."

"What sort of chance?"

"Something in South Africa."

"Something in South Africa has been the will-o'-the-wisp that has ruined lots of young men," she said; "you would do no good there, O. You haven't enough push, originality, or cheek; I believe you would find yourself a tram conductor in Cape Town."

"Then what about India? I might get a billet on some tea estate—yes—and some shooting as well!"

"Tea-planters' assistants, as far as I can gather, don't have much time for shooting. There is the tea-picking to look after, and the coolies to overseer in all weathers. I believe the work in the rains is awful and the pay is poor—you'd be much more likely to get fever than shooting. Have you any other scheme?"

She glanced at her brother, who was lying back in an arm-chair, his hands clasped behind his head, his eyes fixed on the fire. Yes, Owen was undeniably good to look at, with his clean-shaven, clear-cut face, well-knit figure, and length of limb. He shook his head, but after a moment said—

"Now let us have your ideas, Sis. You are always a sure draw!"

"What about matrimony?" she asked composedly, and without raising her eyes.

He turned and surveyed her with a stare of ironical amusement.

"On the principle that what is not enough for one will support two—eh?"

"How can you be so silly! I don't mean love in a cottage; I'm thinking of an heiress. There are several, so to speak, on the market, and I believe I could marry you off remarkably well, if you were not too critical; there is Miss Goldberger—a really good sort—enormously rich, an orphan, and hideous to the verge of fascination. She is in the racing set—and——"

"No, thank you, Sis," he broke in; "I'd rather drive a 'bus or motor any day than live on my wife's fortune. If I married one of your rich friends I should hate it, and I guarantee that she'd soon hate *me*; anyway, I'm not keen on getting married. So, as the young men in shops say, 'and the next article, please?'"

"Of course I know I need not again waste my breath talking to you of business. Martin got you a capital opening in Mincing Lane, and you threw it up; he'd taken a lot of trouble, and he is rather sore about it still. He fancies you look down on the City."

"I? He never made a greater mistake! The City would soon look down on me. I'm no good at figures; I've no business ability or smart alacrity. If I had not taken myself off, I'd soon have been chucked out; besides, I never could stick in an office all day from ten to six. I'd much rather wash plates! I want something that will keep me in the open air all the time, rain or shine; and if I had to do with horses, so much the better. How about a place as groom—a breaker-in of young hunters?"

"Not to be thought of!" she answered curtly.

"No?" then drawing out another cigarette, "do you know, I've half a mind to enlist. You see, I know something of soldiering—and I like it. I'd soon get my stripes, and for choice I'd pick the 'Death and Glory Boys.'"

"Yes; you may like soldiering as an officer, with a fair allowance, a couple of hunters, and polo ponies; but I'm not sure that Trooper Wynyard would care for stables, besides his drill and work, and I may be wrong, but I think you have a couple of troop horses to do up."

"Oh, I could manage all right! I'm rather handy with horses, though I must confess the bronchos I've been riding lately did not get much grooming."

"No, no, Owen, I'm dead against enlisting, remember that," she said authoritatively. "I shall go and interview Uncle Richard to-morrow morning, and have a tooth-and-nail combat on your behalf, find out if he means to stick to his intention, or if I can't persuade him to give you a job on the estate, say as assistant agent, that would suit you?"

"You're awfully clever, Sis," said the young man, now rising and leaning against the chimneypiece, "and in every respect the head of the family. It's downright wonderful how successfully you manage other people's affairs, and give one a push here and a hand there. I am aware that you have immense and far-reaching—er—influence. You have been the making of Kesters."

His sister dismissed the statement with an impatient jerk of her cigarette.

"Oh yes, you have," he went on doggedly. "He was formerly a common or garden wealthy man, whose daytime was divided between meals and business; now he's a K.C.B., sits on all sorts of boards, has a fine place in the country, shoots a bit, is a Deputy-Lieutenant, and I don't know what all—

and *you've* done it! But there is one person you cannot manage or move, and that is Uncle Richard; he is like a stone figure that all the wind and sun and rain may beat on, and he never turns a hair."

"How you do mix your metaphors!" she exclaimed; "who ever saw a stone image with hair upon it! Well," rising to stand beside him, "I shall see what *I* can do in the morning. Now, let us put the whole thing out of our heads and have a jolly evening. Shall we go to a theatre? I suppose you've not been inside one since you were last in town?"

"Oh yes, I was at theatres in Buenos Ayres, the Theatre Doria, a sort of music hall, where I saw some ripping dancing."

"I'll telephone for stalls at something. You may as well have all the fun you can before you start off to plough your lonely furrow."

"It's awfully good of you, Sis. I'm a frightful nuisance to the family—something between a bad penny and a black sheep!"

"No, Owen, you know perfectly well you are neither," she protested, as she lit another cigarette. "You mentioned just now there are only the two of us, and it would be rather strange if we did not stick by one another. And there is this to be said, that although you've been wild and extravagant, and your gambling and practical joking were shocking, all the time you remain a gentleman; and there are two things in your favour—you don't drink— —"

"No, thank God!" he responded, with emphasis.

"As far as I know you have never been mixed up with women—eh, Owen?" and she looked at him steadily.

"No. To tell you the truth, I give them a wide berth. I've seen some pretty awful affairs they had a hand in. To be candid, I'm a little shy of your sex."

"That is funny, Owen," she replied, "considering it was on account of a woman you have just been thrown out of a job."

"You could hardly expect a man to stand by and see a brute like Murcia knocking a poor creature about—half-killing her—and never interfere!"

"No, of course; but you must not make the mistake of being too chivalrous—chivalry is costly—and it is my opinion that it has cost you a good deal already. That detestable de Montfort was not the first who let you in, or persuaded you to pull his chestnuts out of the fire. Come now, own up—confess to the others."

"No—no"—and he smiled—he had a charming smile—"there is such a thing as honour among thieves."

"That's all very noble and generous, my dear brother, but some of the thieves were *not* honourable."

Her dear brother made no reply; he was staring fixedly into the fire and thinking of Hugo de Montfort. How little had he imagined, when he backed Hugo's bill, that the scribbling of his signature would make such an awful change in his own life!

Hugo and he had been at Eton in the same house; they had fagged together, sat side by side in chapel, and frequently shared the same scrapes. Later they had lost sight of one another, as Owen had struggled into the Service and gone out to India. Some years later, when stationed at the depôt, he and de Montfort had come across one another once more.

Hugo de Montfort was a self-possessed young man, with sleek black hair and a pair of curiously unreadable grey eyes: an idler about town— clever, crafty, unscrupulous, and much given to cards and racing.

He welcomed his old pal Wynyard with enthusiasm—and secretly marked him for his own. Wynyard—so said report—was a nailing rider, a good sort, popular, and known to be the nephew and heir of a rich, unmarried uncle; so he played the rôle of old schoolfellow and best pal for all it was worth.

The plausible, insidious scoundrel, who lived by his wits, was on his last legs—though he kept the fact a secret—was seen everywhere, carried a bold front, and owned a magnificent 60 h.p. motor, which was useful in more ways than one. He was staying at the Métropôle at Folkestone, and, struck by a bright idea—so he declared—motored over to Canterbury one fine Sunday morning, and carried off his friend to lunch.

As they sat smoking and discussing recent race meetings, weights, and jockeys, de Montfort suddenly put down his cigar and said—

"I say, look here, Owen, old man. I'm in rather a tight fix this week. I want two thousand to square a bookie—and, like the real sporting chap you are—will you back my name on a bill?"

Owen's expression became unusually grave; backing a bill was an iniquity hitherto unknown to him. Uncle Dick had recently paid up handsomely, and he had given certain promises; and, indeed, had curtailed his expenses, sold two of his ponies, and had made up his mind to keep strictly within his allowance.

"Of course it's a mere form," pursued de Montfort, in his swaggering, off-hand way, "I swear to you. Do you think I'd ask you, if it was not safe as a church! I'll have the coin in a fortnight; but just at the moment I'm terribly short, and you know yourself what racing debts mean. So I come to you, my old pal, before any one; you are such a rare, good, generous, open-handed sort! Don't for a moment suppose that *you* will be responsible," declared this liar; "I'll take up the bill when it falls due; I'd as soon let in my own mother as a pal like you."

In short, Hugo was so urgent and so plausible, that his victim was persuaded and carried away by eloquence and old memories, accompanied de Montfort to a writing-table, where he signed O. St. J. Wynyard—and repented himself before his signature had been blotted!

Two days later Owen received a beautiful silver cigarette-case, inscribed, as a token of friendship from de Montfort, and this was succeeded by an alarming silence. When the time approached for the bill to fall due, Wynyard wrote anxious epistles to his old schoolfellow—who appeared to be one of the crowd who believe that letters answer themselves! Then he went up to town and sought him at his rooms and club; no one could give him any tidings of Hugo beyond the fact that he was abroad—a wide and unsatisfactory address. He sent distracted telegrams to some of the runaway's former haunts; there was no reply. The fatal day arrived, and Owen was compelled to interview his uncle and make a clean breast of the whole business; and his uncle was furious to the verge of apoplexy.

"They used to say," he shouted, "put the fool of the family into the army; but *my* fool shall not remain in the Service! I'll pay up the two thousand you've been robbed of for the sake of my name—and out you go! Send in your papers to-day!"

Lady Kesters was contemplating her face in the overmantle, which also reflected her brother's unusually grave visage.

"Owen," she said, "what a pity it is that I hadn't your looks and you my brains."

They presented a contrast, as they examined one another in the glass. The woman's dark, irregular face, her keen, concentrated expression; the man with clear-cut features, sleepy, deep-set grey eyes, and close-cropped light brown hair.

"I think you are all right as you are, Sis," he remarked, after a reflective pause.

"But you are not," she snapped. "Now, if you had my head. Oh, how I long to be a man! I'd have gone into Parliament. I'd have helped to manage the affairs of a nation instead of the affairs of a family. I'd have worked and slaved and made myself a name—yes, and gone far!"

"What's the good of going far?" he asked, in a lazy voice.

"Ah," she exclaimed, with a touch of passion, "you have no ambition; you don't even know what the word means! Look at the men in the Commons, who have worked themselves up from nothing to be powers in the land, whose influence is far-reaching, whose voices are heard at the ends of the earth. What would be your ambition, come now?" and she surveyed him with sparkling eyes.

"Certainly not to go into Parliament," he answered, "and sit in the worst atmosphere in London for eight months of the year."

"Well, at least it's an electrical atmosphere, charged with vitality! And your ambition?" she persisted.

"To win the Grand National, riding my own horse, since you must know."

"Pooh!" she exclaimed, snapping her fingers with a gesture of scorn, "and what a paltry aim!—the yells of a raving mob, a 'para' in the papers, and the chance of breaking your neck."

"Better than breaking something else! I'm told that a political career, with its incessant work, crushing disappointments, worry, and fag, has broken many a fellow's heart."

"Heart! Nonsense; I don't believe you have one. Well, now, as we are dining early, you had better see about your things from Ryder Street, and I will go and 'phone for stalls for *The Giddy Girl*."

CHAPTER III
THE LAST WORD GOES BEGGING

Sir Richard Wynyard, aged fifty-six, was a little, grey, square-shouldered man, with a good heart and bad temper. His father, the notorious Sir Fulke, had put his two sons into the army, given them small and irregularly paid allowances, and then abandoned them to their own devices, whilst he squandered the family patrimony on horses and cards. When Richard, his heir, was quartered in Dublin, he fell desperately in love with a beautiful Irish girl; but, painfully aware of his own empty purse, he was too prudent to marry—unlike his reckless younger brother, who adventured a runaway match on a captain's pay and debts. Major Wynyard made no sign, much as this silence cost him, and when, after his father's death, he had at last a roof to offer—Wynyard, a stately old place, although somewhat dismantled—he sought his lady-love in haste, but, alas! he was months too late; she had already been summoned to another home,—the beautiful Rose O'Hara, his heart's desire, was dead.

This was said to have been Sir Richard's sole love-affair, and the one grief of his life. The late baronet's reckless extravagance had shattered the fortunes of his descendants; his heir found himself compelled to let the land, close the Hall, sell off the horses, and take up his abode with his mother in the town house in Queen's Gate; where he lived and how, was indifferent to him, he seemed to have no heart for anything. This was attributed to his supreme disgust at inheriting such a legacy of debt; but the real truth was that the loss of the beautiful Rose had temporarily stunned her lover.

Lady Wynyard, once a celebrated beauty, was now a weak and withered old dowager, tyrannically ruled by her servants. When she, too, was carried to the ancestral vault, her son still remained in the gloomy family abode, and, more from apathy than anything else, fell under the thrall of her retainers.

Between his father's and his mother's debts, Sir Richard found himself sorely pressed, and he took Martin Kesters, his schoolfellow and friend, into his confidence.

"I shall be a crippled man all my life," he declared; "it will take years to nurse the property into anything like what it was in my grandfather's day; and, by that time, that young chap, Owen, will step into my shoes."

"Well, Dick, if you don't mind a bit of risk," said his companion, "I know a thing that will set you on your legs and make your fortune; but it's not absolutely certain. Still, if it comes off, you get five hundred per cent. for your money, and become a semi-millionaire. It's an Australian gold-mine, and I believe it's going to boom!"

"Anything is better than this half-and-half existence," said Sir Richard impatiently. "You have a long head, Martin, and I'll take your tip and put on all I can scrape. I'll mortgage some outlying land, sell some of the good pictures and the library, and be either a man or a mouse. For once in my life I'll do a big gamble. If I win, you say it's a big thing; if I lose, it means a few hundreds a year and a bedroom near my club for the rest of my days. I take no middle course—I'll be a rich man or a pauper."

And Sir Richard was as good as his word; he scraped up fifteen thousand pounds, staked the whole sum on his venture—and won.

Subsequently, he cleared the property, invested in some securities, began to feel at ease in the world, and travelled widely. Having known the pinch and humiliation of genteel poverty and practised stern self-denial in his youth, Sir Richard was naturally the last man to have any sympathy with a nephew—a restless, reckless scatter-brain—who was following in the footsteps of his squandering forefathers. The good-looking young scapegrace must have a sharp lesson, and learn the value of money and independence.

Lady Kesters' promised interview with her uncle took place. He was fond of Leila in his own brusque fashion, and secretly plumed himself on having manœuvred her marriage.

"Well, Leila, I suppose you have come about this precious brother of yours?" he began, as she was ushered into the smoking-room.

"Of course I have, Uncle Dick," she replied, as she imprinted a kiss upon his cheek and swept into a chair. "Something must be done!" and she looked at him with speculative eagerness.

"There I agree with you," he answered. "And Owen is the man to do it. God helps those who help themselves!"

"Owen is most anxious to make another start; but it is not easy for a soldier man, brought up as he has been."

"Brought up as a rich man's heir," broke in her uncle, with a quick, impatient movement; "more fool the rich man! I gave the fellow a good education, good allowance, good send-off. I got him into his father's old regiment, and made him a decent allowance; he did fairly well in India, I admit; but as soon as he came home to the depôt, he seemed to have lost his head. Why, I believe the young scamp actually kept racers, and as for his hunters, I never saw finer cattle in my life! One day, when I happened to run down to Canterbury to visit him, I noticed a servant exercising a couple of horses—such a pair! I was bound to stop and admire them, and the groom informed me that they belonged to Lieutenant Wynyard of the Red Hussars; and Mr. Wynyard's uncle hadn't as much as a donkey to his name!"

"But could have thousands if he chose," interposed Leila. "As for racing, it was only his hunters Owen put into regimental steeplechases and that sort of thing."

"And that sort of thing came devilish expensive!" snapped Sir Richard, who was now pacing the room. "I had to pay his debts. I paid them *twice*, and he promised on his word of honour to turn over a new leaf. The next thing he did was to back a bill for an infernal young swindler, and let me in for two thousand pounds—that was the last straw!"

"Yes, I know it was," assented his niece; "but really, Uncle Dick, Owen was not so much to blame as you believe. He was very steady out in India for four years; coming home, as you say, went to his head; he did not realise that money does not go nearly as far here—especially in an expensive cavalry regiment. He kept polo ponies and racing ponies in Lucknow, and could not understand that he could not do the same at home. As to the bill, he is not suspicious, or sharp at reading character, and is staunch to old friends—or those he mistakes for friends—as in the case of young de Montfort. He had never heard what a 'wrong un' he turned out; they were at Eton——"

"Yes, I know—same house—same puppy-hole!" growled her uncle.

"And when Mr. de Montfort looked up Owen and told him a pathetic and plausible tale about his affairs, and swore on his word of honour that his signature was a mere formality—and——"

"Cleared off to Spain and left *me* to pay!" interposed Sir Richard, coming to a halt.

"Owen had to pay too," retorted his sister, with a touch of bitterness.

"You mean that I made him leave the Service? Yes, I could not afford to go on supporting an extravagant young ass."

"Owen is not brilliant, Uncle Dick, but he is no fool."

"A fool and another man's money are soon parted. Life was made too easy for the chap—very different to what *I* found it at his age. I had no hunters, no dozens of silk shirts, and rows of polo boots; *I* never was to be met lounging down Piccadilly as if the whole earth belonged to me."

"Well, at least, Uncle Dick, you were never compelled to give up a profession you adored, when you were barely five-and-twenty."

"I've given up a lot," he answered forcibly, "and when I was older than him; but never mind *me*; we are talking of Owen. After leaving the Hussars, Kesters took him on, and got him a capital billet in the City—a nice soft berth, ten to four, but my gentleman could not stand an office stool and tall hat, and in five months he had chucked——"

Leila nodded. It was impossible to deny this indictment.

"So then it was my turn again; and I thought a little touch of real work would be good for the future Sir Owen Wynyard, and, after some trouble, I heard of a likely opening in the Argentine on the Valencia Estancia, well out of the way of towns and temptation—a horse-breeding ranch, too. You see I studied the fellow's tastes, eh?" And Sir Richard twirled his eyeglasses by the string—a trick of his when he considered that he had scored a point.

"I gave him his passage and outfit, and put a few hundreds into the concern as a spec. and to insure him an interest, and within twelve months here he is back again on my hands—the proverbial rolling stone!" He cleared his throat, and continued: "Now, Leila, my girl, you have a head on your shoulders, and you know that these rolling stones find their way to the bottom, and I am going to block my specimen in good time. I suppose he told you what I said to him yesterday?"

"Yes; he came straight to Mount Street from seeing you."

"He has got to shift for himself for two years, to earn his bread, with or without butter, to guarantee that he does not take a penny he has not worked for, that he does not get into debt or any matrimonial engagement; should he marry a chorus-girl, by Jove I'll burn down Wynyard! If, by the end of that time, he turns up a steady, industrious, independent member of society, I will make him my agent—he shall have an adequate allowance, the house to live in, and most of my money when I am dead!"

Lady Kesters was about to speak, but with a hasty gesture her uncle interposed.

"I may as well add that I think myself safe in offering this prize, for it's my belief that Owen will never win it. He has the family fever in his veins— the rage for gambling—and he is like the patriarch Reuben, 'unstable as water and cannot excel.' At the end of six months he will be penniless, and you and Kesters will have to come to his rescue; for my part I wash my hands of him."

"Uncle Dick," she said, rising, "I think you are too hard on Owen; he would not have come back from South America if he had not had a row with the manager of the Estancia: surely you could not expect an English gentleman—an Englishman—to stand by and see a poor woman nearly beaten to death?"

"Oh," with an impatient whirl of his glasses, "the fellow has always as many excuses as an Irishman!"

"I think you are unjust," she said, with a flash in her dark eyes. "I admit that Owen has been extravagant and foolish, but he was not worse, or half as bad, as many young men in his position. Are you quite determined? Won't you give Owen another chance—or even half a chance?"

"No; his future is now in his own hands, and I stick to what I've said," he declared, with irritable vehemence. "You came here, my clever Leila, to talk me over. Oh, you are good at that, but it's no go this time! I am honestly giving the boy his only remedy. Let me see," sitting down at his bureau, "what is the date? Yes—look here—I make an entry. I give Owen two years from to-day to work out his time—to-day is the thirty-first of March."

"But why not wait until to-morrow, and make it the first of April?" suggested his niece, with a significant and seductive smile.

"Leila," he spluttered, "I'm astonished at you! You jeer at me because I'm not disposed to keep your beloved brother as an 'objêt de luxe,' eh?"

"I don't jeer, Uncle Dick, and I am sorry my tongue was too many for me; but I can see both sides of the question, and it *is* hard that, after indulging Owen as a boy, sending him to Eton, putting him into the Hussars, and letting him become accustomed to the Service, sport, and society, you suddenly pull up and throw him out in the world to sink or swim. What can he do?"

"That is for him to find out, and, since he wouldn't pull up, I must."

"Listen to me," she said, rising and coming closer to him; "supposing Owen were to give you a promise in writing that he would stick steadily to one situation for two years, what would you say then?"

"I'd say that the promise would not be worth the paper it was written on!" he answered, with gruff emphasis. "Give *me* deeds, not documents."

"Oh, so that is your opinion and your last word?"

"It's my opinion—yes—but as to the last word, of course it's *your* perquisite!" and he chuckled complacently.

Lady Kesters stood for a moment looking steadily at her uncle, and he as steadily at her. Then she slowly crossed the room and touched a bell to summon a footman, who presently ushered her out of the house.

CHAPTER IV
LEILA'S IDEA

As Lady Kesters motored home in her smart new Rolls-Royce, her expression was unusually grave; for once Uncle Dick had proved invulnerable, and she was overpowered with surprise; for her ladyship was so accustomed "to push the world before her," to borrow an Irish expression, that any little resistance affected her in the nature of a shock.

Her brother was awaiting her in the smoking-room, and as she entered and threw off her furs, he said—

"So it was no go, Leila! Your embassy was a failure; defeat is written on your face—ahem—I told you so!"

"Now, Owen, I call this base ingratitude. I've wasted my whole morning fighting for you, I am worsted in the battle, and you receive me with grins and gibes!"

"You see, I can understand Uncle Dick's attitude; he is pretty sick of me, and I don't blame him; after all, when you come to think of it, why should he support a healthy, able-bodied duffer simply because he is his nephew?"

"Worse than that," amended his sister, "his heir! *I* can understand his attitude even better than you, Owen. As a young man he never had any real fling, and could scarcely afford cabs and clothes or anything he wanted. He was hampered by a hopelessly extravagant father."

"And now in his old age he is tormented by a spendthrift nephew."

"Yes, and I can't exactly explain; but I grasp the situation. You have had, what as a young man he never enjoyed—that is to say, a splendid time—and chiefly at his expense. He must feel just a little bit sore."

"No; old Dick is a rattling good sort, and I don't agree with you, Leila. It's not so much the money he grudges, but that he thinks I'll never do any good. I've no ballast. I've got to sally out into the world, like the hero in a fairy tale, and prove myself!"

"Yes, my dear brother; you practically start to-day, March the 31st, and do you know that I've got an idea,—and from Purdon, of all people.

He is rather smart looking, and might pass for a gentleman, till he opens his mouth; besides, I happen to know that his mother lives in Fulham, and keeps a small greengrocer's shop."

"Yes, but your idea? You don't want me to start in that line, do you?"

"No," with an irrepressible smile; "I want you to become a chauffeur!"

"A chauffeur!" he repeated, subsiding into an adjacent arm-chair; "but why?"

"But why not?"

"Well, of course, I used to drive a car—and yes—your idea isn't half bad; a chauffeur gets about the world for nothing, has fair pay, and, by all accounts, bar washing the car, a fairly good time."

"You need not be thinking of a good time, Owen; but put all idea of amusement out of your head, and make up your mind that, during the next two years, you will be *doing* time—as a punishment for your crimes! Now, to be practical, you must have a certificate, and you and I will run into the country for the next day or two, and you shall drive the car; of course you are out of practice, and Purdon shall give you tips. I suppose you know all about magnetos, carburetters, and speed? I expect in a week you will qualify and pass, and there you are!"

"Yes, my lady, in a new black leather suit. I'll do my best; I see you've fixed it up."

She nodded assent. He was accustomed to Leila's fixing up of his affairs, and never disputed her authority.

"You can take the car out in the morning, and get accustomed to the traffic. I think you will make an excellent chauffeur, as you have a strong head and no nerves."

"Perhaps I may, and I've a sort of taste for mechanics. As a kid, you remember, I was mad to be an engine-driver."

"Yes; you were always blowing things up, or breaking them down, or taking them to pieces."

"I dare say I'll have something of the breaking down and taking to pieces in my new career."

"Only it's so frightfully risky; you might go in for being an airman—*that's* where you could make money!"

"Yes, with a two to one chance of breaking my neck."

"Think of ten thousand pounds earned in a few hours! All the same it's out of the question, I couldn't bear the anxiety, it's too dangerous; though I see the day coming when airships will displace motors, and I shall be flying over to Paris to dine and do a theatre."

"Meanwhile, give me mother earth and a 60 h.p. car! Well, so it's settled," he said, jumping to his feet and tossing the stump of his cigarette into the fire; "yes, I'll be a chauffeur all right—but what about the pay?"

"I expect you start at two guineas a week, with or without clothes, and find yourself."

"A hundred a year, and an open-air billet! I say, I shall do splendidly. Leila, I feel that Uncle Dick's prize is already in my hand."

"Don't be too sure of that! Bear in mind that some situations may not suit you, that you may not suit them, and be thrown out of employment."

"That's true; it has happened to me twice already—the Army and the ranch—and I've no luck."

"What do you mean, Owen?"

"I mean that nothing comes *my* way; other chaps get all they want in big things, or little. Don't you know the sort that fall across people they wish to meet, that get the best corners at a shoot, the best hands at cards, that win big sweepstakes and lotteries, come in for fine legacies, and, at a good old age, die very comfortably in their beds?"

His sister nodded.

"I have one peculiarity. I can't call it gift, and it's of no earthly value. I only wish it was marketable; I'd pass it on like a shot."

"What is it—second sight?"

"No, that's all bosh! It's—it's—I don't know how to put it—the being on the spot when out-of-the-way affairs come off,—sensational things, accidents, discoveries, deaths. They seem to drop into my day's work in an extraordinary way; sometimes I begin to think I've got the Evil Eye!"

"Now *that's* nonsense if you like! You have knocked about a good deal for the last seven years, and naturally seen far more than people at home."

"Well, anyhow, I wish this queer sort of fate would change, and shove me towards something different—a good post."

"And you believe you'd keep it?"

"Anyway, I'd do my little best. My three weeks as steward were a breaking-in."

"But you were acting all the time, Owen—you know you love it! and you realised that there was a limit to the experience?"

"No, honour bright, I wasn't playing the fool. I am quick and ready, and not afraid of work. I say, look here," and he took his hands out of his pockets and held them up, the palms towards her.

"Oh, oh, my poor dear boy! they are like—like—leather! Like a working man's, only clean!"

"Well, I never was a kid-glove chap, and the reins have hardly been out of them for twelve months. I'm fairly good with my hands, although an awful duffer with my head."

"Just the opposite to me," declared his sister; "I can scarcely sew a button on, and I can't do up a parcel or tie a knot. But to return to our business. Once you have a certificate, the next thing will be to find you a situation. You had better begin in some very quiet country place—a long way from Town and talk—and I will recommend you."

"*You!*" and he burst into a loud laugh.

"Oh yes, you may laugh; but who else is there? We do not wish to invite the world into our family laundry."

"Thank you, Leila."

"Don't be silly! I will give you an excellent character," she continued imperturbably, "as a sober, respectable young man, most careful, obliging, and anxious to please."

"Well, that sounds all right."

"And you must really be, as the French advertisements say, '*un chauffeur sérieux*,' and promise not to play the fool, and I shall get you a nice situation that I happen to know of, with two old ladies."

"O Lord!" he expostulated; "can't you make it a couple of old gentlemen? I'd much rather go to them."

"Yes, no doubt you would," she answered; "but you cannot pick and choose, and this place seems the very one for a start. These are the two Miss Parretts."

"I say, what a name! Any cats?"

"I believe they are an old French family—de Palairet, and have the dark eyes and animation of the race,—but they are so long in England, they have become Parrett."

"De Palairet *is* rather a mouthful. And whereabouts do the old birds nest?"

"In a remote part of Midshire. I came across them when I stayed with our cousins, the Davenants, down at Westmere; when I was a girl I went there every summer, but now the family place is sold."

"Yes, the Davenants are broke. Young Davenant was in the Hussars with me, and was frightfully hard up."

"The two Miss Parretts lived in the village of Ottinge—Ottinge-in-the-Marsh—in a little old red cottage. They had two maids, two cats, and a sweet garden. The original property was in the neighbourhood, and the family manor of the Parretts. The father of these old ladies, Colonel Parrett, married in India, when he was a sub., a planter's daughter, simply because he, they say, was *dared* to make her an offer—and whatever a Parrett is dared to do—they do."

"I say, I think I shall like them! I shall dare them to double my salary."

"The first Mrs. Parrett died and left a baby, your future mistress. Her father sent her home, and married, years later, an Irish girl, and again his wife died and left him with two more girls. One married the village parson, the other lived with her father and sister in the Manor. After the death of Colonel Parrett, it was found that he had squandered all his money putting it into follies: the Manor was mortgaged to the chimneys, the daughters had to turn out, and for years lived in genteel poverty. Now comes a turn of Fortune's wheel! Some distant Parrett relative bequeathed a heap of money to Miss Parrett, and she and Miss Susan have gone back to the Manor. Bella Parrett must be well over seventy; Susan is about fifty, has the youngest heart I ever knew in an elderly body, and is the most unselfish creature in the world. Miss Parrett is an egotistical old person, full of pedigree and importance, but always delightfully sweet and affectionate to *me*. She looks obstinate and self-willed, and I feel positive that some one has dared her to buy a motor! I had a letter from her the other day, asking me to take up the character of a cook; she mentioned that she was about to purchase a most beautiful automobile upholstered in green morocco leather,—think of that! and would soon be looking for a nice, steady, respectable young man as chauffeur, and"—pointing at her brother with an ivory paper knife—"here he is!"

"Is he?" he responded doubtfully, "I'm not so sure."

"Yes. I admit that it will be hideously dull, and I can absolutely guarantee you against any sensational experiences. It is just a sleepy little country place, with few big people in the neighbourhood: no racing, shockingly bad hunting—not that this will affect *you*—but it will be an ideal spot for putting in the time. You will never see a soul you know; I'll keep you well supplied with books, papers, and news, and steal down to see you now and then, 'under the rose.'"

"Don't, don't!" he protested, with a laugh, "think of my spotless character."

"Yes; but I shall come all the same! The place is notoriously healthy, I dare say you may get some good fishing, you will hardly have anything to do—they won't go out much—of course you'll pay a boy to clean the car, and I've no doubt that the old ladies will take an enormous fancy to you and leave you a fortune, and you will be just as happy as the day is long."

"Oh, all right. Then, in that case, my dear Sis, since you say there is a chance of a great fortune and good fishing, you may book me for the situation by the next post."

CHAPTER V
PLANS AND THREATS

When the choice of Owen's future employment was duly imparted to his uncle and brother-in-law, the latter received it with approval, the former with a series of alarming explosions.

"His nephew—his heir—a common chauffeur! Outrageous! Why not enlist, and be the King's servant, if livery he *must* wear?" Then, in a tone of angry sarcasm, "I see—I see his reason. The fellow will be gadding round, making believe to himself it's his own machine; to many young asses, driving a car is an extraordinary pleasure. Yes, that's why he hit on it!" and he slapped his leg with a gesture of triumph.

"You are wrong, Uncle Richard, it was *I* who hit on it," protested the culprit. "Owen never had an idea of being a chauffeur till I suggested it."

"That's likely enough; his ideas are few and far between. Well, now look here, Leila, I forbid him to adopt your plan."

"But, my dear uncle, have you not washed your hands of him for the next two years?" she demanded, with raised brows. "Do you really think you are consistent?"

"But a greasy chauffeur, got up in black leather, like a boot——"

"The pay is not bad, it's a job he can manage, and, after all, you will allow that Owen must live; or are you going to say, '*Je n'en vois pas la necessité*'?"

"Umph! I wonder, Leila, where you got that tongue of yours?"

"And," dismissing the question with an airy gesture, "I know of a nice quiet place in a country village, with two darling old maiden ladies, where he will be, so to speak, out at grass, with his shoes off!"

"Oh yes," he snarled, "I know your quiet, wicked little country village, with the devil peeping behind the hedges and finding plenty for an idle young man to do. Villages are pestilential traps, swarming with pretty girls. Just the place where Owen will fall into the worst scrape of all—matrimony. He is a good-looking chap; they'll all be after him!"

"I don't believe there's a woman in Ottinge under forty, and I never saw a more hard-featured lot—never. You know I stayed in the neighbourhood with the Davenants years ago."

"Another thing—no one can take Owen for anything but a gentleman!" and Sir Richard put up his glasses and surveyed his niece, with an air as much as to say, "There's a poser!"

"Oh yes. He has only to show his hands, worn with manual labour, and I'll tell him to grow his hair long, wear gaudy ties, and hold his tongue."

"Well, have your own way! But, as sure as I'm a living sinner, harm will come of this mad idea; it's nothing more or less than play-acting. He'd much better have gone on the stage when he was about it."

"Unfortunately, there's one objection,—it is the most precarious of all professions; for an amateur it would be hard work and *no* pay. In five years Owen might, with great luck, be earning thirty shillings a week. Oh, I've thought over no end of plans, I can assure you, Uncle Dick, and the chauffeur scheme is by far the most promising."

"Of course you always get the better of me in *talk*; but I've my own opinion. You and Owen will make a fine hash of his affairs between you. Bear in mind that I won't have the Wynyard name made little of in a stinking garage. He is not to use it, or to let any one know he is a Wynyard, and that's flat; and you can tell him that, as sure as he takes service as Owen Wynyard, I'll marry—and to that I stick!" and with this announcement, and a very red face, he snatched up his hat and departed.

Sir Martin Kesters, on the other hand, saw nothing derogatory in his brother-in-law's employment, and warmly applauded the scheme. At twenty-six Owen should be learning independence; moreover, it was his wife's plan, and, in his opinion, everything she said or did was right. "I think it's a sound scheme," he said. "If money is wanted, Leila, you know where to get it."

"No, no; Owen has a little, and he must not touch a halfpenny that he has not earned—it's in the bond; and he will have nothing to spend money on down there. I don't believe there's a billiard-table or a pack of cards in the place."

"The typical hamlet, eh? Half a dozen cottages, a pump, and an idiot—poor devil!"

"Owen or the idiot?"

"Both. All the same, Leila, I feel sure that, now you've taken Owen in hand, he will come out on top."

Wynyard fell in with everything, without question or argument, and cheerfully accepted his sister's arrangements, with the exception of the ties. He drew the line at an orange satin with green spots, or even a blue with scarlet horse-shoes.

No, he declared, nothing would induce him to be seen in them; he was always a quiet dresser. He could wear a muffler, hold his tongue, or even drop his h's if necessary; but he barred making an object of himself, and suggested that she should offer the discarded ties as a birthday present to Payne.

"He'd give notice. Payne, in his unprofessional kit, looks like a chief justice. Well, I won't insist on the ties, but you must promise to be *very* countrified and dense. You know you can take off any one's way of talking in the most remarkable way, and do Uncle Richard to the life!"

"One of my rare accomplishments; and as to being dense, why, it's my normal condition."

"Oh yes, you may joke! But I do hope you won't let the cat out of the bag, Owen, or allow any one to suspect that 'things are not what they seem!' I wonder how you will manage in the kitchen and stables, and if you will be unmasked?"

"Well, I promise to do my best to pick up the local manners and patois, and, my dear Leila, you appear to forget that for the last year I've lived among a very mixed lot, and got on all right."

"Got on all right!" she cried. "How *can* you say so? when you told me yourself that you had half killed a man! However, as you and I are confederates in this most risky enterprise, I feel sure you will do your utmost for my sake. Think of the uproar and scandal if Miss Parrett were to discover that you were *my* brother—late of Eton College and the Red Hussars. Explanation would be impossible; I should be compelled to flee the country!"

CHAPTER VI
FIRST IMPRESSIONS

The train which bore Wynyard to his situation was slow, and lingered affectionately at every station; nevertheless he enjoyed the leisurely journey. He was glad to be in England once more! His eyes feasted greedily on the long stretches of quiet, secluded country, nice hunting fences, venerable villages crowding round a church steeple, and stately old halls buried in hollows, encompassed by their woods.

The afternoon was well advanced when he saw "Catsfield" on a large board staring him in the face, and, realising that he had reached his destination, seized his bag, sprang out, and went in search of his luggage—a corded tin box of a remarkably vivid yellow. His sister had insisted upon this, instead of his old battered portmanteau, as a part of his disguise. A portmanteau, she declared, would give him away at once! For, no matter how dilapidated and travel-stained, a portmanteau conferred a certain position upon its owner!

There were but two people on the platform of the forlorn little station, which seemed to have no business and no belongings, but had, as it were, sat down helplessly to rest in the middle of a sweeping plain of pasture.

Outside the entrance no cabs or vehicles were to be seen, merely an unpainted spring-cart drawn by a hairy bay mare. In reply to the traveller's inquiries, the porter said—

"Oh no, there's no call for flies here, sir, no work for 'em; the cart was sent for a man-servant, and he ain't come. To Ottinge? Yes, sir, he'd take your luggage, I dessay, and you, too, if you wouldn't despise driving with him."

"I wouldn't despise driving with any one; but, as I'm rather stiff and dusty, I'll walk. You say Ottinge is four miles across the fields and seven by the road." "Here," addressing the driver in the cart, "if you are going to Ottinge, will you take my bag and box, and I'll give you a shilling?"

"All right, master; 'eave 'em in, Pete. Where to, sir?"

"Miss Parrett's, the Manor;" then, turning to the porter, "can you point me out the short-cut?"

"Yes, sir, straight over the fields. First you go along this 'ere road to the left, down a lane, then over the water-meadows and a wooden bridge—ye can see the spire of Ottinge Church, and if you steer to that, you can't go far out. Thank you," touching his cap in acknowledgment of sixpence.

As the stranger moved off with an even, swinging stride, the two men stared after him with a gape of astonishment.

"I'm jiggered if I don't believe that's the motor chap after all!" said the driver; "why, he looks like a regular toff, and talks high. I was bid to fetch a young man, so I was, but there was no word of a gentleman—and I know he's boarding at Sally Hogben's."

"It's a queer start," agreed the porter; "he's a likely looking fellow. I expect he'll make rare work among the maids!" as his eyes followed the active figure in tweeds and leather gaiters, till it was lost to sight round a bend in the road.

"That soort o' chap won't be long with them two old women, you may take your oath. Lor' bless ye, he'd cut his throat! Why, you haven't a good glass o' beer nor a pretty girl in the parish."

"I'm none so sure o' that!" retorted the driver, giving the bay a smack with the reins, preparatory to starting; "there's a fair tap at the Drum, and a couple o' rare pretty faces in our church."

"Is that so? I'm not to say busy on Sunday—one down and one up—and maybe I'll just step over and have a look at 'em."

"Eh, ye might go furder and fare worse! Well, I'm off," and he rattled away in his clumsy cart, with the gay new box for its only load.

It was about four o'clock on a lovely afternoon in April; the air was sweet and stimulating, and the newcomer was conscious of a sense of exhilaration and satisfaction, as he looked across the stretch of meadows lying in the sunlight.

Wynyard was country-bred, and the familiar sights and sounds awakened pleasant memories. He noted the bleating of lambs, the cries of plover, the hedges powdered with thorn, and the patches of primroses. Everything was so rural and so restful—such a contrast to the roar of London, the skimming taxis, the hooting and clanking of motors, and the reek of petrol; he had stepped aside from the glare and noise into a byway. As he strode along, steering steadily for the church spire, his spirits rose with every step; he vaulted stiles, leapt lazy little streams, and, coming to a river, which he crossed by a rickety wooden bridge, found that he was within measurable distance of his destination, and paused for a moment to survey it.

The village, which lay under the shelter of some low hills, was long and straggling; red, hunched-up houses and high-roofed, black barns had turned their backs on the pasture, and a hoary church, with a high slated spire and surrounded by a bodyguard of trees, stood sentry at one end of Ottinge-in-the-Marsh. At the other, and almost opposite to where he had halted, was an ancient grey manor house of considerable pretensions, set in creepers and encircled by yew hedges. A stone-faced, sunk fence and a high wooden gate separated him from this property, and, as far as he could judge, the only way he could reach the village was by intruding into the grounds. He looked up and down and could see nothing but a fence abutting on the meadows, and, further on, the backyards and gardens of the villagers. Like the thundering ass he was, he had lost his way! He tried the wooden gate, found it padlocked, and vaulted over—a bold trespasser! As he alighted, a little figure, which had been stooping over a flower-bed, raised itself with a jerk, and he found himself face to face with a bunchy old lady, trowel in hand. She wore a short jacket made of Gordon tartan and a knitted hood with shabby brown strings.

For a moment the two surveyed one another fixedly: she, recognising that she was confronting a tall, handsome young man of six or seven-and-twenty; he, that he was gazing at a little woman, with grey hair worn in loops at either side of a flattish face which was animated by a pair of quick, suspicious eyes—round and black as those of a bird.

"There is no right-of-way through these grounds!" she announced, in a high reedy voice, something like a child's, but more authoritative; and as she opened her mouth it was apparent that she was toothless as a newborn babe.

"I'm awfully sorry," said the interloper, cap in hand, "but I'm afraid I've missed the footpath and lost my bearings. I want to get into the village."

"Well, you're in the village here," she answered tartly. "You've only to go down that avenue," pointing with her trowel; "the Drum is on the left. I suppose you are come about the fishing?"

"Thank you—no—I've nothing to do with fishing."

Once more he took off his cap. She bowed from her waist as if it was hinged, and again indicated his direction.

"The Manor?" echoed a yokel, in answer to Wynyard's question; "why," with a grin, "yer just come out o' it, mister!"

He accordingly retraced his steps down the short drive and rang at the hall door, which was at the side of the dignified old house, and over the lintel of which was the date, 1569, in deeply cut figures. A smart parlour-maid answered the clanging bell, and stared in round-eyed surprise.

"Can I see Miss Parrett?" he asked; "my name is Owen. I'm the new chauffeur."

"The chauffeur!" she repeated, with incredulous emphasis. "Oh!—If you will just step inside, I'll let her know;" and, tripping before him down a long, resounding, flagged passage—which seemingly ran the length of the house—she ushered him into a low-pitched room, with heavy oak beams, and mullioned windows facing south, overlooking the meadows he had recently crossed—a vast, spreading stretch of flat country outlined by a horizon of woods—possibly those of some great demesne.

"I'll tell Miss Parrett," said the maid, as, with a lingering look at the new arrival, she closed the door.

The chauffeur awaited an interview for some time, as it took Miss Parrett at least ten minutes to recover her amazement, and invest herself with becoming dignity. That man the chauffeur! Why, she had actually mistaken him for a gentleman; but, of course, in these socialistic days, the lower orders dressed and talked like their betters; and she registered a mental vow to keep the creature firmly in his place. The fact that she had supposed her new chauffeur to be a visitor who rented the fishing, was an error she never forgave herself—and the origin of her secret animosity to Wynyard.

The room into which he had been ushered was heavily wainscoted in oak; the chimneypiece, a most beautiful specimen of carving—but some ignorant hand had painted the whole with a sickly shade of pea-green! Various tables and chairs, which had seen better days, were scattered about; it was not a show apartment, but evidently the retreat where people did all sorts of odd jobs. A coil of picture wire, curtain rings, and a pile of chintz patterns, were heaped on the round centre table, and a stack of wall-papers littered the floor. A snug, sunny, cheerful sort of den, which would make an A1 smoking-room. Precisely as the chauffeur arrived at this opinion, the door was flung open, and Miss Parrett ambled in.

"So *you* are my new chauffeur!" she began, in a shrill voice, as she surveyed him with an air of acrid self-assertion.

"Yes, ma'am," and Owen, as he looked at her, was conscious of a nascent antagonism.

"Your name, I understand, is Owen. What's your christian name?"

He coloured violently. What *was* his christian name?

"St. John," he answered, after a momentary hesitation. (It was his second name.) "That is—I mean to say—John."

"St. John, what affectation! Of course it's John—plain John. I've engaged you on the recommendation of my friend, Lady Kesters. She says you are steady, efficient, and strictly *sober*," looking him up and down; "she mentioned you were smart—I suppose she meant your clothes, eh?"

Wynyard made no reply, but kept his gaze fixed steadily on a crack in the floor, and the old woman continued—

"Of course Lady Kesters knows you personally?"

"Yes, ma'am."

"I hope I shall find you satisfactory and experienced."

"I hope so, ma'am."

"And not above your place—ahem!"—clearing her throat—"I have recently purchased a most beautiful motor, and I engaged you to drive it, and take great care of it; it is lined with real morocco leather, and cost, second-hand, five hundred pounds." As she paused for a moment to see if he was properly impressed, he repeated his parrot's cry of—

"Yes, ma'am."

"My sister and I propose to use it for paying calls at a distance. You must drive *very* slowly and carefully, and keep the car in perfect order, and spotlessly clean."

"I'll do my best, ma'am," he assented.

"Your wages will be, from to-day, two guineas a week. You will live in the village. We have arranged for you to board with a most respectable woman, and trust you will give her as little trouble as possible, and we shall expect to see you in church at least once on Sunday. You may join the Young Men's Christian Association, and the choir—and——"

But here he interrupted.

"Excuse me, ma'am, but I don't think there's anything about church attendance and singing in our agreement. Sunday, I presume, will be my day off, and I shall be glad of some exercise."

"You never mean to tell me you don't go to church?" she demanded, fixing him with her little beady eyes; "as to exercise, you will get plenty of that in the week—doing odd jobs and going messages. We are only here about six months, and not nearly settled yet."

"I," he was about to add, "go to church when I please;" but at this critical moment the door again opened, and another lady, much younger than his inquisitor, entered briskly. She had a long thin face, a kindly expression, and a pair of bright blue eyes which opened to their widest extent as she looked at Wynyard.

"I heard our new chauffeur had come," she began, rather breathlessly.

"*My* chauffeur, Susan, if you please," corrected Miss Parrett, "seeing that I am paying his wages and he is to drive *my* car."

Miss Susan coloured faintly, and answered with a nervous laugh—

"Yes, yes, dear, of course—of course."

"His name is Owen—John Owen—and I have been telling him of his duties, and how we only require to be driven about the country *quietly*—no dashing, no racing, no touring."

"Yes, my dear sister, that is all very well for you who are nervous; but I do love motoring, and I hope this young man will take me for miles, and let me see something of the country. I wish you would come with us, Bella, won't you?"

"I don't require you to invite me to use my *own* car, Susan," rejoined Bella, with crushing dignity. Wynyard gathered that an increase of riches had not been to the moral advantage of Miss Parrett, and felt sorry for her snubbed relation; but Susan, a valiant soul, took what the gods had given her or withheld, with extraordinary philosophy, was never offended, envious, or out of temper, and recovered from these humiliations with the elasticity of an indiarubber ball.

"You left London early?" said Miss Parrett, turning to him.

"Yes, ma'am, at nine o'clock."

Susan started at the sound of his voice; he spoke like a gentleman!

"Then, no doubt you are ready for something to eat? Susan, you may take the young man down the village and introduce him to Mrs. Hogben, and, on the way, you can show him the motor." Then, to Wynyard, "And as you find it, I shall expect you to *keep* it. I will give you further orders in the morning." Then, in the voice of a person speaking to a child: "Now, go with Miss Susan. You won't be long?" she added, addressing her sister; "there are those letters to be answered."

"No; but anyway I must run up to the Rectory. I've just had a note from Aurea; she came home last night."

CHAPTER VII
MRS. HOGBEN AT HOME

Miss Susan preceded Owen, and as he stalked along the great flagged passage, he noted her trim, light figure, quantity of well-dressed, grizzled hair, and brisk, tripping walk, and he made up his mind—although they had not as yet exchanged a word—that he liked her immeasurably the better of the sisters! How *could* Leila say they were "dear old things!" Miss Parrett was neither more or less than an ill-bred, purse-proud little bully. On their way out he caught sight, through open doors, of other rooms with mullioned windows, and more vague efforts at refurnishing and embellishment.

"We are not long here," explained Miss Susan, reaching for her hat off a peg, and they crossed a vestibule opening into a huge enclosed yard, "though we lived here as children; it's only lately we have come back to our own—or rather my sister's own," she corrected, with a little nervous laugh. "The Manor has been occupied by a farmer for twenty-five years, and was really in a dreadful state of neglect: the roof and upper floors dropping to pieces, and everything that should have been painted was neglected, and everything that should not have been painted, *was* painted."

In the yard a small black spaniel, who was chained to his kennel, exhibited convulsions of joy on beholding Miss Susan. As she stooped to unfasten the prisoner, he instantly rushed at Wynyard, but after a critical examination received him with civility.

"You are highly favoured," remarked the lady; "Joss, although a nobody himself, is most particular as to who he knows. He means to know you."

"I'm glad of that—I like dogs. What breed is he?"

"That is a question we are so often asked. His mother is a prize poodle, his father a small black spaniel. We have never quite decided what we shall bring him up as, sometimes we think we'll clip him and pass him off as a poodle."

"Oh, he is much more of a spaniel—look at his ears and tail," objected the new chauffeur. "Of course he *is* a bit too leggy."

"Yes; I'm afraid poor Joss's appearance is against him, but his heart is in the right place."

"Dogs' hearts always are."

"Joss is so sporting, if he only had a chance," continued Miss Susan. "He swims like a fish and is crazy after water-fowl—that is the spaniel side. The poodle blood makes him clever, sly, inquisitive, and as mischievous as a monkey."

"Is he your dog, miss?"

"No, he belongs to my sister, though she does not care for animals; but she says a dog about the place makes a topic of conversation for callers. We country folk are often hard up; the weather and gardens are our chief subjects. Joss is a capital watch—though I hate to see him chained here day after day. I believe a young dog requires liberty—yes, and amusement—as much as a human being." She glanced at Owen. "You will think me silly!"

"No, miss, I'm entirely of your opinion."

"And poor Joss leads such a dull life; there are no young people to take him out, and no dogs of his own class in the village, and now"—as she began to draw the bolts of a coach-house door, but Owen came forward—"here is the motor;" and, taking a long breath, she ejaculated, "There!"

There indeed was the car, newly painted, and dark green, as described. It was a closed motor brougham to hold four. Owen examined it critically, and with the eye of an expert. Within the last few days he had become rather wise respecting cars. This was an old-fashioned machine, which had seen a great deal of hard wear, and would not stand much rough usage—no, nor many long journeys.

"*Isn't* it nice?" said Miss Susan, "and do look at all the lovely pockets inside," opening the door as she spoke.

"Yes; but I don't see any Stepney wheel," he said.

"Why, it has four—what more do you want?"

To which he replied by another question:

"Where did Miss Parrett get hold of it?"

"Oh, she bought it through an advertisement from a gentleman who had ordered a larger car, and as he didn't want two—indeed, he made rather a favour of selling it—he parted with this one, a bargain."

"Oh—a bargain!" he repeated helplessly.

"Well, I suppose it *was* cheap for five hundred?"

Wynyard made no reply; in his opinion the machine would have been dear at fifty. It was evident that some unscrupulous rascal had foisted an old-fashioned rattle-trap upon these ignorant and unsuspicious ladies.

"My sister is so nervous," exclaimed Miss Susan, "and I don't think she will use the car as much as she supposes. Even in a cab she sits all the time with her eyes closed and her hands clenched. She would never have purchased the motor, only our brother-in-law, the parson here—who is rather a wag in his way—chaffed her, and, just to contradict him, she bought one within a week!"

Miss Susan was evidently a talker, and Wynyard listened in civil silence as, chattering incessantly, she accompanied him down the drive and out into the village street.

"Now I am going to take you to your lodgings, where I hope you will be comfortable," and she looked at him with a kindly little smile. "There is where we lived for thirty years," pointing to a pretty old red cottage, with a paved walk through a charming garden—at present gay with daffodils and crocus.

"Do you know I planted every one of those bulbs myself," she said; "I'm a great gardener—my sister only potters. The gardens at the Manor have run to seed like the house, and it will take a long time to put them straight. After we left it, on my father's death, the tenant was a farmer, and only lately my sister has bought it back. A relative we never saw left Bella all his fortune, and money comes just a *little* strange to her at first. We have always been poor—and so sometimes she—is——"

Miss Susan faltered, blushed, and came to a full stop; she felt conscious that she was forgetting herself, and talking to this stranger—a man-servant—as if he were her equal! Her tongue always ran away with her; unfortunately, she could not help it, and it was absolutely true, as Bella repeatedly told her, "she was *much* too familiar with the lower orders!"

"Ahem! I dare say you will find Ottinge dull after London. Do you know London?" she inquired, after a conscious silence.

"Yes, miss, I know it well."

"There's no one much of your stamp in the village; they are all Ottinge born and bred, and you seem to be a superior sort of young man."

"I don't think I'm at all superior, miss; anyway, I've got to earn my bread the same as other people."

"Here we are at Mrs. Hogben's," she announced, and, opening a gate, walked up the flagged path leading to an old two-storeyed cottage, and a broadly built, elderly woman, with a keen, eager face and a blue checked apron, came to meet them, hastily wiping her wet hands.

"Here is your lodger, Mrs. Hogben; his name is Owen," explained Miss Susan; and Mrs. Hogben's astonishment was so complete that she so far forgot herself as to drop him half a curtsey. "You have given him the top back-room, I understand?" continued Miss Susan, "and, *remember*, it's not to be more than half-a-crown a week; he will arrange about his board himself."

"Yes, Miss Susan; to be sure, Miss Susan."

"And you will do his washing moderately, and cook, and make him comfortable, won't you?"

"Of course, Miss Susan."

"I don't suppose you will eat meat more than once a day," turning to him, "eh?"

"I can't say, miss," he answered, with a slow smile, "a good deal would depend upon the meat."

"Well, I think you will find everything here all right. Mrs. Hogben's son, Tom, is one of our gardeners, and you can come up in the morning with him. Good-evening to you!" Wynyard touched his cap, and she hurried off. He stood and watched her for a moment, the slim, straight-backed figure tripping up the village towards the tall grey church, which dominated the place.

Meanwhile, Mrs. Hogben had looked him over from head to foot; her sharp, appraising eyes, rested with satisfaction on her lodger; taken, womanlike, by a handsome face, she said in a pleasant voice—

"So you're the shover! My word, it do seem main funny, them ladies a-settin' up of a motor—and last year they hadn't as much as a wheelbarrow. Folks do say all the money—and it's a lot—has gotten to Miss Parrett's head, but she was always a terrible hard, headstrong old woman. Now, Miss Susan there is a nice friendly lady; all the place is main fond of Miss Susan."

"She seems—a good sort."

"Yes, and quite girlish still, and gay in herself, though well over fifty, and thinks nothing a trouble. You'll be takin' your meals here?"

"Yes, with your permission, Mrs. Hogben."

"We don't have many high notions of food—just plain and plenty, ye understand?"

"That will suit me all right."

"I'll give you your victuals in the little parlour," and she opened the door into a small gloomy room, with dead geraniums in the window, a round table in the middle, a horse-hair sofa against the wall, and shells upon the mantelpiece. Evidently the apartment was rarely used; it smelt intolerably of musty hay, and was cold as a vault.

"I think, if it's all the same to you, I'll take my meals in the kitchen."

"All right," she assented, "there's only me and Tom. Now come away up, and I'll show you your room."

The stairs, which climbed round a massive wooden post, were so narrow, so low, and so steep, that getting up was by no means an easy performance.

"Eh, but you're a fine big man!" declared Mrs. Hogben admiringly, "and somehow you don't seem to fit in a place of this size; it's main old too—some say as old as the Manor."

"Oh, I shall fit all right," he answered, looking about his chamber.

It was very low and scrupulously clean: the window was on a level with the bare boards, there was a wooden bed, with a patchwork quilt, a chest of drawers, a washstand, and a rush-bottomed chair.

"I shall want a bath," he announced abruptly.

"A bath! Well, I never!"

"Yes; or, if the worst comes to the worst, an old wash-tub."

"Oh," reflecting, "I do believe Mrs. Frickett at the Drum has a tin one she'd lend—no one there wants it."

"I'll carry up the water myself."

"Will you so? I suppose your box is at the house, and Tom will bring it down on the barrow. He will be in to his tea directly. Here he is," as the sound of clumping boots ascended from below.

When confronted with Tom, Wynyard found him to be a man of thirty, in rough working clothes, with one of the finest faces he had ever seen, a square forehead, clear-cut features, and a truly noble and benevolent expression. The general effect was considerably marred by the fact that Tom wore his thick brown hair several inches too long, and a fringe of whiskers framed his face and met under his chin, precisely as his father's and grandfather's had done.

"Tom, here be Miss Parrett's shover," announced his mother, "the man-servant, you know, as will bide with us. You'll take him in hand, and show him about, eh?"

A Rolling Stone | 53

"Ay, ay," agreed Tom, seating himself heavily at table; then, addressing the guest—

"It's very tricky weather?"

"Yes, it generally is in April."

Tom stared hard at the newcomer. The young man used grand words, had a strong look in his face, was well set-up—and clean-shaved of a Wednesday!

"Yer from London, eh? One can see that. Ye must be as hungry as a dog." With an impulse of hospitality, he pushed the loaf towards him, and subsequently experienced a sense of relief and pleasure as he noticed the new chap's hands, the hands of a working man!

The meal consisted of home-made bread, boiled eggs, cold bacon, and tea. The two hungry men made considerable ravages on bread and bacon, and no attempts at conversation. Meanwhile, Mrs. Hogben's sharp eyes and wits were still engaged in taking stock of the newcomer. He did not say much, but when he did speak, it was the pure talk of gentry-folk; yet, he was not uppish, his coat was well worn, and he spoke quite humble-like to Miss Susan.

After a short silence, Mrs. Hogben—a notable gossip—undertook the talking for all three.

"Of course it was Miss Parrett herself as come here about a room for you, Mr. Owen, and says she to me, 'I want you to take a respectable young man on reasonable terms; of course I can't have him at the Manor, on account of the maids.'"

"Why not?" inquired her lodger, with his mouth full.

"'Cause," with a laugh, "she thought you might be making love to them, I expect! And says she, 'Mrs. Hogben, you having no daughters, and no young woman in the house, it will be quite safe.'"

"Oh, I see," he assented, with an amused smile.

"Though for that matter," and she nodded at Tom, "I'm going to have a daughter-in-law one of these days."

Tom buried his face in a mug and spluttered.

"Ay, it's Dilly Topham, and a main pretty girl too; but Tom will mind *her*."

"Miss Parrett is terrible strict," said Tom, recovering his self-possession, "and this do be a model village"; and he winked at Wynyard.

"I'm none so sure!" objected his mother; "there's a good lot of beer and quarrelling at the Drum, especially of a Saturday night; and there was Katie Punnett—well—well—I say no more."

"Oh, the girls are all right, mother."

"Some on 'em; of course that's Missie's doing—she's so friendly with 'em, so nice and so gay; but a good few of the Ottinge girls is of no account. There's Mrs. Watkins with three big young women on her hands; they won't stay in service at no price, and they won't do a turn at home. Their mother holds the house together, and has them, as well as her man, to work for, poor soul!"

"Oh, Watkins, he does 'is share as carrier," protested Tom.

"I don't know what *you* call a share, Tom," said his mother sharply. "I know of a cold winter's morning she gets up and milks the cows, and takes the milk round herself, and comes back, and there's not a fire lit, and them four lazy sacks are all still abed—ay, and asleep. I've gone in of an afternoon, too, and seen Maudie and Brenda stretched on their backs a-reading penny novels—it's all they care for, that and dress, and young men; if I was their mother I'd let out at them!" and she paused for breath. "*I* never had no schoolin', and I'm not sorry; laziness and light readin' is the plague."

"Well, Watkins—he don't read overmuch."

"No, but he smokes and drinks, and is main idle. You know yourself I offered him the good grass off the orchard for the cutting, for his horse— lovely grass it were, too—but it were too much trouble, and he grazes the poor beast along the road in every one's way instead. And there's Jake Roberts—his father left him a fine business as wheelwright and carpenter, and he has let it all go over to Shrapton-le-Steeple 'cause it was too much fag, and he lives on his wife's washing."

"Ye see how my mother is down on Ottinge," said Tom, with another wink, "not being an Ottinge woman herself."

"No, thank the Lord! I'm from another part, and all for work. But I'll say this—that Ottinge is the healthiest spot ye ever put yer foot in. We gets the free air for miles over the pastures, and at the back we're in shelter from the hills between us and Brodfield—that's the big town ten miles off."

"So you have no doctor?" said Wynyard.

"Indeed we have, and a good doctor too; there is not much call for him or for medicines. Ottinge isn't as big as it looks; though so rambling and showy, it's real small."

"Are there many gentry around?" inquired the stranger.

"There's the parson, Mr. Morven—his lady is dead. She wur a Parrett, and handsome. He's a good man, but terrible bookish, and just awful for readin' and writin'. There's Captain and the Honourable Mrs. Ramsay, as live nearly opposite in the house covered with ivy, and three rows of long windows, inside the little brick wall. *They* are not much use; she sells plants and cuttings, and little Pom puppies now and then, and keeps what she calls a 'Dogs' Hotel or Boarding-House'; did ye ever!" and Mrs. Hogben laughed. "Ay, and she advertises it too! She's so terrible busy with dogs, and takes them walking out, and has all sorts o' food for them, and young Bob Watkins as their servant. Her father was a lord they make out, and her husband, the Captain, he got some sort of stroke in the Indies and is queer— some say from drink, some say from a stroke, some say from both. He never goes into no company, but walks the roads and lanes of an evening a-talkin' to himself right out loud. Then he slopes up to the Drum, and though he was an army officer, he sits cheek by jowl with common men, drinkin' his glass, and smokin' his pipe. However, he is quiet enough—quiet as the dead—and Mrs. Ramsay is good pay."

"That's something," remarked her listener, and his tone was dry.

"There's a rare bit o' money in Ottinge, though ye mightn't think it," continued Mrs. Hogben, delighted to have a listener after her own heart; "folks being well left, and mostly having a snug house, and nothing going out but quit rent."

"But who lives round the village? Are there any big places?"

"There's a good few within ten miles. The Wardes of Braske, the Cranmers of Wells Castle, the Woolcocks of Westmere Park—it was the Davenants' for hundreds of years, and Woolcocks' father he was an iron-monger!"

"An ironmaster," corrected her son, with a touch of impatience.

"Well, 'tis all the same. The Davenants were real great folk, and the Hogbens served them for many a day; indeed, the late Sir Henry Davenant shot Hogben's father himself." She folded her arms as she made the announcement, and looked at her lodger as much as to say, "What do you think of *that*?"

"Shot! What do you mean—on purpose?"

"No, 'twas a pheasant he was mistook for—but he killed Tom Hogben stone dead in the top cover, and then sent a carriage to fetch him home. Of course the shooting was given accidental, and the family had a pension; and I will say this, the Davenants were always free and never a mite afraid of spending money, till every stiver was gone."

"What you call open-handed."

"Yes, and the last of the gentlemen, when the place was ate up of a mortgage, lived in a bit of a cottage by the roadside, and was just as proud and grand as if he had forty servants. This Ottinge is a mighty queer quarrelling sort o' place, as you will soon see for yourself. Last year a parson come, when Mr. Morven was in Switzerland with the General—a very gay, pleasant young man, a-visitin' everywhere, and talkin' to every one, and amusin' the parish, and gettin' up cricket, and concerts, so when he left they gathered up to make him a present, and bought him a lovely clock (as he preferred to a bit of a ink-bottle); but it just shows up Ottinge! there was so much wicked jealousy and ill-feelin' that there was no one to *give* it to him— you see, one wouldn't let the other!—and he'd never have got it at all, only, at the last, they stuck in a child—a little girl, as no one wanted to get the better of—and so that settled it, but it may give ye *some* idea of the place."

"Ye see my mother hasn't a good word for it," put in Tom; "but I'm Ottinge, and was born here."

"As to the gentlefolk," continued Mrs. Hogben almost as glibly as if she were reading aloud, "there's the doctor and his wife. She is gayish, and great at theatricals and games—no harm, though. Ay, 'tis a dull place for young folk, and only fit for some to come and end their days. There's the Woolcocks of Westmere Park—terrible rich—they bought the Park when the Davenants were broke, as I tell'd ye. They keep a crowd of servants, and three motors. There's mister and missus, and a son and two daughters—one of them's married. They give a fair lot of employment too—but still, folks 'ud rayther have the old fam'ly."

"My mother goes round telling of folk here and there, and she's left out the one that matters *most*, that starts everything in the village, and is the prettiest girl—bar one—in ten parishes—and that's Miss Aurea!"

"Why, Miss Aurea, of course, she's not to be overlooked," said Mrs. Hogben, "not nowhere—Miss Parrett's niece, and the parson's daughter; but she's not here now, she's a-stoppin' up in London with her father's brother the General—often she does be there—the only child to go round in three families."

Wynyard said to himself that he was actually better posted up in village gossip than Mrs. Hogben; she did not know, as *he* did, that Miss Aurea had returned home!

"She manages her aunt wonderful, that she do; indeed, she manages most things."

"She's awful taken up with settling the Manor House and the garden," added Tom; "she has a lucky hand, and a real love for flowers."

"Ay, and folk do say that Woolcock of Westmere, the only son, has a real love for *her*," supplemented Mrs. Hogben, as she rose and pushed back her chair; "it would be a sensible thing to wed old family to good money."

The newcomer rose also, picked up his cap, and walked to the open door. He had heard the latest news of Ottinge-in-the-Marsh, and now he intended to have a look round the village itself.

"I believe I'll take a bit of a stroll and smoke a pipe," he said, as he put on his cap and went out.

"What do you think of the new lodger, Tom?" asked his mother, as she noisily collected plates and cups.

"I think—it's hard to say yet; but I likes him. He's not our sort, though."

"Why not? He's had a good eddication, that's sure, and talks up in his head like gentry, but his hands is just the hands of a working man; and look at his box—that's no class!"

In the opinion of Mrs. Hogben the box settled the question, and she went off into the scullery and closed the door with a slam of finality.

CHAPTER VIII
OTTINGE-IN-THE-MARSH

Wynyard strolled out into the little front garden along the red brick path to the wooden gate; as he closed this, he observed that it bore in large characters the enticing name of "Holiday Cottage." He smiled rather grimly as he looked back at his new residence, a wood and plaster construction, bowed in the upper storey, with small, insignificant windows. Then he glanced up and down the empty thoroughfare, and was struck by the deathlike silence of the place. What had become of the residents of Ottinge? A flock of soiled, white ducks waddling home in single file from the marshes, and a wall-eyed sheep-dog, were the only live objects in sight.

Ottinge was undeniably ancient and picturesque, a rare field for an artist; the houses were detached—no two alike—and appeared to have been built without the smallest attempt at regularity. Some stood sideways at right angles; others had turned their backs upon the street, and overlooked the fields; many were timbered; several were entirely composed of black boarding; one or two were yellow; but the majority were of rusty brick, with tiled and moss-grown roofs. Wynyard noticed the ivy-clad house or "dogs'" hotel, with its three rows of long, prim windows, and close by another of the same class, with a heavy yew porch that recalled a great moustache. On its neat green gate was affixed a brass plate and the inscription—D. Boas, M.D. Farther on at intervals were more houses and a few scattered shops; these looked as if they were anxious to conceal their identity, and only suffered a limited display of their wares. Chief among them was one double-fronted, with tins of pressed beef and oatmeal on view, and above the door the worthy signboard—T. Hoad, Grocer. "Quality is my Watchword." Next came John Death, Butcher, with a wide window, over which an awning had been discreetly lowered.

Almost every house had its front garden, with a brick wall or palings between it and the road. One, with a flagged path, an arbour, and a bald, white face, exhibited a square board close under the eaves, on which was briefly inscribed the seductive invitation, "Tea." An adjoining neighbour, with absolutely bare surroundings, had affixed to his porch the notice, "Cut

Flowers"; and, from the two advertisements, it was evident that the all-penetrating motor had discovered the existence of Ottinge-in-the-Marsh!

The next object of note—and in daring proximity to the church—was the Drum Inn; an undoubtedly ancient black-and-white building, with dormer windows, an overhanging top storey, and stack of imposing chimneys. It was strikingly picturesque without (if cramped and uncomfortable within), and stood forth prominently into the street considerably in advance of its neighbours, as if to claim most particular attention; it was a fact that the Drum had been frequently sketched, and was also the subject of a (locally) popular postcard.

The tall church, grey and dignified, was a fitting conclusion to this old-world hamlet; parts of it were said to date from the seventh century. Splendid elms and oaks of unknown age sheltered the stately edifice, and close by, the last house in Ottinge, was the dignified Queen Anne rectory. Surrounded by shaven lawns and an imposing extent of garden walls, it had an appearance of mellow age, high breeding, and prosperity. The sitting-room windows stood open, the curtains were not yet drawn, and Wynyard, noticing one or two flitting figures, permitted his mind to wonder if one of these was Miss Aurea, who, so to speak, ran the village, ruled the Manor, and was, according to Thomas Hogben, the prettiest girl—bar one—in ten parishes?

Pipe in mouth, the explorer wandered along for some distance, and presently came to a farmhouse, encircled by enormous black barns and timbered outhouses, with thatched, sloping roofs; but there was no smoke from the farm chimney, no sound from stables or byre; the yard was covered with grass, the very duck-pond was dry. A former tenant and his family, finding the old world too strong for them, had fled to Canada many years previously, and ever since Claringbold's farm had remained empty and desolate. In autumn, the village urchins pillaged the orchard; in winter, wandering tramps encamped in the outhouses. Never again would there be a sound of lowing cows, the humming of threshing gear, the shouts of carters encouraging their horses, or children's voices calling to their dogs.

The newcomer leant his arms upon the gate and surveyed the low, flat country with its distant, dark horizon. Then he turned to contemplate the hills behind the church, dotted with sheep and lambs and scored with lanes; he must learn his bearings in this new locality, as behoved his duty as chauffeur. He had now inspected Ottinge from end to end, from the low-lying grey Manor, projecting into its fields, to the Queen Anne rectory, a picture of mellowed peace.

So here he was to live, no matter what befell. He wondered what would befall, and what the next year held in store for him? For nearly an hour he remained leaning on the stout old gate, giving his thoughts a free rein, and making stern resolutions. Somehow he did not feel drawn to his billet, nor yet to Miss Parrett, but he resolved that he would play the game, and not disappoint Leila. She had, as usual, taken her own line; but had he chosen his fate he would have preferred a rough-and-tumble town life, active employment in some big garage, and to be thrown among men, and not a pack of old women! However, in a town he might be spotted by his friends; here, in this dead-and-alive village, his position was unassailable, and possibly Leila was right — it was her normal attitude.

At last he recognised that the soft April night had fallen, bats were flitting by, the marsh frogs' concert had commenced — it was time to go back to Holiday Cottage, and turn in, for no doubt the Hogbens were early birds.

The ceiling of his room was so low that he hit his head violently against a beam, and uttered an angry swear word.

The place, which held an atmosphere of yellow soap and dry rot, was palsied with age; a sloping, creaking floor shook ominously under his tread; if it collapsed, and he were precipitated into the kitchen, what an ignominious ending!

In a short time Mrs. Hogben's new lodger had stretched himself upon his narrow, lumpy bed, and, being tired, soon fell asleep, and slept like the proverbial log, until he was awoke by daylight streaming in at the window, and the sound of some one labouring vigorously at the pump. He looked at his watch — seven o'clock — he must rise at once and dress, and see what another day had in store for him.

CHAPTER IX
THE NEW CHAUFFEUR

As the new arrival wandered up the street, and inspected the village, he had been under the impression that the place was deserted—he scarcely saw a soul; but this was the way of Ottinge folk, they spent most of their time (especially of an evening) indoors, and though he was not aware of it, Ottinge had inspected him! Girls sewing in windows, men lounging in the Drum, women shutting up their fowl, all had noted the stranger, and wondered who this fine, tall young gentleman might be? An hour later they were amazed to learn that he was no more and no less than the Parretts' new chauffeur, who was lodging with Sally Hogben—Sally, who could talk faster and tell more about a person in five minutes than another in twenty. This intelligence—which spread as water in a sponge—created a profound sensation, and shared the local interest with the news of the sudden death of Farmer Dunk's best cow.

The following morning it was the turn of the chauffeur to be surprised. When he repaired to the Manor, to report himself and ask for orders, he encountered Miss Parrett herself in the hall, who informed him, in her shrillest bleat, that as she did not propose to use the car that day, and as there was nothing else for him to do, he could put in his time by cleaning windows. When Wynyard heard Miss Parrett's order, his face hardened, the colour mounted to his forehead, and he was on the point of saying that he had been engaged as chauffeur, and not as charwoman; but a sharp mental whisper arrested the words on his lips:

"Are you going to throw up your situation within twenty-four hours, and be back on Leila's hands after all the trouble she has taken for you?" demanded this peremptory voice. "You must begin at the bottom of the ladder if you want to get to the top. Let this old woman have her own way, and bully you—and if you take things quietly, and as they come, your affairs will mend."

After what seemed to Miss Parrett a most disrespectful silence, during which she glared at Owen with her little burning eyes, and mumbled with her toothless jaws, he said slowly—

"All right, ma'am. I've never cleaned windows yet, but I'll do my best; perhaps you will give me something to clean them with?"

"Go through that door and you will find the kitchen," said Miss Parrett. "The cook will give you cloths, soap, and a bucket of water. You may begin in the dining-room;" and pointing towards the servants' quarters, she left him. As he disappeared, Susan, who had overheard the last sentence, boldly remonstrated —

"Really, Bella, that young man is not supposed to undertake such jobs! He was only engaged as chauffeur, and I'm sure if you set him to do housework, he will leave."

"Let him, and mind your own business, Susan," snapped her sister. "He is in *my* employment, and I cannot afford to pay him two guineas a week — six shillings a day — for doing nothing. I am not a millionaire! As it is, my hand is never out of my pocket."

"But you engaged him to drive the car, and if you are afraid to go out in it, is that his fault?" argued Susan, with surprising courage.

"Who says I'm afraid?" demanded Miss Parrett furiously. "Susan, you forget yourself. I shall have the car to-morrow, and motor over to call on the Woolcocks."

Meanwhile Owen passed into the back premises, which were old and spacious. Here, in a vast kitchen overlooking a great paved yard, he found a tall woman engaged in violently raking out the range. She started as he entered, and turned a handsome, ill-tempered face upon him.

"Can you let me have some cloths and a bucket of hot water?" he asked in his clear, well-bred voice.

"Yes, sir," she answered, going to a drawer. "What sort of cloths — flannels or rubbers?"

"Something for cleaning windows."

"Oh, laws, so you're the new chauffeur! Well, I never!" And, leaving the drawer open, she turned abruptly, leant her back to the dresser, and surveyed him exhaustively.

He nodded.

"And so that's the sort of work the old devil has set you to? Lady Kesters engaged me for this place, and by all accounts she did the same kindness by you and me! I understood as this was a proper establishment, with a regular housekeeper and *men* — a butler at least and a couple of footmen; there isn't as much as a page-boy. It's a swindle! I suppose you take your meals with us?" (Here, with an animated gesture, she dismissed an inquisitive kitchen-maid.)

"No; I board myself."

Her face fell. This good-looking chauffeur would be some one to flirt with, and her voice took a yet sharper key.

"You're from London, I can see, and so am I. Lord! this is a change"—now casting herself into a chair. "Ye see, I was ordered country air, and so I came—the wages being fair, and assistance given; and thinking we were in a park, I brought my bicycle, and expecting there'd be some society, I brought a couple of ball-gowns, and find this!" and her expression was tragic.

"Have you been here long?" he asked civilly.

"Two weeks too long. I give notice next day, and am going at the month, and you won't be long after me, *I* bet! Do you bike?"

"No," he answered rather shortly.

"Well, anyway, you've the use of your legs! To-morrow is my evening out, so you come round here at five, and I'll give you a nice cup o' tea, and we'll go for a stroll together. We *ought* to be friendly, seeing as we both come from Lady Kesters' recommendation."

To walk out with the cook! This was ten times worse than window-cleaning! Wynyard was beating his brain for some civil excuse when Miss Parrett herself appeared in the doorway—an accusing and alarming figure.

"This is a nice way you waste my time!" she exclaimed, with an angry glance at both. "You and cook gossiping together and idling. Where are the cloths and the hot water, young man?"

The cook, grumbling audibly and insolently, went back to the dresser, and Miss Parrett, with folded arms, waited dramatically in the kitchen till Wynyard was provided for. He then walked off with a brief "Thank you" to his fellow-culprit. As he passed along the flagged passage he caught Miss Parrett's shrill voice saying—

"Now, I'll not have you flirting with that young man, so I warn you! I'll have no carryings-on in *my* house."

Then a door was slammed with thunderous violence, and there was silence.

No, by Jove, he could not stand it, he said to himself as he set down his bucket, and wrung out a cloth; like the cook, he, too, would depart, and in his next situation stipulate for no women. Of course Leila would be disappointed, and he was sorry; but Leila would never ask him to put up with *this*! He would give a week's notice and advertise; he had enough money to keep him going for a while, and his certificate.

Presently he set to work on the dining-room, where there were three old casemented, mullioned windows; to clean these he stood on the lawn, and had begun his job when Miss Susan entered, smiling and radiating good humour.

"I dare say you don't know much about this sort of work," she began apologetically, "and I'll just show you! You have to use lots of clean water, and stand outside on the lawn—no fear of breaking your neck." Then in another tone she added, "I'll see you are not asked to do this again; at present we are rather short-handed, but by and by everything will go smoothly." She was about to add something more, when her sister put her head in at the door, and called out—

"Now, do come away, Susan, and don't stand gossiping with the young man, and idling him at his work. He has wasted half an hour with the cook already!"

Wynyard, as he rubbed away at the panes, whistled gaily whilst his mind dwelt on many matters, amongst others of how strange that he should be down in this queer, God-forsaken village, living in a labourer's cottage, and employed in cleaning windows! Well, he had Miss Susan's word for it that he would not be asked to do it again; she was a good sort, with a nice, cheery face, and such a pair of twinkling blue eyes. Then he thought of the tragic cook, also sent by Leila, and he laughed aloud. The house wanted a lot of servants, and as far as he could gather the staff was short-handed; probably Miss Aurea would see to all this, since she managed every one in Ottinge, did as she liked, and was the prettiest girl within ten parishes!

Wynyard was a handy man, and got through his work rapidly and well. He fetched many cans of water, and presently moved on to the drawing-room—another low room with heavily beamed ceiling and a polished oak floor. The apartment was without carpet or curtains, and scantily furnished with various old chairs, settees and cabinets, ranged against the wall. He was sitting outside on the sill, whistling under his breath, polishing his last casement, when he heard, through the half-open door, a clear young voice talking with animation, and a girl came into the room laughing—followed by an Aberdeen terrier on a leash. As she advanced, he noticed that she had wild rose colouring, wavy dark hair, merry dark eyes, and an expression of radiant vitality. Tom was right! Here, no doubt, was Miss Aurea, the prettiest girl in ten parishes!

As Wynyard looked again at this arresting vision something strange seemed to stir in his heart and come to life. First impressions have a value distinct from the settled judgment of long experience.

"What a floor, Susie!" exclaimed the young lady. "Really, we must get Aunt Bella to give a dance;" and as she spoke she began to hum the "Merry Widow Waltz," and to execute some remarkably neat steps, accompanied by the terrier, who struggled round in her wake, barking indignantly.

"Mackenzie, you *are* an odious partner!" addressing the animal; then to her aunt, "I've brought him on the chain, and he has me on the chain; he is so strong! We have accosted and insulted every single village dog, and frightened Mrs. Watkins' cats into hysterics! However, he can't get loose and murder poor gentlemanly Joss! Oh, we little knew *what* we were doing when we accepted Mac as a darling puppy!"

"I must confess that I never care for these aggressive, stiff-necked Aberdeens, and I don't pretend to like Mac. To tell you the honest truth, I'm mortally afraid of him!"

"But he must be exercised, Susan. And now we must exercise ourselves, and begin on this room. I've sent over the curtains, and they are ready to go up."

Suddenly she noticed the stranger, who was polishing a distant window. "Why, I thought it was Hogben!" she muttered. "Who is it, Susie?" and she looked over at Wynyard with an air of puzzled interest.

"The new chauffeur, my dear," was the triumphant response. "He only came yesterday; his name is Owen."

"Oh!" exclaimed the girl, turning her back to the window and speaking in a low voice. "And didn't he *object*?"

"No; but I fancy he doesn't like it. He seems a nice civil young fellow. Lady Kesters found him for us."

"Did she? I sincerely hope he is a better find than the cook. What a fury! Even Aunt Bella is afraid of her!"

"She has a splendid character from her late mistress."

"I dare say, in order to pass her on at any price. She's a first-rate cook, but a regular demon."

"My dear, they all have tempers—it's the fire, poor things. Now, about the chauffeur——"

At this moment the object of her conversation threw up the sash and stepped into the room—a fine figure in his clean blue shirt, turned up to the elbows, well-cut breeches, and neat leather leggings.

"I've finished this room, miss," he said, addressing himself to Miss Susan. "What am I to do next?" and his eyes rested upon her with respectful inquiry.

"No more windows to-day, thank you, Owen. I expect it is nearly your dinner-hour."

"Shall you require the car this afternoon, miss?"

"No; but it will certainly be wanted to-morrow,—eh, Aurea?"

"Then I'd better take her out and give her a turn;" and with this remark he picked up his bucket and rags, and walked out of the room.

During this brief conversation, Aurea stood by listening with all her ears, and making mental notes. Her aunt's new chauffeur, with his clean, tanned, high-bred face, spoke like an educated man.

"My dear Susie," she inquired, "where did Lady Kesters get hold of such a superior person?"

"I'm sure I can't tell you. She said she had known his family all her life, and that they were most respectable people. Chauffeurs are supposed to be smart, and well-groomed, eh?"

Yes, but there was more than this about the late window-cleaner— something in his gait, carriage, and voice, and, unless she was greatly mistaken, the new employé was a gentleman; but with unusual prudence Aurea contrived to keep her suspicion to herself. Aloud she said—

"Well, now, let us see about the carpet! This room ought to be settled at once—pictures up, and curtains; there's no place to ask visitors into, and you've been here six months. You are lazy, Miss Susan Parrett—this *is* sleepy hollow."

"Oh, my dear child, you know perfectly well it's your Aunt Bella; and she won't make up her mind. What's done one day is taken down another. What *is* that awful row?"

"It's Mackenzie and Joss," cried Aurea, dashing towards the door. Mackenzie, at large and unnoticed, had stealthily followed the chauffeur out of the room, and stolen a march upon his deadly enemy—Miss Parrett's impudent and interloping mongrel. The result of this dramatic meeting was a scene in the hall, where Miss Parrett, mounted on a chair, looked on, uttering breathless shrieks of "Aurea! Aurea! it's all *your* fault!" whilst round and round, and to and fro, raged the infuriated animals, snarling and growling ferociously, their teeth viciously fastened in each other's flesh.

Mackenzie, the more experienced, able-bodied, and malevolent of the two, had Joss by the throat—Joss, for his part, was steadily chewing through Mackenzie's fore-leg.

Here Wynyard came to the rescue, and, though severely bitten, succeeded after some difficulty in separating the combatants; he and Miss Aurea somehow managed it between them, but he had borne the brunt of the fray, the forefront of the battle.

A good deal of personal intimacy is involved in such encounters, and by the time the panting Mackenzie was hauled away by the collar, and the furious Joss had been incarcerated in the dining-room, the new chauffeur and Miss Morven were no longer strangers.

CHAPTER X
AS HANDY MAN

The chauffeur was informed that there were no orders for the car the following morning, as "Miss Parrett was suffering from neuralgia in her face," and also—though this was not mentioned in the bulletin—a sharp pain in her temper.

Aurea, an early visitor, radiating gaiety, was on this occasion unaccompanied by Mackenzie. Mackenzie, aged six years, was the village tyrant and dictator. He also had been accustomed to consider himself a dog of two houses—the Rectory and the Red Cottage; and when the Red Cottage had moved to the Manor, and installed an animal of low degree as its pet, he was naturally filled with wrath and resentment, and on two opportunities the intruder had narrowly escaped with many deep bites, and his life!

Aurea found her Aunt Bella trotting about the premises and passages, with the knitted hood over her head, and key-basket in hand.

"Not going out to-day!" she exclaimed; "but it's lovely, Aunt Bella. The air is so deliciously soft—it would do you no end of good."

"My dear Aurea," she piped, "I know you don't allow any one in Ottinge to call their soul their own, and I must ask you to leave *me* my body, and to be the best judge of my ailments—and state of health."

"Oh, I beg your pardon, Aunt Bella; I meant no harm. Well, then, if you are not going to use the car yourself, perhaps Susan and I could take it over to Westmere? The Woolcocks have a large house-party, and Joey and her husband are there."

Miss Parrett closed her eyes tightly—a sure hoisting of the storm cone—and screwed up her little old face till it resembled an over-ripe cream cheese.

"*Really*, Aurea! I don't know what the world is coming to! How dare you propose such a thing! Take out my car for the first time without *me*! But, of course, I know I'm only a cipher in my own house!"—an almost hourly complaint.

"But do think of the chauffeur, Aunt Bella; is he to have nothing to do?" Here this crafty girl touched a sensitive nerve—a responsive key.

"Plenty for him to do; there's enough work in the house for twenty chauffeurs: unpacking the book boxes and china—never opened since your grandfather's death—staining the floors, and putting up the curtains, and laying carpets. If you and Susan *are* going to settle the drawing-room at last, he may help you. I can't spare Jones or Hogben from the garden."

"Very well, we must have some one to lift the heavy things, and stand on ladders. Where is he?"

"Outside in the hall, awaiting my orders," replied Miss Parrett, with magnificent dignity, folding her hands over what had once been a neat waist, but now measured thirty inches.

Yes, the chauffeur was in the hall, cap in hand, attended by the grateful Joss, and had overheard the foregoing conversation.

Miss Parrett came forth as she concluded her speech, and issued her commands.

"Owen, you are to help my sister and Miss Morven in settling the drawing-room. Be careful how you handle things, and don't break anything; and you may have your dinner here for to-day, with the other servants."

"Very good, ma'am," he assented.

But with respect to dinner with the servants, it was really very *bad*. He would be compelled to fence with the London cook, and keep her and her civil proposals at arm's length—no easy job!

From ten o'clock till half-past one, Wynyard spent an agreeable and busy time in the service of Miss Susan and her niece. His boast to his sister that he was "clever with his hands" was fully justified. He hung the chintz and white curtains with the skill of an upholsterer, he laid the dark blue felt on the floor, stretched it and nailed it neatly in its place, whilst Aurea stood by, and gave directions, and sometimes—such was her zeal—went down on her knees beside him, and pulled and dragged too, exertions which enabled her associate to realise the perfect curve of cheek and neck, and the faint perfume of her glorious hair!

And all this time industrious Miss Susan sewed on rings, fitted loose chintz covers, and talked incessantly. She did not appear to find the presence of the chauffeur the slightest restraint—indeed, he was so quiet and kept his personality so steadily in the background, that as aunt and niece chatted and conferred, measured and altered, they seemed to have entirely forgotten his existence, and as the old drawing-room was full of nooks, angles, and deep windows, he was not only out of mind, but also out of sight. Meanwhile, he enjoyed the rôle of audience, especially in listening to Miss Aurea! What a gay, light-hearted girl! And in her playful arguments with her aunt, he realised the delightful camaraderie that existed between them. Her chaff was so amusing that, although he was not included in the conversation, he often felt inclined to echo Miss Susan's appreciative laugh. Never had he come across any one who had attracted him so much; the more he saw of Miss Morven the more he admired her! Possibly this was because for the last twelve months he had not been brought in contact with a happy, high-spirited English girl—or was it because in this out-of-the-world village he had met his fate?

As Wynyard hung curtains, and put in screws, he stole swift glances at Miss Susan's busy helper, noticed her slim elegance, her infectious smile, and lovely face. It was a ridiculous, but absolutely true fact, that to see a really beautiful, charming, and unaffected girl, one must come to Ottinge-in-the-Marsh!

Meanwhile, as he worked in the background, he gathered up many crumbs of conversation, and scraps of family and local news. He learned that Mr. Morven's great work on *The Mithraic Heresy and Its Oriental Origin* was nearly complete, that the Manor cook had given notice, and that no one had rented the fishing.

"The Woolcocks have a houseful at Westmere," so said Miss Susan, "and their staff of servants had recently enjoyed a sensational turning out. Joey Waring and her husband are there, just back from their winter trip."

"And how is Joe?" inquired Aurea.

"Her hair is twice as fluffy, and she is louder, noisier, and talks ten times more than ever!"

"Now, Susan, you know that is impossible!"

"Yes; Kathleen declares that you can hear her laugh as you pass the park gates."

"What! a whole mile away! She must have mistaken one of the peacocks for Joey, and however loud she laughs and talks, she never says an unkind word of any one."

"No, a good, kind little soul! but I wonder Captain Waring can stand her, and her chatter does not drive him crazy."

"On the contrary, he adores her, and is enormously proud of her flow of animation and conversation. You see, he is so silent himself, Joey is his antithesis; and Joey is worshipped at home, for in a family of large, heavy, silent people, a little gabbling creature is appreciated. Tell me about Kathleen."

"Oh, Kathleen is, as usual, very busy and cheery; she has three new boarders—hungry and quarrelsome."

"And he?"

"Just as usual too, dear. You know he never can be better."

"But he may grow worse!"

"Oh, don't speak of such a thing! Think of Kathleen."

"Yes; and I think Kathleen is a saint—so brave and unselfish. Now, where shall we put the old Palairet mirrors?"

"You had better consult your Aunt Bella."

"My dear, good Susan!" (This was the style in which she addressed her relative.) "Don't you know your own sister by this time? She has been here nearly seven months, and you are not half settled yet—only bedrooms and dining-room—and I have undertaken to help you finish off in three days."

"Yes, but that's nonsense, though I must say you've worked miracles this morning—curtains, covers, carpet; but there was no question of where they had to go. As to pictures, mirrors, and cabinets, it will take your aunt a twelvemonth to decide how to place them."

"I shall decide, and place them to-day," rejoined the girl, with calm decision; "if I ask Aunt Bella, they will be tried on every wall, till our backs are broken, and then taken down after all. The round glass between the windows,"—looking about and speaking with authority—"the other over the mantelpiece, the Chinese cabinet in that niche—they are just made for one another—the Charles the First black bureau from the schoolroom just here, and the screen from her bedroom by the door."

"My dear child, you"—and she broke into a laugh—"you wouldn't *dare*!"

"Would I not? Just wait and see. The room is charming, and when it's finished Auntie B. will be enchanted! You may leave her to me. Oh," in another tone to Wynyard, who had come forward in search of some wire, "you *have* worked well. It must be your dinner-hour. We shall be ready to start again at half-past two o'clock, and then the parlour-maid will help you with the furniture."

"Very well, miss," he answered.

As Aurea walked off, followed by Miss Susan, Wynyard the imposter assured himself that Miss Morven was quicker witted than her aunts. He had noticed her expression of keen attention as he discussed a matter of a curtain pole with her relative, and it was quite possible that she already had an inkling of the truth! He must be careful and wary not to give himself away or utter a word beyond "Yes, miss," and "No, miss." He was already attending closely to the speech of Tom Hogben, and had marked the scantiness and laziness of his vocabulary; how he never said more than he could help, and used the words, "Sure-ly," and "I dunno," and "ye see," and "'ee" for "he," and "I be" for "I am," and resolved to imitate him.

The meal in the servants' hall proved an even more trying ordeal than he anticipated, and was altogether so disagreeable to the new chauffeur that, sooner than face it again, he determined to fast.

The London cook (Miss Hicks) and four maids were present, also the boot-boy—a clumsy yokel, who was in terrified attendance. Owen sat on Miss Hicks' right hand, and received all her attention, the best helpings, and daintiest morsels of a solid and satisfying meal.

She would scarcely suffer the other servants to address him, though the rosy-cheeked parlour-maid made bold and even desperate attempts. She plied him with questions, compliments, and information. For his part, he proved a disappointing guest, and did not afford Miss Hicks much satisfaction; she came to the conclusion that in spite of his fine figure and good looks the chauffeur was a dull sort of chap, and terribly backward at taking a hint. When she nudged him with her elbow, and pressed his foot under the table, there was no response—in fact, he moved a bit away! However, she laid the flattering unction to her soul that the poor fellow was *shy*. He was duly favoured with the cook's candid opinion of the place and their employers, namely, that Miss P. was an old terror, was a shocking one for running after lords and ladies, and talking grand, yet that mean and sneaking she would frighten you! She and Miss Norris, housekeeper at the Rectory, were cuts, only for the Rector; anyway, Norris never came to the Manor. Miss Susan was a lady, but a giddy old thing, so fond of gadding and amusement, and laws! what a one to talk! As for Miss Aurea——

No, he could not sit by and hear Miss Aurea dissected, and with an excuse that he wanted to have a pipe before he went back to his job, the chauffeur pushed away his unfinished cheese, and with a civil farewell took his departure.

The afternoon was a busy one: the mirrors were put up, pictures were hung, but with many incursions and interruptions from Miss Parrett. Joss, the dog, was also in and out, and seemed inclined to attach himself to Wynyard.

Miss Parrett, still hooded, sat upright in an arm-chair, offering irritating criticisms, and quarrelling vigorously as to the position of pictures and articles of furniture; the old lady was altogether extremely troublesome and argumentative, and gave double work. Thoroughly alive to the fact that her niece had good taste, she was jealous of her activities, and yet wished to see the old rooms arranged to the best advantage—as the result would redound to her personal credit.

It was an immense relief to the three harassed workers when the parlour-maid entered and announced—

"If you please, Miss Parrett, Lady Mary Cooper has called, and I've shown her into the study."

"You mean the library," corrected her mistress. "Say I'm coming;" and she trotted over to a glass, removed her hood, and called upon Aurea to arrange her cap.

"Time Lady Mary *did* call!" she grumbled. "We are here seven months."

"She has been abroad," said Susan; "and, anyway, she's not much of a visitor."

"Well, she is our own cousin, at any rate."

"Our cousin—Lady Mary!" repeated Miss Susan. "I do declare, Bella, you have a craze for cousins. Why, we scarcely know the woman!"

"Now, Susan, don't argue! She *is* our relative; her great-great-aunt married a Davenant, and I suppose you will allow that they are our kin? I have no time to explain now;" and she pattered off, abandoning the workers to their own devices.

"Your Aunt Bella is so funny about relations! People I've never heard of she will say are our own cousins."

"Yes, to the tenth generation," agreed Aurea, "if they are well born. Aunt Bella has pedigree on the brain—for myself, I think it a bore."

It was strange that Miss Parrett, who, on her mother's side, was the granddaughter of a rough Hoogly pilot, should be as haughty and exclusive as if she were an Austrian princess. In the neighbourhood it had become a well-established joke that, if any one of importance and old family was mentioned before Miss Parrett, she was almost sure to announce—

"Oh, I don't know much about them personally, but they are our cousins!"

By six o'clock the task of arranging the drawing-room was completed. Wynyard had been assisted by the rosy-cheeked maid in bringing tables, cabinets, and china from other rooms, and they really had, as Miss Susan declared, "worked like blacks."

"It *is* a dear old room!" said Aurea, surveying the apartment with unconcealed complacency. "When the bowls are filled with flowers, and we have a bridge table, and a jigsaw puzzle, we shall be perfect—old-fashioned, and in the fashion."

"Glad you think so!" said a little bleating voice in the doorway. "Lady Mary asked for you, Susan, and I told her you were out, or she'd have wanted to come poking in here. So"—looking about—"you've brought the black cabinet out of the schoolroom! Who gave you leave to do that? And"—she threw out a quivering forefinger—"the blue china bowls from the spare room, and *my* screen! You take too much upon yourself, Aurea Morven! You should have consulted me. I am tired of telling you that I will *not* be a cipher in my own house!"

Aurea coloured vividly. Did her aunt forget that the chauffeur was present? Really, Aunt Bella was too bad. She glanced at the young man, who was standing on the steps straightening a picture; apparently he was absorbed in his task, and to all appearances had not heard the recent conversation.

"Oh, I'm so sorry you don't like the room, Aunt Bella!" said Aurea, seating herself in a high old chair, crossing her neat feet, and folding her hands.

"Sorry!"—and Miss Parrett sniffed—"that's what you always say!"

"Now, my dear, please don't be so cross," she replied, unabashed; "you know, in your heart, you are delighted, and as proud of this drawing-room as a peacock with two tails."

"*Aurea!*" shrieked her aunt.

"You have been here seven months, and you've not a single place in which to receive visitors. Look, now, at Lady Mary—you had her in the musty old study—and why?"—waving an interrogative hand—"simply because for months you could not make up your mind about the arrangement of this room. All the county have called—the first calls—and carried off the first impressions. None of your lovely old things were to be seen, but waiting to be settled."

"Aurea, I will not suffer——"

"Please do let me finish, dear. Before I left, you may remember how you and I talked it all over—cabinets, china, sofas—and settled exactly where everything was to fit. I come back at the end of a month and I find nothing done; so I've made up my mind to work here for several days. I've asked the padré to spare me. This room is finished, and looks extremely nice; the next I take in hand will be the den! Now, as it's after six o'clock, I'm afraid I must be off;" and she arose, stooped down, and kissed her aunt on the forehead, adding—

"Of course I know, dear, that you are immensely obliged to me, and so you need not say anything. Good-bye—good-bye, Susie," waving her hand, and she was gone, leaving Miss Parrett in the middle of the room temporarily speechless.

"Well—up—on my word!" and she took a long breath.

"After all, Bella, Aurea has made the room perfectly charming," said Miss Susan, with unusual courage. "It's the prettiest in the whole neighbourhood; the old things never were half seen before. She sewed the curtains herself, and, until to-day, we've never had any decent place to ask visitors to sit down in."

"Oh yes, it's all very well, but if she hadn't my nice old things to work with, she couldn't have made up such a room. Yes, I'm always just—every one says my sense of justice is my strong point—and I admit that she helped; what I object to is Aurea's way—her way," she repeated, "of just doing exactly whatever she chooses, and smiling in your face. She leads the whole of Ottinge by the nose, from the parson, her father, down to Crazy Billy." And Wynyard, who was listening to this declaration, told himself that he was not surprised.

Miss Parrett was not particularly attached to her niece, although she was by no means indifferent to her fascinating personality, and a sunny face that brought light and gaiety into the house; but this wizened old woman of seventy-four grudged the girl her youth, and was animated by the natural antagonism of one who has lived, towards one who has life before her!

CHAPTER XI
THE TRIAL TRIP

At last, with considerable pomp and circumstance, after a whole week of procrastination, Miss Parrett ventured to inaugurate her motor.

She appeared in a long fur cloak and gigantic sable stole—a shapeless bundle, resembling a well-to-do bear, with a cross human face. Susan, who, after all, was but fifty, looked unusually trim and young in a neat tailor-made, and becoming toque, whilst Aurea—who had been permitted to share in the triumph—was so pretty herself, that one scarcely noticed what she wore, merely that she exercised marvellous dexterity in the matter of introducing a large black hat into the interior of the car.

The household were collected for this supreme event: the cook, scowling and scornful, three maids, Hogben, Jones the head gardener, and the boot-boy, all assembled to witness the start—even Joss was in attendance. The motor (in truth a whited sepulchre) had been recently done up, and with its good-looking driver in smart leather coat and cap, presented an imposing appearance as it sped down the drive.

Miss Parrett closed her eyes, and when it swung out of the gate with a slight lurch, she gave a loud scream, but as it glided up the street, and she noticed that all eyes were on her car (there was Mrs. Ramsay at her door, and the doctor's wife too), she became comparatively composed. At the gate of the Rectory the Rector awaited the great sight, and waved a valedictory stick; then they sped along easily, and, being now out of the village, Wynyard put on the second speed, but was instantly arrested by Miss Parrett's protesting cries.

"Tell him to stop!" she called to her sister. "Supposing we met something. There!" as they passed the local carrier's cart within three yards.

"Owen, you are not to go so fast!" commanded Susan. "Miss Parrett is nervous."

He obediently slowed down to eight miles an hour, and as the old machine joggled along, bumping and shaking, the window-glasses rattling, the chauffeur was conscious of a feeling of angry contempt, instead of the usual partiality which a driver reserves for his own car. He had heard that a driver should be in tune with his machine, but how could any sane man be in sympathy with this bone-shaker? He was confident that after a long journey, or any extra strain, the old thing would collapse and fall to pieces.

After many directions, and not one poor little adventure, they entered a long avenue leading to an imposing Tudor house with picturesque chimney-stacks, situated in a great park. This was once the family seat of the Davenants—cousins of the Wynyards; and as she saw the end of her journey, Miss Parrett's courage mounted. When the car was crawling, or, better still, at a full stop, she was extremely fond of motoring and not the least nervous.

As the visitors approached the hall door, they overtook a large and lively house-party, who were returning from the golf links to tea. They included Mr. Woolcock—a burly figure in knickerbockers, and brilliant stockings,—his vivacious married daughter, Mrs. Wade Waring, commonly known as "Joey," her husband, and half a dozen guests—altogether a smart and cheerful crowd.

After the first noisy greetings had subsided, Mrs. Waring seized upon Aurea; she, to use her own expression, "*adored* the girl." Aurea Morven was so pretty to look at, so gay, and so natural, it was a sin to have her buried in Ottinge; and she secretly designed her for her future sister-in-law. Aurea was just the wife for Bertie. He was heavy, dull, and stodgy—a complete contrast to herself, with her animated face, lively gestures, wiry figure, and ceaseless flow of chatter.

As, arm in arm, she was conducting her friend indoors, she halted for a moment to look back.

"So that's the wonderful new motor!" she exclaimed dramatically. "I say, where did you find such a tophole chauffeur? Why," she screamed, "I know him! It's *Owen*; he was a saloon steward on the *Anaconda*!" and Wynyard, seeing that he was recognised, made a virtue of necessity, and touched his cap.

"Why, Owen," hastily descending the steps as she spoke, "fancy you on dry land! So you've given up the sea, and taken to a new trade. How do you like it?"

"It's all right, thank you, ma'am," he answered, with an impassive face.

"I hope you got the beautiful white-covered umbrella I left for you?"

"Yes, thank you, ma'am."

"I was afraid the stewardess might bag it! I thought it would be useful to you in Buenos Ayres, when you were walking in the Calle Florida with your best girl!" and she surveyed him with twinkling eyes.

"Come, come, Joey!" expostulated her father; "you are blocking up the gangway, and we all want our tea. Let the man take his car round."

"But only think, dad, he was my pet steward coming home," declared his lively daughter; "on rough days he brought me chicken broth on deck, and was *so* sympathetic—just a ministering angel! Toby will tell you what a treasure he was, too. He always had a match on him, always knew the time, and the run, and was the best hand to tuck a rug round me I *ever* knew!"

Long before the conclusion of this superb eulogy, (delivered in a high-pitched voice from the steps), its subject had found a refuge in the yard.

"Isn't it extraordinary how one comes across people?" continued Joey, as she led Aurea indoors. "Fancy your chauffeur being one of the stewards on the *Anaconda*!"

"What's that you say about my chauffeur?" demanded Miss Parrett, with arrogant solemnity, who had been a disapproving witness of the recent scene. (She considered Joey Waring a shockingly fast, vulgar little person, who absorbed far too much of the general conversation and attention; but as she was the wife of a wealthy man, and the sister of a notable *parti*, she dissembled her dislike, or believed she did. But Joey was aware that the eldest "Polly" considered her a terribly inferior, frivolous sort of person.)

"I'm only saying how odd it is to find a steward turned into a chauffeur! I do hope he is experienced, dear Miss Parrett, and that he won't bring you or the car to grief. I call him quite dangerously good-looking, don't you?"

To this preposterous question Miss Parrett made no reply, merely squeezed up her eyes, tossed her head, and as she followed Mrs. Woolcock into the drawing-room her feathers were still quivering.

After tea Mrs. Waring carried Aurea off to her room to enjoy a good gossip, and to exhibit some of the treasures she had collected during her recent trip. Joey and her husband were enterprising travellers; he, a big, silent man—the opposite of his lively little wife—was also a mighty sportsman.

"Now, let me hear what you have been doing with yourself, Aurea," said the lady, after a long and animated description of her own experiences in the West Indies and Buenos Ayres. "You have been up in town, I know. Do tell me all about your love-affairs—I know they are legion. Do confide in little Joey!"

"My love-affairs!" and the girl laughed. "I have none; and if I had, Joey, you are about the worst confidante I could find. All particulars would be given out no later than at dinner to-night, and you'd put my most heart-breaking experience in such a light, that every one would be shrieking with laughter."

"Well, anyway, you are heart-whole so far, eh?"

"Yes; I think I may admit that."

"And so your Aunt Bella has set up a motor; what possessed her?" And she stared into the girl's face, with a pair of knowing, light grey eyes. "She's as nervous as a cat!"

"Aunt Bella was possessed by the spirit of contradiction. And, talking of the car, do tell me some more about the chauffeur."

"Or the waiter that was," lighting another cigarette. "He was awfully quick and civil; every one liked Owen."

"Did it strike you, Joey, that he was something above his class—er—in fact, a gentleman?" And as Aurea asked the question she coloured faintly.

"No, my dear," rejoined her friend, with decision. "I have not a scrap of imagination, or an ounce of romance in my composition. Such an idea never dawned on me. You see, Toby and I go about the world so much; although we have two big houses, we almost live in hotels, and I am accustomed to being served by men with nice voices and agreeable manners, who speak several foreign languages. *So* sorry to dispel your illusions, but Owen waited to the manner born. He may have been trained in some big house, and been a gentleman's gentleman. I fancy he is a roving character. I think some one said he had been on a ranch up-country."

Aurea looked out of the window, and was silent. Joey knew the world, and Joey, for all her free-and-easy ways and her noisy manners, was *au fond* a sensible, practical, little person.

"I dare say you are right, Joey," she remarked at last.

"Why, of course I am! I grant you that the man is rather an unusual type of chauffeur, to come down to a dull situation in a dull little village; but, for goodness' sake, don't run away with the idea that he is some swell in disguise, for he is *not*; he is just 'off the cab rank'—no more and no less. I admit his good looks, but that's nothing. One of the handsomest young men I ever saw was a London carriage groom. I give you my word, his eyelashes were half an inch long! In these days, too, there are such hideous scandals about women and their smart chauffeurs, that one cannot be too reserved or too careful."

"Joey!" cried Aurea, turning on her with a crimson face.

"Oh, I'm not thinking of you, darling; you are as cold and austere as Diana herself. I do wish you were not so icy to some one—you know who I mean."

But Aurea's expression was not encouraging, and her vivacious companion continued—

"Isn't this a darling old place?" rising and looking over the Italian gardens and sloping lawns. "Somehow I always feel sorry for those Davenants, and as if we had no business here, and it was still theirs. We have their heirlooms too—the Davenants' Vandyke, the lacquered cabinets, the Chippendale chairs. Dad bought them, as they matched the place; but *we* don't fit in. Dad and mum were far happier in London; keeping up a great estate and a great position is an awful strain when one was not caught young. Do you know, the servants are a frightful trial; they find the country dull. And at the last ball we had, nearly all the hired waiters were intoxicated; they drank most of the champagne, and one of them handed a lemonade to Lord Mottisfont, and said there was no fiz left! The mum was so mortified she wept, poor dear."

"Well, everything always seems to go smoothly, quite London fashion, and without a hitch," said Aurea consolingly.

"Yes, but not behind the scenes; and the Mum sometimes makes such horrible blunders in etiquette, such as sending in a baronet's wife before a countess—and the countess looked pea-green! Altogether it's a fag. When Bertie marries I expect pater will make him over the place. I wouldn't mind reigning here myself—would you, Aurea?"

"What a silly question, Joey! I'm not cut out for reigning anywhere."

"Only in people's hearts, eh?" stroking her cheek with a finger. "Isn't that a pretty speech? Well, come along, I want to show you the pretty things I collected abroad—my fans and lace and embroideries."

But just at this moment a maid entered, and said—

"If you please, ma'am, I was to say that Miss Parrett's car is at the door, and she's waiting for Miss Morven."

The drive home was made by another road (in spite of Miss Parrett's querulous protestations, and it was evident that the sooner she could abandon the motor the better she would be pleased). Susan, on the other hand, was anxious to see more of the country, and make a detour round by a little town, eight miles away.

"Why, it's nothing," she protested; "it's not worth taking out the car for a run over to Westmere—one might as well walk!"

"One would think it was *your* car, to hear you talking, Susan;" and Miss Parrett threw herself back in the corner, and closed her eyes, only to open them again immediately, as they sped along the empty, country roads between hedges already green.

"There's Hopfield Hill!" she exclaimed, suddenly sitting bolt upright. "I'm not going down that in a motor, so don't suppose it, either of you."

"But it's three-quarters of a mile long, and you have a blister on your heel," expostulated her sister. "Come, Bella, don't be foolish."

"*Don't* argue; if it was twenty miles I'd walk it. This thing gives me palpitation as it is."

In spite of Aurea's and Miss Susan's prayers, vows, and assurances, Miss Parrett descended at the top of a long hill, insisted that her companions should accompany her, and together the trio tramped down in the mud, whilst the chauffeur sped along merrily, and awaited them at the base. On their way home by a narrow byroad they nearly met with a nasty accident. A cart, drawn by a young horse, was coming out of a gate as the motor approached, and there was an exciting scene. The boy who was driving lost his head, the horse reared and plunged, Miss Parrett shrieked, and the motor—which was jammed into the bank—shuddered all over; but, after a moment—a critical moment—all was well—all but Miss Parrett, who collapsed into her corner, and announced that she had spasms of the heart, and was dying!

Ultimately they reached the Manor without further trouble; the dying lady was restored with brandy and water, and Owen the chauffeur spent the next two hours in cleaning the muddy car. This was the part of the job he loathed. Just as he had completed his task, he beheld, to his discomfiture, the cook stepping delicately across the yard, carrying a black bottle in one hand, and a wineglass in the other.

"Good-evening to you, Mr. Owen. My word! you do look hot after all your fag with the car. Beastly work, ain't it? I've just run over with a glass of ginger wine—it's my own."

"Thank you, Miss Hicks. It's awfully good of you, but it's a thing I never touch," he answered politely.

"Then what do you say to a pint o' beer, or a cup o' tea?"

"No—er—I'm about done," pulling down his sleeves; "and I'm going."

"The old girl seems a bit upset," remarked the cook, who had come out for conversation; "she's awful frightened of the car."

"She needn't be," he answered shortly.

"Not with *you* a-driving, I'm sure, Mr. Owen. I wish I could have a run in it, eh? There was a chauffeur as I knew in London—rather a pal of mine—that used to give his friends fine drives, as much as down to Brighton, when the family was out of town. He were a treat, I can tell you!"

"Was he? I'd say he was a thief—unless he used his own petrol."

"Oh, come now, you're mighty strict and proper, I can see. Chapel, I suppose?"

"No; you're wrong there."

"Look here, what's the use of being so stand-off and so stiff—it's downright *silly*; you and me, as it were, coming to this cruel place from the same reference. Won't you call round and take me for a nice walk on Sunday afternoon?"

"No; you're very kind—but I can't."

"Why, what else have you to do?" her eyes kindling. What else had he to do? Lie on his bed and smoke, and read Leila's papers. And there were other alternatives; he could take a long stretch, say ten miles out and back, or he might go to evening service and gaze at Aurea Morven!

"My word! you are a stupid!" declared Miss Hicks; "even if you have a young woman up in town, she won't mind. *Have* you a young lady?" and her bold eyes were searching.

Had he? He had! His young lady was Miss Aurea, her mistress's niece—Aurea or no other; and as he put on his coat he looked his tormentor steadily in the face and answered—

"Yes, I have."

"Oh, so that's it! I see! And you're hurrying off to write to her? Well," — spitefully—"I can tell you one thing for yer comfort, there's no post out of Ottinge before Monday morning!"

"Isn't there? That's a pity. Well, good-evening to you, Miss Hicks;" and he walked off, leaving Miss Hicks gaping after him. She, however, consoled herself with a couple of glasses of ginger wine, before re-entering the house.

CHAPTER XII
THE DOGS' HOTEL

The morning succeeding the motor's first trip proved depressingly wet; thick mists of cold spring rain shrouded the outlook from the Manor, beat down upon the pleasure ground, and made pools in the hollows of the drive.

Miss Parrett, who was, as the servants expressed it, "dodging" in and out of the sitting-room, issuing commands and then withdrawing them, fastened upon the chauffeur the moment he came for orders.

No, the car would not be required, and he could go some errands into the village.

"Mind you don't go loitering and gossiping," she added. "I know your sort, chattering with the maids. Remember that your time belongs to me;" and she pointed a stumpy forefinger at her knitted jacket. "I've a note for Miss Morven at the Rectory, and another for Ivy House, and I want some things at Topham's shop. I'll give you a list. You can go into the schoolroom and wait."

Calm with excessive rage Wynyard entered the schoolroom, where he found Miss Susan with a handkerchief tied over her head, and an apron over her dress, unpacking dusty china from a battered case.

"Such a day!" she exclaimed cheerfully; "and they say it's going to last—so we shall be very busy, and make use of you."

"All right, miss," he assented shortly; the accusation of "chattering with maids" still left its sting.

"We are going to get up the cases of old books and china, and unpack them here. The carpenter is putting shelves in the library; but he is such a lazy fellow, I don't expect he will come out in this weather."

"There you are as usual, Susan, talking and idling people," said her sister, entering with two notes and a list; and in another moment Wynyard had been dispatched.

First of all he went to the Rectory, and here the door was opened by Mr. Morven himself, attended by Mackenzie, who immediately stiffened from head to tail, and growled round the chauffeur's legs, evidently recognising in him the ally of his mortal foe. Mr. Morven was a squarely built elderly man with a grey beard, a benevolent expression, and the eyes of the dreamer.

As he took the note he glanced at the messenger, and his eyes dilated with the intentness of a surprised stare. Wynyard's type was not common in the parish; somehow Mrs. Hogben's lodger did not correspond with his surroundings.

"I see this is for my daughter," he said, and beckoning to a parlour-maid he handed it to her. "Just come into my study, will you, till the answer is written," leading the way across a wide hall panelled in oak. Through an open door Wynyard caught a glimpse of the drawing-room, and was conscious of a faded carpet, fresh chintz, books, old china, a glowing fire, and a fragrant atmosphere. The general impression of the Rectory, with its oaken staircase, family portraits, and bowls of potpourri, was delightful but fleeting; it seemed a peaceful, flower-scented old house, of spotless neatness.

"You're a newcomer, I believe?" said the Rector, preceding him into a room lined with books from floor to ceiling, and seating himself at a writing-table. "Miss Parrett's chauffeur?" and he smiled to himself at some reminiscence. "I see they are making use of you. Church of England?"

"Yes, sir."

"If you have any sort of voice—tenor, baritone, or bass—we shall be glad to have you in the choir; our tenor is getting on; he must be close on seventy."

"I'm afraid I'm not much good, sir."

"Well, if you don't sing, you look like a cricketer, eh? I must get something out of you, you know;" and he laughed pleasantly.

"Oh yes, I can play cricket all right."

"If you can bowl a bit, with Miss Parrett's leave, I'll put you into the village club; we rather fancy ourselves, and a young man of your stamp will be an acquisition." At this moment Aurea entered, carrying an enormous cardboard box.

"Good-morning," she said. "I see aunt sent you for the lampshade, and here it is."

"What a size!" exclaimed her father. "Why, you must have robbed your best hat! I declare it's not fair to a man to ask him to be seen with such a thing going through the village."

A Rolling Stone | 85

"Not half so bad as seeing people go down the street with a black bottle in either hand!" retorted his daughter.

"I don't mind, sir," said Wynyard, taking up the box as he spoke.

"Please tell Aunt Bella I will be after you in two or three minutes," said Aurea; then to her father, "She wants to unpack grandpapa's books at last!"

"You mean that she wants you to unpack the books," corrected Mr. Morven; "you might steal a few for me, eh? I suppose you will be away all day?" and he looked at her rather wistfully.

"No, no, dear, I'll be back soon after tea." To Owen: "Straight on, it's an easy door."

As Wynyard turned in the hall and backed out, box in hand, he had a vision of pretty Miss Aurea perched on the arm of his chair, with her arm round her father's neck. Lucky old beggar!

His next errand was to the shop—Topham's—and as he lingered irresolutely in the rain, staring up and down the street, he was overtaken by a brisk figure in an aquascutum and motor cap.

"I see you are searching for our emporium," she began, "and I'll show it to you—in fact, I'm going in myself to get some brass-headed carpet nails."

The shop stood sideways to the street, as if anxious for concealment, and was the most astonishing place of its kind that Wynyard had ever entered. A stall in an Indian bazaar was tame and tidy in comparison. The house was old and low, the shop of narrow dimensions; it widened out as it ran back, and lost itself in a sort of tumbledown greenhouse. The smell was extraordinary, so varied, penetrating, and indescribable—and small wonder, he said to himself, when he had inspected the stock!

An oldish woman with a long nose (the Ottinge nose) stood stiffly behind the counter; at her left the window was full of stale confectionery, biscuit tins, sticky sweets in glass bottles, oranges and apples in candle boxes; heaps of Rickett's blue, and some fly-blown advertisements.

Behind Mrs. Topham were two shelves dedicated to "the library," which consisted of remarkably dirty and battered sixpenny novels; these she hired to the village at the generous price of a penny a volume for one week. To the left of the entrance were more shelves, piled with cheap toys, haberdashery, and china; and here ended the front of the shop. Concealed by a low screen were tins of oil, a barrel of ginger ale on tap, and a large frying-pan full of dripping. The remainder of the premises was abandoned to the greengrocery business on a large scale—onions, potatoes, and cabbages in generous profusion.

"Good-morning, Mrs. Topham," said Miss Morven. "What a wet day! How is your cough?"

"Oh, I'm amongst the middlings, miss. What can I do for you?"

"I want some brass-headed carpet nails, and my aunts have sent a list;" and she motioned to Wynyard.

Mrs. Topham seized upon it with her long, yellow fingers (they resembled talons)—the Manor were good customers.

"You can send over the things, Mrs. Topham; but I want the nails now."

"I'm sure, miss, I've got 'em, but I can't just rightly think where they be."

As she spoke, she turned out a drawer and rummaged through it violently, and then another; the contents of these gave one an idea of what is seriously understood by the word "chaos": wool, toffee, night-lights, dog biscuits, and pills were among the ingredients.

"Try the blue box," suggested Aurea, who was evidently acquainted with the resources of the establishment.

The blue box yielded nothing but a quantity of faded pink ribbon, a few postcards of the church and Drum, a dozen tennis balls, some small curling-pins, and several quires of black-edged paper.

"Why, if that isn't the very thing I was looking for last week!" exclaimed Mrs. Topham, as she pounced on the paper. "And now Miss Jakes she's bin and got it over at Brodfield; 'tis a cruel chance to be near a big town—and so there's for you!"

As the search for nails promised to be protracted, Miss Morven turned to Wynyard and said—

"You need not wait; please take the lampshade on, and say that I'm coming."

But before returning to the Manor he had yet another errand to fulfil—a note for Mrs. Ramsay at Ivy House. Here he rang repeatedly, he even gave heavy single knocks with the bulbous brass knocker, but received no reply beyond the distant barking of indignant dogs. At last he went round and discovered a large paved yard, but no human being. Then he ventured to approach one of the sitting-room windows and peered in—a comfortable dining-room with a cheerful fire, but empty. No, just underneath the window on a sofa lay an elderly man fast asleep. He wore grey woollen socks on his slipperless feet, an empty tumbler stood on a chair beside him—and this at eleven o'clock in the morning. (True, O. Wynyard, but it had contained no stronger drink than hot water.)

He had the intention of rapping at the pane, but changed his mind and retired to the door, and as he waited he heard a voice above him calling out in a rich brogue—

"Bad scran to ye, Fanny, if there isn't a young gentleman below wid a big band-box, and he is afther pullin' out the bell by the roots; 'tis a shame to lave him standin' in all the pours of rain! An' such a lovely big man!"

At this moment the hall door was opened by a tall dark woman in a mackintosh and motor cap, with two frantic fox-terriers on the lead, and a self-possessed French bulldog in dignified attendance.

"I'm afraid you've been waiting," she said, in a soft brogue. "I was away at the kennels, the servants were upstairs, and the Captain is asleep." Then, opening the note (as well as the fox-terriers would permit), she glanced over it, and the messenger glanced at her—a woman of thirty-five, with a thin, well-bred face, black hair, and very long lashes. When she lifted them, he saw that her eyes were of a blue-black shade, both sad and searching—the whole expression of her face seemed to be concentrated in their pupils.

"Please tell Miss Parrett I'll come to tea. I've no time to write. I have to take the dogs out." The fox-terriers were straining hard at their leash. "They must have exercise; and when these come back, there are three more."

As she spoke, Wynyard could hear the injured yelping of their disappointed companions.

"Now, don't open the little dogs' room," she called to an elderly woman in the background, who gave the amazing answer—

"And what would ail me?"

"And mind that the Captain has his broth at twelve." Then she stepped out into the beating rain, and Wynyard was surprised to find that Mrs. Ramsay was about to accompany him.

"I'm going your way," she explained; "it's the safest. These two are new dogs, and I'm rather afraid to go near the Rectory; their Aberdeen is such a quarrelsome beast—always trailing his coat."

"Mackenzie?"

"Ah, and so you know him?" she said, with a smile; "you weren't long in making his acquaintance."

Wynyard exhibited his left hand, and a severe bite.

"I suppose he was trying to kill Joss; that's his profession—a killer of other dogs."

"You seem to have a good many of them," as an afterthought, "ma'am."

"Yes; they are not all my own. I take in boarders—only six at a time, and they must be small, no invalids accepted. I look after them for people who go abroad, or from home for a few weeks. I am fond of dogs, so I combine business and pleasure."

"Yes, ma'am; but they must be a trouble and a responsibility—other people's pets."

"I have to take my chance! Some are so nice, it just breaks my heart to part with them. Indeed, there's Tippy here, the bulldog, I'm pretending he is sick—isn't it a shame of me? Some are surly, others so sporting, that half my time is spent in scouring the country, and looking into rabbit holes. Others are quarrelsome, or chase, snap, and kill fowl and get me into great trouble. I never keep *them* on an hour after their time is up. You are the Miss Parretts' chauffeur, aren't you?"

"Yes, ma'am."

"Is this your first situation?" eyeing him keenly.

"Yes, ma'am."

Why did she ask such a question? Did she, to use the good old expression, "smell a rat"?

"I'm afraid you will find Ottinge terribly dull. I wonder how you discovered a place so far from everywhere—just the back of beyond?" and she looked at him interrogatively—her dark blue eyes were extraordinarily piercing.

To this impertinent remark no reply was necessary, as it brought them precisely to the Manor gate. The lady nodded, and walked on quickly—a slim, active, resolute figure, with the straining fox-terriers dragging at her hands, the little bulldog trotting sedately at her heels. The group passed steadily out towards the open country, with the light rain drifting down upon them. What queer people one came across in Ottinge! Miss Parrett, the ill-tempered old bully, the Hon. Mrs. Ramsay, with her soft voice and expressive eyes, eking out a living by making herself a slave to strangers' dogs.

"Oh, so she sent a verbal message, did she?" snorted Miss Parrett. "Well, when *I* was a girl,"—turning to her sister—"and people asked me out, I always wrote them *a proper note*; but manners are not what they were in my day. Oh, if my dear, courteous father could only know of some of the things that are done, he would turn in his grave!"

Miss Parrett was fond of quoting the old Colonel, and insisting upon his devotion to herself; whilst, if the truth were known, they had been bitterly antagonistic to one another during his lifetime, and the Manor was the frequent scene of acrimonious quarrelling, unfilial gibes, and furious rejoinders.

It was fully a quarter of an hour later when Miss Morven arrived with the brass-headed carpet nails.

"I *knew* she had them!" she declared triumphantly; "for she got a lot for us last winter, so I ransacked the shop, and, after a long search, where do you think I found them, Susan?"

"In her pocket, to be sure!"

"No, not quite—probably I shall next time. In one of the brown teapots she has on sale! She *was* surprised—I wasn't! She is getting quite dotty, and won't have help; and there is Dilly, her pretty, flighty granddaughter, with nothing to do but flirt!"

All that day Wynyard worked zealously, assisting the carpenter (who had come after all) and in unpacking and dusting books that had not seen daylight for thirty years. On this occasion, in spite of Miss Parrett's condescending invitation, he dined at Holiday Cottage.

That very same evening Mrs. Ramsay came to tea at the Manor, and was fervent in her admiration of the drawing-room, which praise Miss Parrett absorbed with toothless complacency, saying in her quavering bleat—

"I'm so glad you like it. Of course it was *my* taste, and my ideas, and they are my things; but Aurea and Susan helped me—yes, and the chauffeur made himself useful."

Wynyard, who was working close by, felt inclined to laugh out loud. It seemed to him that he was everything but a chauffeur: window-cleaner, carpet-layer, messenger, and assistant carpenter—a good thing he was naturally pretty handy. And although all these extra burdens had been laid upon him, the first impulse to throw up the situation had died away; he did not mind what jobs the old lady set him to do, but would take them as all in the day's work, for he had no intention of leaving Ottinge at present—he must have some consideration for Leila!

After tea, when Miss Parrett was engaged in scolding her domestics and writing violent postcards to her tradesmen, Mrs. Ramsay drew Aurea into the drawing-room.

"Well, me dear," and her dark eyes danced, "I did not say a word before your aunts, but I've *seen* the remarkable chauffeur! I assure you, when I opened the door and found him standing there with a large box, you might have knocked me down with the traditional feather! I was taking the new dogs out for a run, and so we walked together to this gate."

"What do you think of him?" asked Aurea, carelessly, as she rearranged some daffodils in a blue bowl.

"What do I think? I think—although he scarcely opened his lips—that there is some mystery attached to him, and that he is a gentleman."

"Why do you say so?" inquired the girl, anxious to hear her own opinion endorsed. "He is not a bit smarter than the Woolcocks' men."

"Oh, it's not exactly smartness, me dear, it's the 'born so' air which nothing can disguise. His matter-of-course lifting his cap, walking on the outside, opening the gate, and, above all, his *boots*."

"Boots!"

"Yes, his expensive aristocratic shooting boots; I vow they come from Lobbs. Jimmy got his there—before he lost his money."

"Perhaps the chauffeur bought them second-hand?" suggested Aurea.

Mrs. Ramsay ignored the remark with a waving hand.

"I cannot think what has induced a man of his class to come and bury himself here in this God-forsaken spot."

"Ottinge-in-the-Marsh is obliged to you!"

"Now, you know what I mean, Aurea. You are a clever girl. I put the question to him, and got no satisfactory answer. Is it forgery, murder, piracy on the high seas, somebody's wife—or what?" She rested her chin on her hand, and nodded sagaciously at her companion. "I understand that he has been working indoors a good deal, and helping you and Miss Susan." She paused significantly. "You must have seen something of him. Tell me, darling, how did you find him?"

"Most useful, wonderfully clever with his hands, strong, obliging, and absolutely speechless."

"Ah! Does he have his meals here?"

"No."

"Dear me, what a cruel blow for the maid-servants! Did he come from a garage?"

"No; a friend of Aunt Bella's found him."

"A woman friend?"

"Yes; she gave him an excellent character."

"And what of hers?"

"Oh, my dear Kathleen, she is Lady Kesters, a tremendously smart Society lady, awfully clever, too, and absolutely *sans reproche!*"

"Is that so?" drawled Mrs. Ramsay. "Well, somehow or other, I've an uneasy feeling about her protégé. There is more than meets the eye with respect to that young man's character, believe me. My woman's instinct says so. I'm sorry he has come down and taken up your aunt's situation, for I seem to feel in me bones that he will bring trouble to some one."

"Oh, Kathleen! You and your Irish superstitions!" and Aurea threw up her hands, clasping them among her masses of hair, and stared into her friend's face and laughed.

"Well, dear, if he does nothing worse, he will have half the girls in love with him, and breaking their hearts. It's too bad of him, so good-looking, and so smart, coming and throwing the 'comether' over this sleepy little village. Believe me, darlin', he has been turned out of his own place; and it would never surprise *me* if he was just a nice-looking young wolf in sheep's clothing!"

"Oh, what it is to have the nice, lurid, Celtic imagination!" exclaimed Aurea. "I don't think the poor man would harm a fly. Joss has taken to him as a brother—and——"

"Miss Morven as—a sister?"

"Now, what are you two conspiring about?" inquired Miss Susan, entering, brisk, smiling, and inquisitive.

"I'm only discussing your chauffeur, me darlin' Miss Susan. I notice that several of the village girls drop in on Mrs. Hogben—you see I live opposite—and they expose their natural admiration without scruple or reserve."

"Owen is a useful young man, if he is a bit ornamental—isn't he, Aurea? I'm going to get him to help me in the greenhouse, for I don't believe, at this rate, that we shall *ever* use the car."

CHAPTER XIII
THE DRUM AND ITS PATRONS

Mrs. Hogben had lost no time in giving her lodger explicit instructions as to what was expected of him in Ottinge! Her lecture assumed a negative form. He was not to take out any one's girl, or there'd be trouble; he was not to talk too much politics, or there'd be more trouble; he was not to drink and get fuddled and fighting, or there was the Bench and a fine; as to amusement, there was cricket, Mrs. Topham's Library, and the Drum Inn, for his evenings.

The good woman said to herself, "The motor is always washed and put away by six o'clock, and if he comes here, he must either sit in his room or in the kitchen, and *she* wasn't a-goin' to have that blocked up with young girls, and never a chair for herself and her own friends."

Wynyard readily took the hint; at Ottinge one must do as Ottinge did, and he cheerfully accompanied Tom over to the Drum a few evenings after his arrival.

"What sort of liquor do they keep, Tom?" he asked, as they crossed the street.

"Well, some be better nor some, but there's no bad beer; the old stuff here is rare and strong, but it comes pretty dear."

The low, wainscoted taproom, with its sanded floor, was full of day-labourers, herds, ploughmen, cow-men, and carters taking their bit of pleasure, talking loudly and disjointedly, drinking beer in mugs, or playing the ever-popular game of "ring." Here, for the first time in his life, Wynyard was brought into personal contact, as man to man, with the agricultural world as it is. In the more exclusive bar were to be found farmers, owners of certain comfortable red houses scattered up and down the street, the organist, the schoolmaster, the grocer—in short, the moneyed patrons of the hostelry. Several were talking over village affairs, discussing politics, racing, artificial manures, or cattle. Some were playing draughts, some were reading the daily papers, others were doing nothing. Of these, one was a bent, gentlemanly individual in a grey tweed suit, with a grey moustache, a grey, sunken, vacant face, who sat aloof smoking a brier pipe—his eyes staring into vacancy. Another was a white-haired, shrunken old man, who wore green carpet slippers, and occupied a cushioned arm-chair, and the best seat near the fire. This was Joe Thunder, the oldest inhabitant, ninety-three years of age his last birthday. Once upon a time he had seen the world—and other worlds; now he was comfortably moored in a fine, substantial cottage with a garden back and front, kept bees, was an authority on roses, and filled the post of the patriarch of Ottinge.

All newcomers were formally presented to Daddy Thunder, and as Tom pushed Wynyard in his direction he said—

"This be the Parrett ladies' new man, daddy." To Owen, "Daddy, here, he knows the place well, and can tell ye all about it, better nor any, though he wasn't Ottinge born."

Daddy slowly removed his long clay pipe, and inspected the stranger with a pair of shrewd little grey eyes. He had rosy cheeks, a benevolent, even sweet expression, and looked fifteen years younger than his age.

"Ye come fra' London?" he began agreeably.

"Yes, sir, three days ago. It's a good long journey."

"Ay, mister," nodding his white head expressively. "Ye don't belong to *us*. Yer speech—like the Bible chap—bewrayeth ye—y're no working man!"

"I am, indeed," rejoined Wynyard quickly, "and working for my bread the same as the rest of the company; it's all I have to look to—my two hands."

"Nay, is that so?" and he glanced at him incredulously. "Well, I've bin here a matter o' twenty year, and I never see one o' your make a-comin' in and settin' in the Drum. There's 'im," and he indicated the bent figure in the corner, whose pipe was in his hand, his eyes riveted on the stranger with a look of startled inquiry.

"That's the Captain, but 'e's no account. 'E comes in and 'e sits and maybe listens; 'e never speaks. They do say 'e 'ad a soort o' stroke in India, and 'is brain 'as melted like, but 'e is 'armless enough—anyhow, 'is lady won't put 'im away."

"I suppose you've lived here a long time?" said Wynyard, drawing forward a chair, and placing it so as to sit with his back to the said Captain, whose stare was disagreeably steady.

"Twenty year, more or less. I am a south country man, and my daughter she married and settled 'ere, and 'er 'usband died; an' as there was only the two on us, I come along to keep 'er company, and to die 'ere, since I was gettin' pretty old, being over seventy; but, Lor' bless ye! that's twenty-two year ago, and 'ere I be still gettin' about, and doin' a bit o' gardenin'. The air is grand—nothing ails me but gout," holding out a crippled hand. "This isn't the place to die in—it's the place to live in. It keeps ye alive. Why, I'm ninety-three. Oh, it's what ye may call a terrible lively place."

This was not his listener's opinion, who would have instituted instead the word "deadly."

"You must have seen a great deal in ninety-three years," said Wynyard, lighting his pipe.

"Lor' bless ye, yes; and I've a wunnerful memory."

"Do you remember the days of Napoleon?"

"What—old Bony! Nay," a little offended, "I'm not as old as *that*; but I do mind a talk o' 'is funeral in France."

"I beg your pardon, I'm an awful duffer at dates. You remember Wellington?"

"Oh ay, 'e was only the other day, so to speak."

"And what else do you remember?"

"Well, as a lad, I remember I was terrible afeerd o' the press gang."

"The press gang?"

"Ay; that come pokin' round after able-bodied men for the Navy, and kidnappin' 'em away to sea, and keepin' them there, whether or no, for years, and their families at home starvin'."

"I say, what times!"

"Ay, so they was. I've seen two men 'angin' in chains on Camley Moor when I was about ten—it were for sheep-stealin', and put the fear o' death on me. Surely I can 'ear them chains a-clankin' now!"

Wynyard felt as if he had been suddenly precipitated into another world. Here he was, sitting talking to a live man, who discoursed familiarly of hanging in chains, and the press gang!

"Would you take something, sir?" he asked. "I'd like to drink your health."

"Ay, ay, I don't mind 'avin' a glass wi' ye. Ginders! Ginders!" raising his voice, "give us a taste of yer old beer, the *best*—two half-pints;" and, as they were brought, he looked at Wynyard, and said, "To ye, young sir, and good luck to ye in Ottinge; may ye live as long as I do!"

"Thank you; have you any prescription for your wonderful health?"

"Ay, I have so. Look 'ere, I've not tasted medicine for fifty year. I don't hold wi' doctors. I only eat twice a day—my breakfast at eight, and my dinner at two. My daughter she do mike me a cup o' tea at six, but I don't want it, and it's only to oblige *her*. Work—work's the thing when yer young. I mind bein' in the train one day, and a great heavy man complainin' o' his pore 'ealth, and 'is inside, and another says, 'I can tell ye o' a cure, master, and a sure one.' 'What's that?' ses 'e, all alive. 'Rise of a mornin' at four o'clock, and mow an acre before ye break yer fast, and go on mowing all day—that will cure ye—ye'll be a new man.' 'I'd be a dead un,' ses 'e. *My* advice is: no medicine, short commons, lots of work, and there ye are, and ye'll live to maybe a hundred."

"But what about cuts and wounds? How do you doctor them?"

"Oh, just a plaster o' earth, or a couple o' lily leaves. One is as good as t'other. Well, I'm a-goin'," struggling to his feet; "an old gaffer like me keeps early hours."

As Wynyard handed him his stick, he slapped him smartly on the back, and it was evident from this accolade that the "shover" was now made free of the Drum.

The newcomer looked about him, some were playing dominoes, some cards, one or two were reading the day's papers, and all the time the Captain sat immovable in a corner, and his eyes never moved from Wynyard. Such cold, impassive staring made him feel uncomfortable, and settling his reckoning he presently followed old Thunder's example and went home.

Captain Ramsay, whose fixed attention had made the stranger so uneasy, had once been a popular officer in a popular regiment, and when quartered in India had fallen in love with and married the Hon. Kathleen Brian (daughter of an impoverished viscount) who was on a visit to relatives in Simla. The first year was rapturously happy for both of them, and then one day, when out pig-sticking near Cawnpore, Captain Ramsay had his topee knocked off, and in the excitement of the chase galloped on, with the result that he was knocked over by a sunstroke. Sunstroke was followed by brain fever, and he nearly died. Ultimately he was invalided home, and, owing to ill-health, obliged to leave the Service. Nor was this all. He seemed to become another man, his character underwent a complete change; he was quarrelsome and morose, fought with his own family, insulted his wife's people, and developed into an Ishmael. He invested his money in the maddest ventures, and rapidly dispersed his entire fortune (Kathleen was penniless), and now nothing remained but his small pension. Year by year he became more disagreeable, restless, and strange. The couple wandered from place to place, from lodging to lodging. Vainly his wife's relatives implored her to leave him; he was "impossible," her health was suffering; she, who had been so pretty, at twenty-seven looked prematurely faded and haggard; but Kathleen was obstinate, and would go her own way and stick to her bad bargain. Her brothers did not know, and would never know, the Jimmy she had married—so clever, amusing, good-looking, the life of his company, a first-rate officer, and a matchless horseman; the man who got up the regimental theatricals, ran the gymkhana, was editor of the regimental paper, and so devoted to her always. No, no, she would never abandon him, though every year he grew worse, and more brusque, excitable, and unsociable; and every year saw them sinking still further in the social scale.

At last an aged uncle died, and left Captain Ramsay Ivy House, Ottinge, with its old-fashioned furniture, linen, books, and plate. This windfall, with his pension, would keep them going, and at best it afforded a retreat and a hiding-place. The neighbourhood with flattering alacrity had called on Captain and the Hon. Mrs. Ramsay, and she was declared to be charming, so agreeable and still handsome. She duly returned their visits in a hired fly, left her husband's cards, Captain J. V. Ramsay, and made his excuses.

It soon was evident that the Ramsays were desperately poor, and did not intend to keep a trap or entertain; that he was queer, and only to be met about the fields and lanes, or in the Drum; but by degrees the neighbours came to know Mrs. Ramsay better, and to like her extremely. She had travelled, was a brilliant conversationalist, and a sound bridge player; she was also an Honourable—one of the many daughters of Lord Ballingarry of Moyallan Castle—so the neighbours bought her little 'Poms,' recommended the hotel to their friends, lent her carriages or motors, sent her game and books, and did their best for her. But Captain Ramsay was beyond any one's assistance; he refused to see people, or to know Ottinge. He went abroad generally with the bats and the owls, along lonely roads and footpaths; his daily paper and the Drum were his sole resources, and only that, at long intervals, a shrivelled figure was caught sight of shuffling up the High Street, the neighbourhood would have forgotten that Captain Ramsay existed.

Lady Kesters sent papers and wrote weekly letters to J. Owen, Holiday Cottage, Ottinge. But her brother's replies were short, vague, and unsatisfactory, and in answer to a whole sheet of reproaches, he dedicated a wet Sunday afternoon to his sister. He began:—

> "Dear Leila,—I had your letter yesterday, and it's a true bill
> that I am a miserable correspondent, and that my notes are
> as short and sweet as a donkey's gallop. I only got twenty
> marks in composition when I passed. Now, however, I'm
> going to put my back into this letter, and send you a long
> scrawl, and, as you command me, all details—no matter

how insignificant. I am writing in my room, because the kitchen is full of young women—Mrs. Hogben's at-home day, I suppose! The parlour windows are never opened, the atmosphere is poisonous, and thick with the reek of old furniture. So here I am! I've faked up a table by putting blocks under the yellow box, for the washstand is impossible. This room is old and low; if I stand upright in some places, my head is likely to go through the ceiling, and in others my legs to go through the floor; but I know the lie of the land now. The window looks into a big orchard, and beyond that are miles of flat country; but you've seen Ottinge, so I spare you local colour. I am all right here. Mrs. Hogben is a rare good sort, and does me well, washing included, for twenty-three shillings a week, and I make out my own bills—as she neither reads nor writes, but takes it out in talking. When I had a cold, she made me a decoction called 'Tansie Tea' and insisted on my swallowing it—the fear of another dose cured me. Her son Tom is a decent chap, and we are pals; he works at the Manor as second gardener of two. As to the ladies there, I am disappointed in Miss Parrett; you told me they were *both* 'old dears.' Susan really is an old dear, but, in my opinion, Miss P. is an old D. Possibly you only knew her as a tea-drinking, charming hostess, full of compliments and sweetness; the real Miss Bella is a bully, vain of her money, and shamelessly mean.

"The Manor is a nice, sunny house, flat on the ground, with great oak beams and rum windows, and a splendid garden enclosed in yew hedges run to seed; they are trying to get it in order, clipping the yews and digging out the moss, but two men and a boy are not enough, and Miss P. is too stingy to employ more. As I've little to do, I sometimes lend a hand. The motor is a faked-up old rattle-trap, all paint and smart cushions; but its inside is worn out. Miss Parrett is under the impression that petrol is not a necessity, and I have such desperate work to get it, and she always cross-examines me so sharply, and gives the money as such a personal favour, that one would suppose I wanted the beastly thing for my own consumption. It is a riddle to me *why* she ever bought the car. She is afraid to go out in it, and won't let her sister use it alone. I've been here four weeks; it's been out six times, always at a crawl, and within a four-mile radius. Miss Parrett likes to pay visits to show off her 'beautiful' car; but I feel like a Bath-chair man!

"One day we went over to Westmere, the Davenants' old place, where you used to stay. The Woolcocks, who have it now, are enormously rich, go-ahead people, and the married daughter pounced on me as Owen the steward on board ship! No one here has any idea who I am, and I keep a shut mouth; and when I do talk, I try to copy Tom Hogben. There are few gentry about,—that is, in Ottinge; the parson, Mr. Morven, the Parretts' brother-in-law, comes in sometimes and gives advice about the garden. He is a cheery sort, elderly, a widower, and a splendid preacher—thrown away on this dead-and-alive spot. His sermons are sensible and modern, and you've something to carry away and think of, instead of wanting to shy hymn-books, or go to sleep. The church is a tremendous age, and restored—the Ottinge folk are very proud of it. In one chancel, the north chancel, lie our kin the Davenants; there is a fine window, erected by a certain Edward Davenant to the memory of his wife, the lady in a pink scarf—quite a smart get-up of, say, a hundred years ago, is represented as one of the angels, and he himself is among the disciples. Both were copied from family portraits. What do you think of the idea?

"Mr. Morven has let me in for singing in the choir; you should see me in a surplice—it barely comes to my knees, and makes me feel so shy! Thanks to the choir, I've got to know the organist, and the schoolmaster—a very decent chap; I go and smoke a pipe there of an evening, and also a young farmer who has promised me some fishing when I can get off—that's not often. There is no village club, as you may remember, and the men of the place assemble at the Drum Inn. I drop in there sometimes, though, just as often, I take a tramp over the country, accompanied by the Manor dog, who has adopted me, and often does 'a night out.' Mrs. Hogben leaves the door on the latch. She also told me I should go to the Drum along with Tom, as she thought I was a bit dull; so to the Drum I go, to show I'm not above my mates, and I have a glass of beer and a pipe, and hear all the village news, and the village elders discussing parish rates, socialism, free trade, the price of stock, and how Jakes' Bob is going into the grocery, and Harry Tews' spring cabbage has failed!

"There is one queer figure there: a broken-down, decrepit officer, Captain Ramsay, whose wife lives in the village and keeps a dogs' hotel. He looks as if he drank, and is always muddled, or else he is mad. He speaks to no one, but he never takes his eye off *me*. I tell you, Sis, I don't half like it—though I swear he has never seen me before.

"Well, I hope Martin is better. I'm sorry he has been feeling a bit cheap; it's a pity I can't send him some of this air— splendid; there's an old chap of ninety-three in the place— still going strong.

"Your papers are a godsend. I pass them on to the schoolmaster, and he lends me books; but although I seem to do little, I never have much time for reading. I'm getting on all right, and intend to stick to the old birds, the green car, and Ottinge; though, as it said in the Psalms this morning, it does seem to be a 'land where all things are forgotten.' At any rate our ways are primitive and virtuous—we have one policeman, he sings bass in the choir,—and we hold little conversation with the outer world. Indeed, news—other than local—is despised. The sweep is our postman, and the village softy limps round with the papers when he thinks of it. I'm about to be enrolled in the Ottinge Cricket Club, and I'm looking forward to some sport. They little guess that I played in the Eton eleven! Here endeth this epistle, which must count as a dozen and thirteen.—Your affectionate brother,

"O. St. J. W."

Lady Kesters read this letter quickly, then she went over it very deliberately; finally she handed it to her husband.

"He seems perfectly happy and satisfied, though he detests Miss Parrett and says the car is an old rattle-trap. He has no pals, very little to do, and has taken to gardening and singing in the choir." She paused expressively. "Somehow I don't see Owen in *that* picture, do you?"

"Can't say I do," replied her husband.

"Just the last sort of life to suit him, I should have thought. Martin, do you suppose that's a faked-up letter, and he wrote it to relieve my mind?"

"No; the chap hasn't it in him to fake anything. I'd rather like to hear his attempts at the local dialect!"

"Then tell me what you really think; I see you have something in your head."

"My dear, I'm astonished you don't see it for yourself! You are ten times as clear-sighted as I am," and he hesitated; "why, of course, there's a young woman in the case."

"He never mentions her!" objected his wife.

"A deadly symptom."

"Some village girl—no. And he is bound not to think of any love-affair or entanglement for two whole years."

"How long has he been at Ottinge—four weeks, eh?" She nodded.

"Well, I believe that, in spite of your uncle and you, Owen is in love with some one already."

CHAPTER XIV
LIEUTENANT WYNYARD

It was an undeniable fact that the chauffeur spent much more time in the Manor grounds than driving the car. The car was rarely used, and anything was better than loafing about the yard or the village with his hands in his pockets—one of the unemployed. Wynyard liked the fresh smell of the earth, and growing things, the songs of birds—especially of the blackbird, with his leisurely fluting note.

The garden, which lay to the left of the house, overlooked meadows, and was evidently as ancient as the Manor itself. It was also one after the heart of Bacon, "Spacious and fair, encompassed with a stately hedge." The farmer, who had neglected the roof and upper floors of the dwelling, had suffered these same yew hedges to grow as they pleased; and they now required a great deal of labour in trimming them to moderate proportions. The soil was rich—anything and everything seemed to flourish in the garden, which was intersected by broad gravelled walks that crossed one another at regular intervals; these were lined by a variety of old-fashioned plants—myrtle, lavender, and sweetbrier, grown to gigantic dimensions; here were also Madonna Lilies, London Pride, Hollyhocks, Sweet-William, and bushes of out-of-date roses, such as the "York and Lancaster," and other Georgian survivals. Precisely in the middle of the garden, where four walks met, was a hoary sundial, which bore the inscription, "Time Tries All." A path, leading direct from the sundial to an ancient bowling-green, was enclosed with rustic arches, and in the summer time the Manor pergola was a veritable tunnel of roses, and one of the sights of the neighbourhood.

And here it was that the unemployed chauffeur spent most of his time, clipping intractable hedges, planting, pruning, and digging. Such occupation removed him effectually from the orbit of his enemy—Miss Parrett—who merely pottered about the beds immediately surrounding the house. This was Miss Susan's realm—she was the family gardener; his volunteered labour also afforded Wynyard the now rare and priceless privilege of seeing Miss Morven when she ran in to talk to her aunt and help in the greenhouse—since, thanks to her active exertions, the Manor had been set in order, and her visits were no longer of daily occurrence.

Now and then he caught sight of her, walking with Mrs. Ramsay and her "guests," motoring with Mrs. Waring, or riding with her father. Once or twice they had passed him in the lanes at a late hour, riding fast, pursued by the panting Mackenzie. His best opportunity of meeting the young lady was at choir practice, and here he admired Miss Morven, not only for her sweet, clear voice, but her marvellous tact and admirable skill, the way she pacified Pither, the cranky old organist (a fine musician), and smoothed down rivals who claimed to sing solos, applauded the timid, and gently repressed the overbold. It was delightful to watch her consulting and advising and encouraging; but how could any one escape from the effect of that girl's beauty and contagious spirits? or withstand the influence of the subtle power called charm?

On Sundays she sat in the Rector's pew, facing the square enclosure of the Woolcocks, over which hung stately hatchments and memorials of the Davenant family; and from his corner in the choir Wynyard noted, with secret uneasiness and wrath, how the heir of Westmere—a squarely built, heavy young squire—kept his worshipping eyes fastened upon Aurea's clear-cut profile. After all, what was it to him? he asked himself furiously. Young Woolcock was heir to twenty thousand a year, and what was *he* at present? but her aunts' servant!

There had been a good deal of excited speculation in the village respecting Wynyard—as to who he really was, and where he came from. But although some swore he had been a soldier, and others vowed he had been a sailor, no one was any the wiser than the first day that he had arrived at Mrs. Hogben's, followed by his yellow tin box. "Ay, he could hold his tongue, that was sure; and was always ready enough to lend an ear to other people's affairs—but tight as an oyster with regard to his own."

Miss Susan, who felt towards him a kindness that was almost maternal, tormented by curiosity, had done her utmost to pump him. One day, in the greenhouse, she had seemed to see her opportunity. He had read off a French name on a label, and his accent and glibness were perfection.

"Ah! I see you have had a good education, Owen," she remarked, beaming at him over her glasses.

"Oh, middling, miss."

"You keep a boy to clean the motor, I hear!"

"Only once or twice, miss, when my hand was sore. His people are poor, and a shilling doesn't come amiss."

"I feel certain," clearing her throat, "that you are not accustomed to this sort of life, Owen." As she spoke, she kept her clear blue eyes on his face, and looked at him with the direct simplicity of a child. "I am interested in you, Owen. Do tell me about yourself, you know I wish you well."

"Miss Susan," and he straightened his shoulders and set down the pot he was holding, "you received my reference from Lady Kesters—and I believe it was all right?"

Miss Susan became very red indeed, and the garden scissors slipped from her thumb. There was something unusual in the young man's tone and glance.

"If you or Miss Parrett find that I am not giving satisfaction——"

"Oh no, no, no!" she broke in breathlessly, "I—I'm afraid I'm rather inquisitive—but I take a real interest in you, and you have been *such* a help to me—and I feel so friendly towards you—but, I won't ask you any more questions."

This little scene was subsequently related to Aurea, as she and her aunt drank tea together at the Rectory, and Miss Susan imparted to the girl— between bites of buttered toast—her own eager speculations. Mystery has a wonderful charm! A handsome young man, who was both reserved and obliging, who, it was known, was respected in the Drum, and kept to himself, and whom she believes to be one of her own class—offers a dangerous attraction for a girl of twenty! Aurea debated the puzzle in the abysmal depth of her own heart, and when a girl once allows her thoughts to dwell persistently upon a man—no matter what his station—her interest in him is bound to develop far beyond the bounds of everyday acquaintance!

Aurea was startled to discover that her mind was dwelling on the chauffeur more than was desirable; he occupied too large a share of her thoughts, though she did her utmost to expel him, and fill them with other matters—such, for instance, as the parish almshouses, the clothing club, and the choir—but a taciturn, mysterious young man, figuratively, thrust himself head and shoulders above these commonplace matters. Owen had a good voice, and had been impressed into the choir—a rollicking hunting song, sung at the Drum, had betrayed him. It was customary there, on certain nights, to sit round in a circle and call upon the members for entertainment, and Owen's "John Peel" had established his reputation.

Aurea was secretly annoyed by the way that girls on practice nights set their caps at the newcomer—boldly attracting his attention, appealing to his opinion, nudging one another significantly, and giggling and simpering when they spoke to him. And he? He met them half-way, shared hymn-books, found places, and talked, and seemed to be entirely happy and at ease in their company. Why not? He was ostensibly of their own class. He had not flinched from accepting a peppermint from Lily Jakes,—on the contrary, had received it with effusion,—and the overblown rosebud, tossed at him by Alexandra Watkins, had subsequently decorated his buttonhole.

Aurea contemplated these signs of good fellowship with stifled irritation. Was she envious, because the chauffeur, her aunts' servant, usually so monosyllabic and self-contained, could laugh and talk with these village girls? At this appalling arraignment her face flamed, she shrank in horror from her own thoughts. No, no, no, a hundred thousand times no!

Still, it must be confessed that, strive as she would, she could not help wondering and speculating about Owen, the chauffeur—whether she saw him vigorously washing the car, or trundling a wheelbarrow in the garden; zealously as he worked, it seemed to her observant eye that he looked as if he had not been accustomed to such employment. Who was he? The answer to this question came to her unexpectedly, and in a most unlikely place.

Aurea and her Aunt Susan went to Brodfield one afternoon, in order to execute various commissions for the Manor; the car was grudgingly lent for the occasion. There would have been no expedition, only that Miss Parrett was out of a certain shade of pink wool, the new cook was out of tapioca, and Miss Susan was a little out of sorts, and declared that "a drive in the air would cure her." The car waited at the post office, whilst the ladies accomplished their different errands in different shops. Aurea was the first to finish, and was sauntering slowly up the street, when she noticed that rare sight—a soldier in uniform—a smart Hussar on furlough, with a friend in mufti, coming towards her. As they passed the car, they glanced at it, and the soldier started, made a sort of halt, stared stupidly, and brought his hand to the salute! Yes, and the chauffeur gave him a little nod, and put his finger to his cap! (apparently unconscious of Miss Morven's vicinity).

As the two men approached, talking loudly, she overheard the Hussar say, as he strutted by—

"Well I'm damned, if that fellow on the car wasn't Lieutenant Wynyard! I was in his troop at Lucknow—a rare smart officer, too. What's his little game?"

"You'd better go back and arsk 'im," suggested the other, with a loud laugh.

"Not *me*," and they were out of earshot.

Aurea felt dumbfounded, as she moved on and got into her place. Susan, of course, was lingering as usual, chattering and last-wording to acquaintances, and she was not sorry to have a few moments to herself, to sit and meditate on her surprising discovery. So Owen's real name was Wynyard—and he had been an officer in a Hussar regiment. What *was* his game?

And her first impressions were justified; he was a gentleman, in spite of Joey's authoritative verdict and Mrs. Ramsay's gloomy forebodings. What dreadful thing had he done to be compelled to live under an assumed name, and bury himself, of all places, in Ottinge?

Aurea was now more deeply interested and puzzled than ever! She and Susan had no secrets from one another—for Susan was so young in her mind and heart that she seemed to be almost Aurea's contemporary!

From the first they liked the chauffeur, and though they had not said much, each was conscious of the other's opinion. Now that Aurea knew his name and former status for a fact, strange to relate, she resolved to have just this one little secret from Susan—and keep the knowledge to herself!

On the way home she proved an unusually silent and unsympathetic companion. Her conversation was jerky and constrained; she was not in the least interested in the scraps of local news that her aunt had collected in street and shops, but appeared to be lost in a maze of speculation and abstraction.

CHAPTER XV
BY WATER

Miss Parrett felt slightly embarrassed and uncomfortable when people remarked how seldom her motor was seen! "Was it not satisfactory?" they inquired. The old lady also recognised that her chauffeur was doing the work of a really capital gardener, and was Susan's right hand; this annoyed her excessively. She disliked the idea that her employé was slaving to please her sister; and accordingly changed her tactics, gave instructions for the car to go out twice a week with Miss Susan and Miss Morven, or Miss Susan and Mrs. Ramsay.

Susan and her niece had promptly availed themselves of this permission, and seized the opportunity of penetrating into far-away villages and to distant country seats; and the poor old motor, at their request, was racketted along at its best speed, as they were bound to be in Ottinge before dark, in order that the car might be washed. If they, by any chance, were a little late, they were received at the hall door by Miss Parrett, in cold silence, watch in hand.

After the recent heavy rains, the low, marshy country was flooded, and, returning one afternoon from a twenty-mile expedition, at a sharp turn in the road where the ground sloped steeply, the motor ran into a wide sheet of water—a neighbouring river had burst its banks. There was no going back, that was impossible. Miss Susan for once lost her nerve, and, putting her head out, asked the chauffeur piteously—

"What shall we do?"

"There's only one thing for it, miss," he answered promptly. "I don't think the water is deep, and I'll keep straight on—as near as I can guess—in the middle of the road; you see, there are ditches at either side, and I can't turn; but you need not be nervous—as long as the water doesn't reach the magneto you are all right."

But, as they crept forward cautiously, the water was gradually rising; it rose and rose, till it stole in under the door, and then the motor came to a full stop.

"*Now*, what's going to happen?" demanded Miss Susan excitedly.

"I see the road is not more than fifty yards ahead, and the water is shallower. We have stuck in the worst part."

"But what is to become of us, my good man? Are *we* to sit here all night—and the motor may blow up?"

"I'll go to a farmhouse and borrow a couple of horses, and I dare say after a bit I can start her again."

"And are we to remain here, Owen, and be half-drowned? You know my sister will be *crazy* if we are not home by seven."

"There's one thing I could do, Miss Susan," he replied, "that is if you have no objection; I can carry you and Miss Morven through the water, and put you out on the road high and dry. I think I might get a trap in Swingford village; you could drive home, and I'll bring the car along to-morrow. It seems the only thing to be done."

After this suggestion there ensued a long and animated consultation between aunt and niece; at last Miss Susan, raising her voice, said—

"Very well, Owen, I see no alternative; you can take me first—I am a light weight."

Owen now descended from his place and waded to the door, which he opened.

"All right, Miss Susan, you may depend on me. I won't drop you."

"How am I to manage?" she asked shame-facedly.

"It's quite easy! Just put your arms round my neck, miss, and hold tight."

After a moment's coy reluctance—it was the first time in her life she had ever put her arms round a man's neck—Miss Susan timidly embraced him.

"Hold on," he commanded, and, lifting her bodily out of the car as if she were a child, waded away, striding and splashing up to his middle in water. When he had carefully deposited her on dry land, the chauffeur returned for the young lady, who, it must be confessed, awaited him with a wildly beating heart; it seemed to her that in his air there was actually a look of mastery and triumph. If he had been an ordinary chauffeur, such as the Woolcocks', she would not have minded; but this man—this Lieutenant Wynyard, who was of her own class—oh, how she shrank from this enforced ordeal; she felt deeply reluctant and ashamed.

However, she asked no questions, made no hysterical protests, but rose as he appeared, put her arms on his shoulders—though she would rather have waded up to her neck—and was borne into the stream, upon which a laggard moon had recently arisen. Little, little did Aurea guess that, as she leant her head upon his leather shoulder, how Owen, the chauffeur, had to fight with a frantic, almost overmastering, desire to kiss her! And what an outcry there would have been, not merely from the young lady herself, but the sole witness, her maiden aunt!

Fortunately, with a superhuman effort, he pulled himself together, steadied his racing pulses, and thrust the dreadful idea behind him, as he struggled to the end of his task, and presently placed Miss Morven high and dry on the road beside her relative. Then, leaving the rescued ladies to one another's company, he set off to a village two miles distant to hunt up some conveyance.

As Wynyard tramped along in his wet clothes, he had it out with his ego. For all his youth and hot blood, he had always a cool power of judgment— as far as his own acts were concerned—and he was now prepared to discuss the present situation with himself. Since he had held Miss Aurea's light form in his arms, felt her sweet breath on his cheek, he knew there was no use in playing the ostrich, and that he was hopelessly in love—had been in love since the very first time he had set eyes upon her! Looking back at the matter, calmly and dispassionately, he realised that it was not on account of Leila's disappointment that he stayed on, and did not throw up his situation—as Miss Parrett's exasperating behaviour so often tempted him to do. He remained at Ottinge solely to be near Aurea; it was for Aurea that he kept his temper, slaved in the garden, and sang in the choir; yet he could not say a word to Aurea, or endeavour to ingratiate himself like other more fortunate young men; he had his bond to remember, and his hands were tied—yes, and his tongue too. Was ever any fellow in such a fix? And such was the contrariness of life, he had gone about the world when he was free, and had never once met a girl he thought of twice—and here he was always thinking of Aurea, yet dared not disclose his feelings; meanwhile, some luckier fellow would come along and make up to her and marry her! And at the thought he stopped and ground his heel into the earth with savage force.

There was Bertie Woolcock, rolling in money, heir to that fine place; and he would have one year and ten months' start, whilst *he* was left at the post! Oh, it was enough to drive him mad to think of! Well, Bertie had never held her in his arms, at any rate,—he had; how she had trembled, poor darling! Yes, he was that to the good.

"Mean beast!" apostrophising himself; "when you know that the girl could not help herself, and would have given everything she possessed to get out of such a dilemma!" What would Leila say? Should he tell her? No;

she would only laugh (he could hear her laugh) and ask, "What are you going to marry on, even if Uncle Dick lets you off?"

He had two pounds two shillings a week, and if he made love to her niece, Miss Parrett would naturally and properly send him about his business. Oh, it was all an infernal muddle—there was no way out of it— nothing to do but hide his feelings and bide his time; the wild, haunting refrain of an old negro camp hymn came into his head, "And hold the Lion down! and hold the Lion down!" Well, he was holding the lion down, and a thundering hard job he found it!

He had no reason to suspect that Aurea ever thought of him—why should she? She was always polite, gracious—no more. His only little scrap of comfort lay in the fact that he believed Miss Susan liked him—liked him really, in a nice, sentimental, proper, old-maid fashion! She was romantic, so said her niece, who bantered her on her passion for promoting love-affairs and love-matches—he had heard her taunt her playfully with the fact. Undoubtedly Miss Susan was his good friend, and that was the sole morsel of comfort he could offer himself!

Presently Wynyard reached a sleepy little village, unearthed a carrier's cart, horse, and man, and returned to the place where the two ladies were awaiting him with the liveliest impatience.

That evening, at nine o'clock, Miss Susan, who had deposited her niece at the Rectory, arrived at home in a carrier's cart—the sole available mode of conveyance. Her sister, who had been roaming about the hall and passages, accompanied by Mrs. Ramsay, wringing her hands and whimpering that "Susan had been killed," was considerably relieved. But, as soon as her fears were subdued, she became frightfully excited respecting the fate of her beautiful motor, which, by all accounts, had been left standing in the middle of a river—five miles from home.

"Oh, I assure you it will be all right, Bella; please don't worry yourself. Owen will manage."

"Owen, indeed!" she echoed angrily; "it's my opinion that he manages *you*—you think a great deal too much of that young man; there's something at the back of him—it would never surprise me if some day he went off with that motor, and we never saw him again."

"My dear sister! You know you are overwrought, or you would never talk such rubbish."

"If the motor was stuck in the middle of a river, I should like to know how you and Aurea got out of it without being half-drowned?" she demanded judicially.

"Oh, we got out of it very simply, and it was as easy as kiss my hand," rejoined Miss Susan, with a gay laugh. "The only person that got wet was Owen; he carried us."

"*What!*" cried Mrs. Ramsay, with dancing eyes; "carried you and Aurea—how?"

"Why, in his arms—where else? First he took me, then he took her; and we were no more trouble to him than if we had been a couple of babies."

"Well, upon my word," snorted Miss Parrett, casting up her hands, "I think the whole thing is scandalous! You and Aurea flying about the country, and spending most of your time in the motor, going here and going there, coming home at night alone in a carrier's cart, and telling me you left the motor in the middle of a river, and that you were carried out of it in the arms of the chauffeur! and that without a blush on your faces! Upon my word, Susan Parrett, I don't know what's coming to you! Either you are going mad, or you are falling into your second childhood."

Miss Parrett was profoundly relieved to see her valuable car arrive on its own horse-power the following afternoon. It certainly looked rather limp and sorry for itself, and did not recover from its adventures in the river for some time. Water had a fatal effect upon its organisation; indeed, its condition became so serious that it had to be sent to a garage, there to be overhauled—and a bill, which was the result, proved one of Miss Parrett's favourite grievances for the ensuing six months.

CHAPTER XVI
TWO PRISONERS

By the middle of June Miss Susan had departed to visit friends in the south of England, escorting her niece as far as London, where she was to spend some weeks with General and Mrs. Morven. The motor was in hospital at Brodfield, and Owen, the chauffeur, had absolutely nothing to do; no gardening, no greenhouse, no car. Miss Parrett was now the undisputed ruler of Ottinge—manor and village—and he kept out of her way in a crafty, not to say cowardly, fashion; when at home, Miss Susan and her niece had intervened as buffers between him and Miss Parrett's despotic rudeness. Doubtless her bullying and browbeating were a legacy from her burly grandfather, the Hoogly Pilot; indeed, she was positively so insulting with regard to repairs, his bill for petrol, and the extraordinary— the incredible quantity he wasted, that sooner than face her and have rows, he more than once paid for it out of his own pocket! But do not let it be for a moment supposed that the chauffeur was afraid of the old lady; he was afraid of himself—afraid that if she became altogether insupportable, he might lose, in one and the same moment, his temper, and his situation!

When Bella Parrett reigned alone, it was a sore time for the Manor, and especially for Joss. The old lady did not care for any animals or pets, save a venerable green and blue parrot—her own contemporary. She had accepted Joss, a gift from Mr. Woolcock, as she was assured that, having no man living at the Manor, a dog was a necessity in case of robbers, but chiefly because Miss Parrett half suspected that the Martingales—neighbours of the Woolcocks—were anxious to possess the said amusing little puppy. Joss was often in disgrace; but what could one expect of an idle young dog, without companions, education, or pursuits? When Susan was at home all went well; she looked after him and screened his failings, and took him out—though her sister frequently expostulated, and said—

"Now, I won't have the creature attaching himself to you, Susan; he must learn to know that he is *my* dog!"

All the same, she never troubled about "her dog's" food or sleeping quarters, and it was actually Susan who paid for his licence!

Now Susan was absent, also his good friend Aurea—and Joss was in confinement and deep disgrace; even before his friends' departure he had been under a black cloud. His youthful spirits were uncontrollable; Joss had inherited the keen sporting instincts of his father, with the intellectual faculties of his accomplished mother, Colette, the poodle, and was both bold and inquisitive. Recently, the wretched animal had chewed off the tail of a magnificent tiger-skin, and concealed it, no one knew where! Miss Parrett hoped he had eaten it—as it was cured with arsenic—but more likely it had been stored in one of his many bone larders. He had poked his nose into a valuable jar, upset, and smashed it! he had come in all wet and muddy from a rat-hunting excursion in the river, and recouped his exhausted energies by a luxurious siesta in Miss Parrett's own bed—and there was also a whispered and mysterious communication respecting the disappearance of a best and most expensive *front*, which had undoubtedly gone to the same limbo as the tiger's tail!

"The brute is worse than a dozen monkeys," declared his furious mistress, and he was accordingly bestowed on a farmer, who lived miles away near Catsfield, merely to return, accompanied by a piece of rope, the same evening. After this, the word "poison" was breathed; but luckily for Joss, Ottinge did not possess a chemist. Finally he was condemned to a fare of cold porridge, and solitary confinement in an empty stable—being suffered to roam loose at night after the house was closed.

The chauffeur and the brown dog had a good deal in common; they were both young and both captives in their way. Oh, those long, endless summer days, when the young man hung about the yard, with nothing to do, awaiting orders, unable to undertake any job in case the car should be wanted. When he called each morning for Miss Parrett's instructions, and to ask if she would require the motor, the invariable reply was that "she would let him know *later*."

The first time they met, Miss Parrett had taken a dislike to the chauffeur, and this dislike had recently been increased by an outrage of more recent date. She had seen Owen, her paid servant, in convulsions of laughter at her expense; yes, laughing exhaustively at his mistress! This was on the occasion of a ridiculous and distressing incident which had taken place one sultry afternoon in the garden. The Rector and his daughter were helping Susan to bud roses—a merry family party; the chauffeur was neatly trimming a box border, Hogben raking gravel, Miss Parrett herself, hooded like a hawk, was poking and prowling around. All at once she emerged from a tool-shed, bearing in triumph a black bottle, which she imprudently shook.

"I'd like to know what *this* is?" she demanded, in her shrillest pipe. The answer was instantaneous, for the liquor being "up," there was a loud explosion, a wild shriek, and in a second Miss Parrett's identity was completely effaced by the contents of a bottle of porter. The too inquisitive lady presented a truly humiliating spectacle. Hood, face, hands, gown, were covered with thick cream-coloured foam; it streamed and dripped, whilst she gasped and gurgled, and called upon "Susan!" and "Aurea!"

As the stuff was removed from her eyes by the latter—anxiously kind, but distinctly hysterical—almost the first object to catch the old lady's eye was the chauffeur, at a little distance, who, such was his enjoyment of the scene, was actually holding his sides! He turned away hastily, but she could see that his shoulders were shaking, and told herself then that she would never forgive him. She bided her time to award suitable punishment for his scandalous behaviour—and the time arrived.

The malicious old woman enjoyed the conviction that she was holding this too independent chauffeur a prisoner on the premises, precisely as she kept the detestable Joss tied up in the stables. Joss rattled and dragged at his chain, and occasionally broke into melancholy howls, whilst the other paced to and fro in the red-tiled yard, thinking furiously and smoking many more cigarettes than were good for him.

Accustomed from childhood to a life of great activity, to be, perforce, incarcerated hour after hour, awaiting the good—or evil—pleasure of an old woman who was afraid to use her motor, exasperated Wynyard to the last degree. The car was ready, he was ready; usually about six o'clock Miss Parrett would trot out in her hood and announce in her bleating voice—

"Owen, I shall not require the car to-day!"

Sometimes she would look in on a humble, fawning culprit in the stable, and say, as she contemplated his beseeching eyes—

"Hah! you bad dog, you *bad* dog! I wish to goodness you were dead—and you shall wish it yourself before I've done with you!"

It was not impossible that these amiable visitations afforded Miss Parrett a delicious, and exquisite satisfaction.

The Drum Inn closed at ten o'clock, and even before the church clock struck, the Hogbens had retired; but the former Hussar officer, accustomed to late hours, and with the long summer night seducing him, found it impossible to retire to his three-cornered chamber—where the walls leant towards him so confidentially, and the atmosphere reeked of dry rot. No, he must breathe the sweet breath of the country, have some exercise, and walk himself weary under the open sky.

Mrs. Hogben—who had now absolute confidence in her lodger, and told him all her most private family affairs—entrusted him with the door-key, that is to say, she showed him the hole in which—as all the village knew—it was concealed. Sometimes it was one in the morning when the chauffeur crept upstairs in stockinged feet, accompanied by Joss—yes, *Joss!* There were a pair of them, who had equally enjoyed their nocturnal wanderings. The dog slept on a bit of sacking, in his confederate's room, till Mrs. Hogben was astir, then he flew back to the Manor, and crept through the same hole in the yew hedge by which, in answer to a welcome whistle, he had emerged the preceding evening. Behold him sitting at the kitchen door when the kitchen-maid opened it, the personification of injured innocence—a poor, neglected, hungry animal, who had been turned out of doors for the whole long night.

These were delightful excursions: over meadows and brooks, through deep glens and plantations, the two black sheep scoured the country, and, as far as human beings were concerned, appeared to have earth and heaven to themselves. Wynyard roamed hither and thither as the freak took him, and surrendered himself to the intoxication that comes of motion in the open air—a purely animal pleasure shared with his companion.

They surprised the dozing cattle, and alarmed astonished sheep, sent families of grazing rabbits scuttling to their burrows; they heard the night-jar, the owl, and the corn-crake; bats flapped across their path, and in narrow lanes the broad shoulders of Wynyard broke the webs of discomfited spiders. The extraordinary stillness of the night was what impressed the young man; sometimes, from a distance of four or five miles, he could hear, with startling distinctness, the twelve measured strokes of Ottinge church clock.

During these long, aimless rambles, what Joss' thoughts were, who can say? Undoubtedly he recalled such excursions in ecstatic dreams. Wynyard, for his part, took many pleasure trips into the land of fancy, and there, amidst its picturesque glamour and all its doubts, distractions, and hopes, his sole companion was Aurea! Nothing but the hope of her return sustained and kept him day after day, pacing the Manor yard, in a sense *her* prisoner! His devotion would have amazed his sister; she could not have believed that Owen, of all people, would have been so enslaved by a girl, could have become a dumb, humble worshipper, satisfied to listen to her laugh, to catch a radiant glance of her dark eyes, and, when he closed the door of the car, to shield her dainty skirt with reverent fingers.

Presently there came a spell of bad weather, the rain sweeping across the country in great grey gusts and eddying whirls, moaning and howling through the village, making the venerable trees in Mrs. Hogben's orchard quite lively in their old age, lashing each other with their hoary arms, in furious play.

It was impossible for Wynyard to spend the entire evening indoors over Mrs. Hogben's fire, listening to tales of when "she was in service," though he was interested to hear that Miss Alice Parrett as was—Mrs. Morven—"was the best of the bunch, and there wasn't a dry eye when she was buried." He also learned that Mr. Morven was rich for a parson, and had once kept a curate, well paid, too; but the curate had been terribly in love with Miss Aurea, and of course she wouldn't look at him—a little red-haired, rat-faced fellow! and so he had gone away, and there was no more regular curate, only weekends, when Mr. Morven went abroad for his holiday. And now and then Mrs. Hogben would fall into heartrending reminiscences of her defunct pigs.

"Afore *you* come, Jack, I kep' pigs," she informed him; "one a year. I bought un at Brodfield—a nice little fellow—for fifteen shillings to a pound, and fattened un up, being so much alone all day, I could never help making sort of free with the pig, and petting un. He always knew me, and would eat out of my hand, and was a sort of companion, ye see?"

"Yes," assented Wynyard, though he did not see, for in his mind's eye he was contemplating Aurea Morven.

"Well, of course, he grew fat, and ready for the butcher, and when he was prime, he had to go—but it just broke my heart, so it did; for nights before I couldn't sleep for crying," here she became lachrymose; "but it had to be, and me bound to be about when the men came, and the cries and yells of him nigh drove me wild; though, of course, once he was scalded and hung up, and a fine weight, it wor a nice thing to have one's own pork and bacon."

Her companion nodded sympathetically.

"Howsomever, the last time I was so rarely fond of the pig, and his screams and carryings-on cut me so *cruel*, that I made a vow, then and there, I'd never own another, but take a lodger instead—and you, Jack, be the *first!*"

"I'm sure I'm flattered," rejoined Wynyard, with an irony entirely wasted on his companion, who, with her skirt turned over her knees, and her feet generously displayed, sat at the other side of the fire, thoroughly enjoying herself.

"Tom is out," he said, and this remark started her at once into another topic, and a series of bitter complaints of Dilly Topham—Tom's girl.

"The worst of it is, she's mighty pretty, ain't she?" she asked querulously.

"She is," he admitted. Dilly was a round-faced, smiling damsel, with curly brown hair and expressive blue eyes—a flirt to her finger-tips. It was also true that she did lead poor Tom a life, and encouraged a smart young insurance agent, with well-turned, stockinged calves, and a free-wheel bicycle.

"I'd never put up with her," declared Mrs. Hogben, "only for her grandmother."

"Why her grandmother?" he questioned lazily.

"Bless your dear heart, old Jane Topham has been a miser all her life. Oh, she's a masterpiece, she is, and lives on the scrapings of the shop; she hasn't had a gown this ten year, but has a fine lump of money in the Brodfield Bank, and Dilly is all she's got left, and the apple of her eye. Dilly will have a big fortune—only for that, I'd put her to the door, with her giggling and her impudence, yes I would, and that's the middle and the two ends of it!"

When Wynyard had heard more than enough of Dilly's doings and misdoings, and the biographies and tragedies of his predecessors (the pigs), he went over to the Drum, listened to discussions, and realised the prominent characteristics of the English rustic—reluctance to accept a new idea. Many talked as if the world had not moved for thirty years, and evinced a dull-witted contentment, a stolid refusal to look facts in the face; but others, the younger generation, gave him a new perspective—these read the papers, debated their contents, and took a keen interest in their own times.

Wynyard generally had a word with old Thunder, and played a game of chess with Pither, the organist. Captain Ramsay was established in his usual place—smoking, silent, and staring. So intent was his gaze, so insistently fixed, that Wynyard invariably arranged to sit with his back to him, but even then he seemed to feel the piercing eyes penetrating the middle of his spine!

One evening Captain Ramsay suddenly rose, and shuffled out of his corner—an usual proceeding, for he remained immovable till closing time (ten o'clock). He came straight up to where Wynyard was bending over the chess-board, considering a move, and laying a heavy hand on his shoulder, and speaking in a husky voice, said—

"I say—*Wynyard*—don't you know me?"

CHAPTER XVII
LADY KESTERS HAS MISGIVINGS

At this amazing question the chauffeur started violently, looked up into the anxious, sunken eyes gazing into his own, and answered—

"No, to the best of my belief, I've never seen you before—never till I came here."

The man's worn face worked with violent emotion—which he vainly struggled to subdue.

"What!" he demanded, in a high, hoarse key, "have you forgotten Lucknow?—and Jim Ramsay of the Seventh? Impossible!"

Wynyard glanced at him and again shook his head.

After a long pause, expressive of indignant incredulity—

"Why, man alive, you and I were at school together! Don't you remember your poky little room over the churchyard, and how we fagged for Toler, and played hard rackets?"

As Wynyard still remained irresponsive, suddenly, to his horror, the questioner burst into tears and tottered unsteadily towards the door, wringing his hands, uttering loud convulsive sobs, and exclaiming, "As a dead man out of mind! As a dead man out of mind! Tell them to sound the Last Post!"

There was a loud murmur from the card-players, and old Thunder, turning about and addressing the company, said—

"Poor old chap, 'e's worse nor ever. At school together"—to Wynyard— "Lor' bless me! why, ye might be his son! I suppose 'e's a stranger to ye, mister?"

"Yes; I never laid eyes on him before."

"He's a-going off his nut," declared a voice from the nap table; "he did ought to be put away—he did."

"Ay," agreed the organist, addressing Wynyard, "his good lady won't hear of it; but it's my opinion that he is no longer safe to himself or others—

it's the loose and at-home lunatics that commit these awful crimes ye read of in the papers, and makes your blood run cold."

Wynyard made no reply. He had more than once heard Pither himself spoken of as a madman and a crazy fellow; but *he* was merely eccentric. As for Captain Ramsay, he was lost in conjecture as to how that unfortunate and afflicted gentleman had got hold of his *real* name?

This mystery was solved no later than the next evening. In the lovely, soft June twilight he was walking past the Claringbold's empty farm, and here came upon the captain, who was leaning over the gate, and signalled imperatively to him with his stick.

"Look here!" he called out, and Wynyard stood still. "You've been a puzzle to me for nearly six weeks—and at last I've got you."

"Got *me!*"

"Of course you are Owen Wynyard; you and I knew one another long ago. Why, man! we were schoolfellows, almost like brothers, and afterwards, when our two regiments lay in Lucknow—why, God bless me! it's over thirty years ago!"

Captain Ramsay had got hold of his right name, but otherwise he was a raving lunatic.

"You are Owen Wynyard, aren't you?" he asked impatiently.

"Yes, I am, but I don't use the Wynyard here; and I must beg you to keep it to yourself."

"Oh, all right; in one of your old scrapes, my boy! Money scarce! Ha ha!" and he laughed hysterically. "So you're lying doggo from the Soucars, but why *here?*"

"That's my business," he answered sharply.

"Come, come, don't be so grumpy and short with me, Owen. You were always such a rare good-tempered chap. What has changed you, eh? Now, come along home with me, and we will have a good 'bukh' over old times," and, as he spoke, his grasp—a fierce, possessive clutch—tightened painfully on his prisoner's arm.

"But," objected the victim, "I was going for a turn."

"No, you are not; you are coming straight home with me. My wife will be glad to make your acquaintance. I forget if you've met her?" and he touched his forehead. "I'm a little funny here, Owen. India, my boy! she takes it out of all of us one way or another—teeth, hair, liver, brains. Come on now—right about turn!" he concluded facetiously.

There was no use in resistance or in having a violent personal struggle with the lunatic—nothing for it but to submit; and, in spite of his reluctance, Wynyard was conducted, as if in custody, right up to the door of Ivy House. Were he to refuse to enter, he knew there would only be a scene in the street, a gaping crowd, and an unpleasant exposure.

"Look, look, Tom!" cried Mrs. Hogben, pointing to the opposite house, "if the captain hasn't got hold of our young fellow, and a-walkin' him home as if he had him in charge—he has took a fancy to him, I do declare!"

"There's more nor one has took a fancy to Owen," remarked Tom, with gruff significance; "but, as to the captain—well—I'd rather it was him—nor me."

The captain entered his house with a latchkey and an air of importance; there was a light in the square hall, and a door at one side was ajar. He called out—

"Katie, Katie, come and see what *I* have found for you!"

A door was opened wide, and there stood Mrs. Ramsay in a tea-gown, with a little black Pom. in her arms. She looked amazed, as well she might, but instantly dissembled her surprise, and said—

"Good-evening—I see my husband has invited you in for a smoke?"

"Smoke!" said Captain Ramsay, passing into the drawing-room, and beckoning Wynyard to follow him. As he did so, he glanced apologetically at the lady of the house, and it struck him then that he was looking into a face that had seen all the sorrows of the world.

The room was furnished with solid old furniture, but Mrs. Ramsay's taste—or was it Miss Morven's—had made it a charming and restful retreat, with pretty, soft wall-paper, rose-shaded lamps, flowers, a quantity of books, and a few Indian relics—such as a brass table, a phoolcarrie or two, and some painted Tillah work which he recognised as made near Lucknow.

"Katie," resumed her husband, after a pause, "I know you will be pleased to hear I've met a very old friend," and he laid his hand heavily on Wynyard's shoulder. "Let me introduce Captain Wynyard—Owen Wynyard of the Red Hussars. He and I were quartered together in Lucknow, a matter of thirty-three years ago—why, I knew him, my dear, long before I ever set eyes on *you!*"

As he concluded, he gazed at her with his dark shifty eyes, and Wynyard noticed the nervous twitching of his hands.

"I'm sure I'm delighted to make your acquaintance," she said, with the utmost composure, though her lips were livid. Jim was getting worse—this scene marked a new phase of his illness—another milestone on the road to dementia.

"We were inseparable, Katie, I can tell you, and went up together for our leave to Naini Tal, and stayed at the club, rowed in the regatta, had a ripping time, and went shooting in Kumaon. I say, Owen, do you remember the panther that took your dog near Bhim Tal—and how you got him?"

Wynyard nodded assent—in for a penny, in for a pound! He was impersonating a dead man, and what was a dead dog more or less?

"Do you remember the cairn we raised over him, and he was so popular, every one who knew him, that passed up or down, placed a stone on it?"

"Wouldn't you like to go and smoke in the dining-room?" suggested Mrs. Ramsay. "Jim, I'll ring for Mary to light the lamp, she does not know you are in."

"No, no, I'll go myself," and he shuffled into the hall.

"He has taken you for some one else, of course, poor fellow!" she said, turning quickly to Wynyard, and speaking under her breath.

"Yes," he answered, "for my father—but please keep this to yourself—I've always heard I am extraordinarily like him."

"Then humour him, humour him, *do*. You see how bright and happy this imaginary meeting has made him. Oh, it will be so kind of you to talk to him of India—he loves it—how I wish you knew the country—you must pretend, and I will coach you. Lucknow is very hot, and gay, not far——"

"But I needn't pretend," he broke in, "I know the country—yes—and Lucknow too. I was there with my father's old regiment."

She stared at him for a moment in bewildered astonishment.

"I say, you won't give me away, will you?" he added anxiously.

"No; is it likely? If you will only come and talk to him of an evening now and then, it will be truly one of the good deeds that will be scored up to you in heaven. Ah, here he is, and the lamp."

"Now come along, Owen," he said briskly. "Here you are, I've got my best tobacco for you. Let's have a bukh!"

And what a bukh it was! Captain Ramsay carried on most of the conversation, and as he discoursed of old friends, of shikar, of camps and manœuvres, racing and polo, his sunken eyes kindled, he became animated; it was another personality to that of the silent, drooping figure known to Ottinge. Wynyard, as he listened and threw in a word or two, could now dimly realise the good-looking smart officer in this poor stranded wreck.

Mrs. Ramsay, who had brought her work and her little dog, sat somewhat apart, beyond the shaded lamp's rays, listened, wondered, and inwardly wept. What vital touch to a deadened mind had kindled these old memories? What a mysterious organ was the human brain!

And the taciturn chauffeur, he too was changed—it was another individual; he sat there, smoking, his elbow on the table, discussing army matters (now obsolete), notable generals, long dead and gone, the hills and plains of India, the climate—that, at least, was unchanged—with extraordinary coolness and adaptability. The guest was playing the rôle of being his own father, with astounding success. And what a good-looking young fellow! she noticed his clear-cut features, the well set-on head, the fine frame, the distinguished looking brown hand that lay carelessly on the table. The scene was altogether amazing; this sudden recognition seemed to have aroused Jim from a long, long mental slumber. Was it a sign of recovery—or was it a symptom of the end?

When at last Owen rose to go, Captain Ramsay made no effort to detain him, but sat, with his head thrown back and his eyes fixed on the opposite wall, lost in a reverie of ghastly vacuity.

It was Mrs. Ramsay who accompanied her guest into the hall, and inquired, in her everyday manner—

"And when is the motor of Ottinge coming back?"

"I am to fetch it to-morrow."

Then, in another voice, almost a whisper, she added—

"I am so grateful to you. My husband and your father seem to have been like brothers—and you really managed wonderfully. You have given Jim such pleasure, and, poor fellow, he has so little!" Her eyes were dim as she looked up, "Even I, who am with him always, see a change. I am afraid he is growing worse."

"Why not better?" asked Wynyard, with forced cheerfulness. "Have you seen a mental specialist?"

"Oh yes, long ago; his condition is the result of sunstroke, and they said he—he ought to be—put away in an asylum; but of course his home is his asylum."

Her visitor was not so clear about this, and there was no doubt that now and then the captain's eyes had an alarmingly mad expression.

"Can you manage to come and see him occasionally, or is it asking too much?"

"I'll come with pleasure; I have my evenings off—the car never goes out at night, as you may know; but I'm only Owen Wynyard, late of the Red Hussars, in this house, if you please, Mrs. Ramsay."

"Of course; and I shall be only too thankful to see you whenever you can spare us an hour," and she opened the door and let him out.

From this time forth there commenced an intimacy between the chauffeur and the Ramsays. He not only spent an hour now and then with the captain, smoking, playing picquet, and talking over old times, but he gave Mrs. Ramsay valuable assistance with her boarders, treated bites, thorns, and other casualties with a practised hand; on one occasion sat up at night with a serious case of distemper; on another, traced and captured a valuable runaway. He admired her for her unquenchable spirit, energy, and pluck, and helped in the kennel with the boy she employed, and undertook to exercise the most boisterous dogs of an evening. These thoroughly enjoyed their excursions with an active companion, who, however, maintained a strict but kindly discipline; and, of a bright moonlight night, it was no uncommon sight to meet the chauffeur, four or five miles from Ottinge, accompanied by, not only Joss, but by several of Mrs. Ramsay's paying guests.

The friendship between the captain and the chauffeur naturally did not pass unnoticed, and the verdict of the Drum was that the young fellow, having spare time on his hands, had been "took on as a sort of keeper at Ivy House, and gave a help with the kennel and the old man—and the old man was growing worse."

Leila had arranged to pay a flying visit to Brodfield when her brother went there to fetch the motor, and he found her awaiting him in a gloomy sitting-room of that once celebrated posting-inn—the Coach and Horses.

"Three months are gone!" she said, after their first greetings, "so far so good, *ce n'est que le premier pas qui coute!*"

"There are a good many *pas* yet! It's awfully nice to see you, Sis, and be myself for once in a way," and then he proceeded to unfold his experience with Captain Ramsay.

"Oh, how ghastly! The poor lunatic talking away to you, and taking you for our father! Imagine him recognising you by the likeness, and skipping thirty-three years! No one else suspects you, do they?"

"His wife knows my real name, and that's all; I had to tell her, but she is safe as a church. Miss Susan has been curious."

"Bless her dear simple heart!"

"I say amen to that; but of all the mean, purse-proud, tyrannical old hags, give me Bella Parrett! She's always bragging of her family, too, and her crest—in my opinion it ought to be a civet cat!"

"Oh, Owen," and she laughed, "it's not often that you are stirred to such indignation."

"Ah, you don't know her."

"Apparently not. Well, what do you say to a move, and to better yourself? I believe I could find you a capital place in Somersetshire, not so retired, more in the world, and with quite smart people."

"No, thanks, I'll stick to this now—anyway till Christmas."

"But, Owen, when the old woman and the motor are so objectionable—by the way, I must inspect it before you start to-morrow—why remain?"

"Oh, I've got the hang of the place now. I know the people, I've comfortable quarters—and—er—I like Miss Susan——"

"Do you like any one else, Owen, come?"

"I like the parson, and the schoolmaster, and Tom Hogben."

"Well, well, well!" throwing herself back, "I see you won't give me your confidence! I am positively certain there is some one in Ottinge you like much better than the parson and the schoolmaster—or even Miss Susan."

"I swear there is not," he answered, boldly confronting her. (Aurea was not in Ottinge, but visiting her rich London relatives, doing a bit of the season with, to borrow the native term, "Mrs. General Morven.")

Leila was puzzled. Owen, she knew, was a hopelessly bad liar, and his face looked innocence itself.

"I've got a box for the theatre here—a company on tour. We may as well go—you can sit in the back," she said, rising.

"All right; it's to be hoped none of the Ottinge folk will be there, and spot me!"

"Not they! Don't you know your Ottinge by this time? Is it likely that any one of them would come all this way to see a mere play?"

"Miss Susan might, she loves an outing and any little bit of amusement; but she's not at home, and if she was, she would not get the use of the motor."

"The theatre is only across the square—it's quite near, so we may as well walk;" and they did. Lady Kesters in a high black dress, her brother in a dark suit, passed unnoticed among the crowd, and enjoyed the entertainment.

The next morning Lady Kesters left Brodfield by the ten o'clock train for London, having previously inspected the celebrated green gem at the garage. She even got into it, examined it critically, and laughed as she descended.

"Oh, what a take in! What a shame to have cheated those poor old women! Why, Owen, I believe it must be years and years old!"

"And a bad machine always; strong when you want it to be weak, and weak when it should be strong. Some of these days it will play me a trick, I'm sure."

"What, that old bone-shaker! No, no. Well, I'm afraid you must soon be starting—as you say Miss Parrett awaits you, watch in hand—and so must I. It's been awfully good to see you, and find you are getting on so well—'a chauffeur almost to the manner born.' Martin takes a profound interest in our enterprise."

"He keeps me supplied with lots of tobacco and A1 cigars. Tell him that Miss Susan asked me if I got them in the village? and Miss Parrett, who is as sharp as a razor, inquired how I could *afford* to buy them? I ventured to offer a couple to the doctor—I told him they were a present; he took them like a lamb, and asked no questions."

"What! does a lamb smoke? Well, I'll tell Martin how much his offerings are appreciated, and that you really are fit—and quite happy, eh?"

"Yes, tell him that neither of you need worry about me; I'm all right at Ottinge."

But when, an hour later, Lady Kesters gazed meditatively on the flying Midlands, with her thoughts concentrated upon her brother, she was by no means so sure, that he *was* all right at Ottinge!

CHAPTER XVIII
THE REASON WHY

Whilst Ottinge had been dozing through lovely summer days, Aurea Morven was enjoying a certain amount of the gay London season. General and Mrs. Morven had no family — Aurea was their only young relative, the Parretts' only niece, the parson's only child; and, though she was the light of the Rectory, he was not selfish, and shared and spared her company. Besides, as Mrs. Morven said, "Edgar had his literary work, his large correspondence, his parish, and Jane Norris to look after him, and it was out of the question to suppose that a girl with such beauty and attractiveness was to be buried in an out-of-the-way hole like Ottinge-in-the-Marsh — although her father and her aunts *did* live there!" Mrs. Morven, a masterful lady on a large scale, who carried herself with conscious dignity, looked, and was a manager — a manager of ability. She was proud of the general's pretty niece, enjoyed chaperoning her and taking her about, and anticipated her making a notable match; for, besides her pretty face, and charming, unspoiled nature, Aurea was something of an heiress.

It seemed to this clear-sighted lady that her niece was changed of late, her spontaneous gaiety had evaporated, once or twice she had sudden fits of silence and abstraction, and, although she laughed and danced and appeared to enjoy herself, refused to take any of her partners seriously, and shortened her visit by three weeks!

Miss Susan had arrived at Eaton Place for a couple of days. It was arranged by the girl that she and her aunt were to leave town together — though the general and his wife pleaded for a longer visit, offering Aurea, as a temptation, a ball, a Windsor garden-party, and Sandown — the filial daughter shook her head, with smiling decision; she had promised the Padre, and, besides, she wanted to get back to the garden before the best of the roses were over! Theatre dinners were breaking up at the Ritz, and a stream of smart people were gradually departing eastward. Among the crowd in the hall, awaiting her motor, stood Lady Kesters, superb in diamonds and opera mantle. She and Miss Susan caught sight of one another at the same moment, and Miss Susan immediately began to make her way through the throng.

"So glad to meet you!" gasped the elder lady. "I called yesterday afternoon, but you were out."

"Yes, so sorry—I was down in the country. Do come and lunch to-morrow."

"I wish I could, but, unfortunately, we are going home. Let me introduce my niece, Aurea Morven—Lady Kesters."

Lady Kesters smiled and held out her hand. Could this extremely pretty girl be the reason of Owen's surprising contentment? She looked at her critically. No country mouse, this! her air and her frock were of the town. What a charming face and marvellous complexion—possibly due to the Marsh air!

"I have known your aunts for years"; and, though addressing Miss Susan, she looked straight at Aurea, as she asked, "And how is the new chauffeur suiting you?"

The girl's colour instantly rose, but before she could speak, Miss Susan flung herself on the question.

"Oh, very well indeed—most obliging and civil—has been quite a treasure in the house and garden."

Lady Kesters raised her delicately pencilled eyebrows and laughed.

"The chauffeur—*gardening*! How funny!"

"You see, Bella is so nervous in a motor, it is not often wanted, and Owen likes to help us. We find him rather silent and reserved about himself; he gives the impression of being a bit above his place?" and she looked at Lady Kesters interrogatively.

"Really?"

"I suppose you can tell me something about him—as you said you'd known him for years?" continued Miss Susan, with unconcealed eagerness. "I am, I must confess, just a little curious. Where does he come from? Has he any belongings?"

"Oh, my dear lady, do you think it necessary to look into your chauffeur's past! I believe he comes from Westshire, his people—er—er—lived on my grandfather's property; as to his belongings—ah! there is my husband! I see he has found the car at last, and I must fly! So sorry you are leaving town to-morrow—*good*-bye!" Lady Kesters now understood her brother's reluctance to leave Ottinge—she had seen the reason why.

Miss Susan and her niece travelled down to Catsfield together, were met in state by the motor and luggage-cart, and created quite a stir at the little station. Miss Morven had such a heap of boxes—one as big as a sheep trough—that the cart was delayed for nearly a quarter of an hour, and Peter, the porter, for once had a job:

The ladies found that, in their absence, the neighbourhood had awakened; there were large house-parties at Westmere and Tynflete, and not a few smart motors now to be seen skimming through the village. It was a fact that several tourists had visited the church, and had "tea" at Mrs. Pither's, and patronised her neighbour's "cut flowers." The old church was full on Sundays, dances and cricket matches were in prospect, and Miss Morven, the countryside beauty, was immediately in enviable request.

Miss Parrett had relaxed her hold, so to speak, upon the car, and lent it daily, and even nightly, to her niece and sister; indeed, it seemed that she would almost do anything with the motor than use it herself; and though she occasionally ventured to return calls at a short distance, it was undoubtedly pain and grief to her to do so—and, on these occasions, brandy and heart-drops were invariably secreted in one of its many pockets.

Owen, the automaton chauffeur, was the reluctant witness of the many attentions showered upon his lady-love, especially by Bertie Woolcock, who was almost always in close attendance, and put her in the car with many voluble regrets and urgent arrangements for future meetings. He would linger by the door sometimes for ten minutes, prolonging the "sweet sorrow," paying clumsy compliments, and making notes of future engagements upon his broad linen cuff. He little suspected how dearly the impassive driver longed to descend from his seat and throttle him; but once he did remark to the lady—

"I say, what a scowling brute you have for a chauffeur!"

Meanwhile, Miss Susan looked on and listened to Bertie's speeches with happy complacency. Bertie was heir to twenty thousand a year, and it would be delightful to have her darling Aurea living at Westmere, and established so near home.

One evening, returning from a garden-party, Miss Susan and her niece had a narrow escape of being killed. Aurea was seated in front—she disliked the stuffy interior, especially this warm weather; they had come to a red triangle notice, "Dangerous to Cyclists," and were about to descend a long winding hill—the one hill of the neighbourhood. Just as they commenced the descent with the brake hard on, it suddenly broke, and in half a second the car had shot away!

Wynyard turned his head, and shouted, "Sit tight!" and gave all his mind to steering; he took the whole width of the road to get round the first corner, and then the hill made an even sharper drop; the car, which was heavy, gathered momentum with every yard, and it seemed impossible to reach the bottom of the hill without some terrible catastrophe. Half-way down was another motor. Wynyard yelled, sounded the horn, and flashed by; a pony-trap, ascending, had a narrow escape of being pulverised in the green car's mad flight. Then, to the driver's horror, he saw a great wagon and horses on the road near the foot of the hill, and turned cold with the thought that there might not be room to get by. They missed it by a hair's-breadth, and continued their wild career. At last they came to the level at the foot of the slope, and Wynyard pulled up, after the most exciting two minutes he had ever experienced. He glanced at his two companions; they were both as white as death—and so was he! Miss Susan, for once, was speechless, but at last she signed that she wished to get out, and Wynyard helped her to the bank, on which she collapsed, inarticulate and gasping.

"It's a good thing Aunt Bella was not with us," said Aurea, and her voice sounded faint; "*this* time she really would have died! What happened?" turning to Owen.

"The brake rod broke, miss—the old car is rotten," he added viciously.

"Old car!" repeated Susan, who, though her nerves were in a badly shattered condition, had at last found utterance.

"Very old and crazy—and you never know what she is going to do next, or what trick she will play you—and you ladies have been giving her a good deal of work lately."

"If you had lost your head, Owen!" exclaimed Miss Susan.

"I hope I don't often do that, miss," he answered steadily.

"If you had not had splendid nerve, we would all have been killed; why, we just shaved that wagon by a hair's-breadth—that would have been a smash! We were going so fast."

He made no reply, but moved away to examine the machine.

"Of course it would have been death, Aurea, and I don't want to go like that!"

"I should hope not, Susie."

"I don't think I shall be afraid when it comes—I shall feel like a child whose nurse has called it away to go to sleep; but I'd prefer to go quietly, and not like some crushed insect."

Wynyard, as he worked at the car, could not help overhearing snatches of the conversation between aunt and niece; the latter said—

"The other day I was watching a flock of sheep in the meadows; the shepherd was with them, and they were all collected about him so trustfully. By his side was a man in a long blue linen coat. I said to myself, 'There is death among them; poor innocents, they don't know it.' That's like death and us—we never know who he has marked, or which of the flock is chosen."

"He nearly chose us to-day—but he changed his mind."

Aurea nodded, and then she went on—

"As to that odious motor, every one says Aunt Bella was shamefully taken in; but she would not listen to advice, she would buy it—she liked the photo. The car is medieval, and, what's more, it's unlucky,—it's malignant! and you remember when we met the runaway horse and cart near Brodfield; I was sitting outside, and I declare it seemed to struggle to get into the middle of the road, and *meet* them! you remember what Goethe said about the demoniac power of inanimate things?"

"Now, my dear child, that's nonsense!" expostulated Miss Susan. "I had a poor education, and I've never read a line of Goethe's; if he wrote such rubbish, I had no loss!"

"Well, you will allow that the car did its very best to destroy us to-day! And Mrs. Ramsay told me a man she knew recognised it by its number—and that it once ran over and killed a girl on a bicycle, and the people sent it to auction, where some one bought it for a song, passed it on to Aunt Bella, and here it is!"

"The car will be all right now, Miss Susan," announced the chauffeur, touching his cap; "there are no more hills, we are on the flat, and I can take you home safely; but I'm afraid she will have to go to Brodfield again to-morrow."

"Owen, do you believe in a motor being unlucky?" she asked, rising as she spoke.

"I can't say I do, miss; I don't know much about them."

"What do you mean?—not know about motors!"

"Oh," correcting himself, "I mean with respect to their characters, miss; it's said that there are unlucky engines, and unlucky ships, and submarines—at least they have a bad name. I can't say that this car and I have ever, what you may call, taken to one another."

And with this remark, he tucked in Aurea's smart white skirt, closed the door, mounted to his place, and proceeded steadily homewards.

CHAPTER XIX
OWEN THE MATCHMAKER

Undoubtedly it was hard on Wynyard that, at a time when his own love-affair was absorbing his soul and thoughts, he should be burthened with the anxieties of another—in fact, with two others—those of Tom Hogben and Dilly Topham.

For some weeks Tom had been unlike himself, silent, dispirited, and almost morose, giving his mother short answers or none; yet, undoubtedly, it *is* galling to be accused of a bilious attack when it is your heart that is affected.

Mrs. Hogben was dismayed. What had come over her boy? Her lodger, too, was concerned, for Tom, hitherto sober, now brought with him at times a very strong suggestion of raw whisky! At last he was received into his confidence—the communication took place over an after-dinner pipe in the Manor grounds.

During the dog-days, the atmosphere of Mrs. Hogben's little kitchen was almost insupportable—such was the reek of soap-suds, soda, and the ironing blanket; and Wynyard suggested that he and Tom should carry their dinner, and eat it in the old summer-house on the Manor bowling-green.

"We'll be out of your road," he added craftily, "and save ourselves the tramp here at midday."

At first Tom did not see precisely eye-to-eye with his comrade; he liked his victuals "conformable"—and to be within easy reach of the loaf, pickle jar, and—though this was not stated—the Drum!

But after one trial he succumbed. There was no denying it was rare and cool in the old thatched tea-house, and his mother, who was thankful to get rid of "two big chaps a-crowding her up—so awkward at her busiest laundry season,"—provided substantial fare in the shape of cold meat and potatoes, home-made bread, and cheese—and, for Tom, the mordant pickles such as his soul loved. The pair, sitting at their meal, presented a curious contrast, although both in rough working clothes, and their shirt-sleeves.

The chauffeur, erect, well-groomed, eating his bread and cheese with the same relish, and refinement as if he were at mess.

The gardener, exhibiting a four days old beard, and somewhat earthy hands, as he slouched over the rustic table, bolting his food with the voracity of a hungry dog.

They were both, in their several ways, handsome specimens of British manhood. Hogben, for all his clownish manners, had good old blood in his veins; he could, had he known the fact, have traced and established his pedigree back to King Henry the Sixth!

Wynyard's progenitors had never been submerged; their names were emblazoned in history—a forebear had distinguished himself in the tilting ring, and achieved glory at Agincourt.

Possibly, in days long past, the ancestors of these two men had fought side by side as knight and squire—who knows?

Having disposed of his last enormous mouthful, closed his clasp-knife, and produced his pipe, Hogben threw himself back on the seat, and said—

"Look here, mate, I want a bit of a talk with 'ee."

"Talk away, Tom," he replied, as he struck a match. "You have fifteen minutes and a clear course."

"Oh, five will do me. As fer the course, it bain't clear, and that's the truth. It's like this, Jack, I'm in a mort o' trouble along o' Dilly Topham."

Wynyard nodded, the news had not taken him by surprise.

"An' you, being eddicated, and having seen London and life—and no doubt well experienced with young females—might give me a hand."

Wynyard nodded again—Tom was undoubtedly about to make a clean breast of it. So he lit his cigarette, and prepared to listen.

"Dilly and I was children together—I'm five year older nor she—and my mother, being a widder, I had to start to work when I was ten, with a milk round—and indeed long afore—so my schoolin' wasn't much, as ye may know! 'Owever, Dilly and I was always goin' to be married for fun; and she grew up a main pretty girl, and then it was agreed on in earnest. Well, now she gives me the go-by! Most days she won't look near me, and she never comes 'ere; she's got a gold bangle from some other chap, and when I ask about it, she gives me a regular doing, and says I'm to mind me own business! What do ye say to that? It's the insurance fellow, I'll go bail, from Brodfield; if I catch him—I'll—I'll bash 'is 'ead in—so I will—'im and 'is legs! What am I to do—I ask you as a friend?"

"Well, Tom, I'm not as experienced as you suppose," said Wynyard, after a thoughtful pause, "but, if I were in your shoes, I'll tell you just exactly my plan of operations."

"Ay, let's have 'em right away."

"First of all I'd have my hair cut, and trim myself about a bit."

"What! an old blossom like me?"

"Yes; shave that fringe of yours altogether, and wear your hair like mine," running his hand over his cropped head. "I declare, I could not live with a mop like yours! And you may not know it, Tom, but you are an awfully good-looking fellow."

"Eh—am I?" with slow complacency. "They do say so of Ottinge folk; they are mostly of fine old blood, come down in the world—and the only thing that's stuck is the features—especially the nose."

"I can't tell you anything about that, but I'm certain of one thing—you must give up whisky."

"Ay"—reddening—"must I so?"

"Don't let it get a hold, or it may never leave you."

"Ay, but sometimes when I'm down, the devil 'e comes, and 'e says, 'You go and 'ave a *drink*, Tom, it will do you good'; and 'e keeps on a-whisperin' 'Go and 'ave a drink, Tom, go and 'ave a drink, Tom,' and so I goes at last, and 'as three or four!"

"Tell the devil to shut up, and do you go to the barber."

"'E's away this week thatching," was the amazing reply.

"Well, when he comes back get shaved, and you won't know yourself! Then I'd like to give you one of my old coats, and a tie, and a few collars— we are about the same size—and Miss Dilly won't recognise you; and after that, mind you take no notice of her; but share your hymn-book with Nellie Hann—ask her out walking of an evening, and I bet you anything you like, you will have Miss Dilly after you like a shot!"

"Well, mate, I'll do it," said Tom moodily; "but it's a tricky business walkin' with another girl—she might take notions—and if it falls out badly with Dilly, I'll drown myself, but thank you all the same."

After a long and brooding silence, Tom struggled to his feet and scratched his head—

"If ye understood what it was to be *set* on a girl—you would know what a misery I feel; but you are not built that way, as any one can see—and now

I must go back to my job, or I'll have the old lady on to me. She stands in the landing window, a-watching like a cat at a mouse-hole. It's not so much the work—as that she likes to see us *a-slaving*. Well, I'll take yer advice, and I am much obliged to ye." And, shouldering his spade, Tom lurched away, with long uneven strides.

"Now, what did you do that for?" Wynyard asked himself. "You silly idiot! giving advice and putting your finger in other people's pies. Why should you meddle?"

No answer being forthcoming from the recesses of his inner consciousness, he rose and stretched himself, and presently returned to his struggle with a contrary old lawn-mower.

By chance, the very next evening, on the road to Brodfield, Wynyard came upon Dilly and the insurance agent; they were evidently about to part, and were exchanging emphatic last words. He accosted them in a cheery, off-hand manner, and after a few trivial remarks about the weather, and the heat, said—

"As I suppose you are going back, Miss Topham, we might as well walk together. May I have the honour of your company?"

Dilly beamed and giggled, the agent glowered and muttered inarticulately; but he was a little in awe of the chauffeur chap, with his quiet manners, steady eye, and indefinable suggestion of a reserve force never exerted—and with a snort and a "So long, Miss Dilly!" he mounted his bike, and sped homewards.

Dilly was both amazed and enchanted. So, after all, she had made an impression on this quiet, good-looking Owen chap! and for him, did he wish to "walk out with her," she was ready—to speak the brutal, naked truth—to throw over both Ernest Sands and Tom Hogben.

"I'm glad to have met you like this," he said, as they proceeded side by side.

"Oh yes," she responded eagerly, "so am I—awfully glad!"

"Because I want to have a word about Tom."

"Oh—*Tom*," with inexpressible scorn, "I've just about done with Tom!"

"Done for him, you mean! You're breaking his heart; he's a topping good chap, I know, for I live in the house with him."

Here, indeed, was a bitter disappointment for Miss Dilly. So the smart chauffeur was merely talking to her as a friend of Tom's!

"I say," he continued, "do you think it's playing the game to be carrying on with this other chap, if you are engaged to Tom?"

"Who says so?" she demanded sharply.

"He does—Ottinge does."

"Laws! A lot of jangling old women! Much I care what they say!" and she tossed her head violently.

"You need not tell me that."

"Why?" she snapped.

"Because you meet a young man you are not engaged to, and walk miles with him through the lanes after sundown."

"Well, I'm sure! Why mayn't I have a friend if I choose?"

"It is entirely a matter of opinion; if I were in Tom's shoes, Miss Dilly, and knew of this evening's outing, I'd give you the chuck at once, and have nothing more to do with you."

"Oh—*you!*"—insolently—"they say you're a sort of half gentleman as has got into some trouble. Why don't you mind your own affairs? Come now!"

"Tom is my friend and my affair."

"Bah! a working man and a gentleman—friends! Go on!" and she stared at him defiantly.

"Yes, he is; and I won't stand by and see his life spoiled, if I can help it."

"Well, then," and she burst into sudden tears, "it's his mother as is spoiling it—not me."

"How do you make that out?"

"Wasn't we pledged four year ago, and I took his ring, and there's Maggie Tuke engaged years after me, and nicely set up in her own house now, with a gramaphone and a big glass—yes, and Nellie Watkin too; and I've got to wait and wait till Mrs. Hogben pleases. *She* won't give up Tom, so there it is! Oh, of course she's all butter and sugar to a good lodger like you, but she's as hard as a turnpike, and she's waiting on till my grandmother comes forward—and that she'll never do. Why, she grudges me a bit of chocolate, let alone a fortin'."

"Oh, so that's it, is it?"

"Yes, that's it, since you must know; and I tell you I'm not going on playing this 'ere waiting game no longer—I'm about fed up, as they say; I'm twenty-six, and I've told Ernest as I'm going to break it off with Hogben."

"Come now, which do you like the best?" asked Wynyard, amazed at his own impertinence, "Tom or Ernest?"

"Why, Tom, of course, but what's the good?"

"Look here, will you promise not to hate me—and will you let me see what I can do?"

For a moment she gazed at him with an air of profound mistrust; at last she muttered in a peevish voice—

"Yes, you can't make things no worse, anyway—and that's certain sure."

This was not a very gracious permission, but Miss Topham wiped her eyes and held out her hand; at the moment, by most provoking bad luck, the Rector and his daughter dashed by in a dog-cart, and the former, recognising him, called back a cheery "Good-night, Owen!"

"Is it possible that the fellow has cut out Tom Hogben, and is making up to Dilly Topham?" he said to his daughter.

"I'm sure I don't know," she answered stiffly.

"I should not have thought she was *his* sort; but one never can tell! At any rate, she was crying and holding his hand—there must be an understanding between them, eh?"

But Aurea made no reply; apparently she was engrossed in watching a long train of rooks flying quickly homewards—drifting across the rose-tinted sky—and had not heard the question. Her father glanced at her; her pretty lips were very tightly compressed, one would almost suppose that something had annoyed Aurea!

That evening, when Tom was at the Drum, Wynyard had a serious conversation with Mrs. Hogben—a really straight and private talk, respecting her son and his love-affair. "If Leila were to see me now!" he said to himself, "trying to engineer this job, how she would laugh!" To his landlady he pointed out that one was not always young, and that Tom and Dilly had been engaged four years. (He had a vague idea that Tom's wages and Tom's company all to herself, were considerable factors in his mother's reluctance to name the wedding-day.)

And for once Wynyard was positively eloquent! He put down his pipe, and spoke. He pleaded as he had never in his life pleaded for himself—he felt amazed by his own arguments! Mrs. Hogben was thunder-struck; generally, the fellow had not a word to throw to a dog, and now to hear him talk!

"Think, Mrs. Hogben," he urged, "what is Tom to wait for? He has his twenty-five shillings a week and this house—it's his, I understand," and he paused. "If Dilly gives him up who will blame her? She has waited—and for what?" Another dramatic pause. "*You* are waiting for Mrs. Topham to die. She is likely to hold on another ten or twenty years. You say this is a healthy place—and she may even see you out; it's a way old people have—they get the living habit, and hold on in spite of no end of illnesses. And I tell you plainly that if Dilly throws over Tom—as she threatens—Tom will go to the bad; and then perhaps you will be sorry and blame yourself when it's too late."

By this time Mrs. Hogben was in tears.

"And so I'm to turn out, am I?—out of the house I was in ever since I married and the house where my poor husband died of 'roses on the liver'" (*cirrhosis*) "and let that giddy girl in on all my good china and linen," she sobbed stertorously.

"No, not by any means—there's room for all! I shall not always be here, you know. Well, Mrs. Hogben," rising, "I hope you will forgive me for intruding into your family affairs, but just think over what I have said to you; you know I mean well, and I'm Tom's friend," and with this declaration her lodger bade her good-night, and climbed up the creaking stairs into his crooked chamber.

The immediate result of the chauffeur's interference was the transformation of Tom into a smart, clean-shaven young man—who openly neglected his lady-love, actually escorted her hated rival from evening church, and remained to share the family supper of pig's cheek and pickles. Owen's prescription had a marvellous effect; for, three weeks after this too notorious entertainment, it was officially given out at the Drum that Tom and Dilly Topham were to be wed at Christmas—and to make their home with Sally Hogben. On hearing this, so to speak, postscript, various maids and matrons were pleased to be sarcastic respecting the two Mrs. Hogbens, and wished them both "joy."

CHAPTER XX
SUDDEN DEATH

There had been an outbreak of festivities in the neighbourhood of lethargic Ottinge; the climax of these was a grand ball given by Mrs. Woolcock at Westmere, to celebrate her youngest daughter's engagement to Lord Lowestoff. Every one who was any one—and indeed not a few nobodies—were bidden as guests; Mrs. Woolcock liked to see her rooms crammed to suffocation. No expense was spared—the arrangements were made on a lavish scale. On this occasion the extra waiters and other luxuries were imported from London by special train, and a carefully selected house-party provided the bride-elect with a ready-made court that intervened between the future peeress and the vulgar herd. Dancing took place in the great drawing-room (in old days it was called the White Saloon), and through its wide, open windows humble spectators—such as coachmen and chauffeurs—were at liberty to look on, to wonder, and to criticise.

The Misses Parrett and their niece were present. Miss Parrett—who had nerved herself for the ordeal with a glass and a half of port—had motored to Westmere through the darkness, with great, flaring lamps—a truly heart-shaking experience! but she was determined to exhibit her new velvet gown and her new diamonds. Her satisfaction with her own appearance was such that, before she embarked on her venture into the night and the motor, her household were summoned to a private view—precisely as if she were a young beauty or a bride!

The old lady, who bore an absurd resemblance to a black velvet penwiper, enjoyed the ball immensely, and took a number of mental photographs; she also "took the wall" of various obnoxious people who had dared to patronise her in her days of poverty. Her particular satellites, stout widows and anxious-looking spinsters, rallied around her, ardently admiring her toilette, and listened patiently to her boring recollections of the balls she had attended years ago; but, in point of fact, they were more keenly interested in the ball of to-night and their prospects respecting escorts to the supper-table.

Much as she was engrossed in herself and her own importance, Miss Parrett could not help noticing that her niece was singled out for special attention by Bertie Woolcock. This, though a genuine satisfaction to her, was no pleasure to her chauffeur, who, from a coign of vantage on the lawn, commanded a capital view of the gay scene—the illuminated room, the constant circulation of black and white, and sometimes coloured, figures. Among these Miss Morven was pre-eminent—the undisputed beauty of the evening—wearing a filmy white gown, with a sparkling ornament glittering in her dark hair; she looked radiantly lovely and radiantly happy, as she floated lightly by.

The chauffeur's watchful eyes noted that she had (quite unnecessarily) bestowed three waltzes on that blundering elephant, Bertie Woolcock; how red and hot he looked—more as if he were threshing than dancing! What would *he* not give for just a couple of turns with the belle of the ball! The band was "Iffs" and the floor seemed to be ripping! Well, there was nothing for it but to wait as an outsider, and to hold on to his patience with both hands.

After the great ball—its glories, shortcomings, surprises, and failures—had died away into a nine days' wonder, there were several cricket matches, and Ottinge discovered, to its supreme elation, that they had a notable man in Miss Parrett's chauffeur! (This became evident when the local eleven assembled for their evening practice in the Manor fields.) The fame of Owen's batting actually brought old Thunder on the scene; for he, too, had been a fine cricketer, long before gout had seized upon him and he had subsided into carpet slippers.

"Ottinge *v.* Westmere" was a two days' match, and the last day at the park included a garden-party, arranged, as Mrs. Woolcock murderously expressed it, "to kill off all the neighbours!"

"I say, Miss Morven," said Bertie Woolcock, greeting her and her father on their very late arrival. "We are catching it hot now, though Ottinge was nearly out at three o'clock; that chauffeur fellow of your aunts' has made sixty runs for his side. I hope you sympathise with us—we shall lose the match."

"No, no indeed, Ottinge for ever!" she replied. "Where is the chauffeur?" glancing round.

"Out in the field now."

For some time she did not discover him, standing, a good way off, bareheaded, and in well-fitting flannels. He looked every inch a gentleman!

What a contrast to poor Bertie, who seemed, in comparison, a great slouching yokel.

"He's a good-looking chap, isn't he?" said the Rector, with the complacency of a man who is alluding to one of his own parishioners.

"Yes," admitted young Woolcock in a grudging tone, "I suppose he is—a ladies' beauty! One hears such a lot of sultry stories, in these days, about women being mashed on their chauffeurs, and runaway matches. For my part, I call a chauffeur a rank idler—a chap who sits all day, looks as solemn as an undertaker, and gets spoiled by the ladies." Then to Aurea, "Now, come over to the tent, Miss Morven, my mother has kept a place for you."

The match proved close and exciting. Westmere had a strong team, and Aurea looked on with intense interest; the Park was in, and out in the field were Dr. Boas, Hogben, Jones, Owen, and others. Time went on, the last man was in, and making runs—the fate of the match hung in the balance, when it was brought to an end by a capital catch; Owen had not merely to run at top speed, but to stoop suddenly to catch the ball—a fine effort—which was loudly and deservedly applauded.

"*He* knows all about it," remarked a man who was standing beside Aurea. "He is a public school boy, I'll bet my hat. What is he doing in Ottinge? A chauffeur! Good Lord! Some young swell in disgrace with his family."

Miss Morven mentally endorsed this speech; but actually she shrugged her shoulders.

Miss Susan beamed at the victory—Owen's triumphs were hers. She felt as proud of his cricket and his songs at the Parish Hall Concerts as if he had been her own flesh and blood—other elderly spinsters have been known to take young men into the recesses of their empty and innocent hearts.

When the match was over, she kept her eye on the hero of the occasion, and, seeing him getting into his coat and preparing to depart, she beckoned eagerly, and then hurried towards him with outstretched hands.

"Congratulate you, Owen! I do feel so proud of you!"

"Thank you, miss. I'm going to fetch the car—it's getting late."

"Can you tell me the time?"

He pulled out his watch from his breast-pocket, and hastily touched—as luck would have it—the wrong spring; the back flew open, and a small photograph, no bigger than a finger-nail, fell upon the grass. In a second Owen had put his foot upon it, swooped, and snatched it up. Whether from stooping or otherwise, his colour was higher than usual, as he boldly confronted Miss Susan, whose face had become unusually grave—for, unless her eyes deceived her (and she had capital sight) the treasure was a photograph of her niece Aurea, cut out of a group of "First Aid" recently taken at the Rectory! She had recognised it in one lightning glance!

However, the chauffeur met her eyes imperturbably, as he replaced the little scrap, opened the face of his watch, and announced, with staggering self-possession—

"Half-past six, Miss Susan."

Miss Susan turned hastily away, her maiden mind in a violent commotion. So Owen, the chauffeur, carried Aurea's photograph about with him in his watch! What did it mean? Well, of course, it could only mean one thing, he was—and who could wonder—in love with the girl! Yes, and the conviction gave Miss Susan a violent shock; she was scandalised, she was pleased, and she was *not* pleased—a peculiar and contrary state of mind. She determined to keep the amazing revelation to herself. Aurea must not be told on any account—it might put disturbing ideas into her head—it would not be proper; and for one whole week Miss Susan contained her mighty secret, which secret disagreed with her both mentally and physically. She was short and snappy—a new phase of her character—ate little, avoided the garden, and mainly subsisted on tea. At the end of seven long days she found her endurance had reached its limits, and, sitting with her back to the dim light of the Rectory drawing-room, Susan Parrett solemnly divulged to her niece the tale of her significant discovery.

Was she shocked? Did she turn red and white? No, indeed; Aurea received the astonishing information with a peal of laughter.

"Oh, my dearest Susie, what a tale! Why, it was no more my photograph than yours! Am I the only young woman that is known to Owen, the chauffeur?"

This clever girl was so insistent and so amused that she actually persuaded her deluded aunt that her eyes had deceived her, and she had made a ridiculous and silly mistake—yet all the time the girl's own heart sang to the tune that the story was *true*.

This silent chauffeur was a gentleman who had been in the Service, and he carried her picture inside his watch. These two facts were of profound interest to Aurea Morven, and she turned them over in her mind many, many times a day; the result being, that she held herself as much as possible aloof from her aunts' employé. When she did avail herself of the car, it was never to sit, as heretofore, outside by the driver, but within the stuffy interior. She shrank from coming into contact with a man who was seldom, to tell the honest truth, out of her thoughts. To garden-parties and tennis tournaments she now hailed her father, instead of accompanying Susan; and together they drove in the Rectory dog-cart—this arrangement entailing not a few excuses and pleadings, that were not too firmly based on the truth—and the poor forsaken car remained in the coach-house, or took Miss Parrett out for a brief and agonising airing.

In consequence of all this, the car's driver had more time than ever on his hands! The summer days are long, and, when off duty, he saw a good deal of the Ramsays. The captain seemed of late to have sunk into a further depth of mental lethargy, and to have lost much of his affectionate interest in his old schoolfellow, Owen Wynyard.

"I am giving up the dogs for the present," announced Mrs. Ramsay one morning at the kennels, as he brought back three leg-weary companions. "I find I must not continue what absorbs so much of my time and carries me from home—though you are so good, and have undertaken the three worst characters—they're just as wild as goats."

"But I like them," he declared; "they are capital company, and give me an object for my tramps—these two fox-terriers and the little beagle and I are great chums. We have done a fine round this morning—they have had the time of their lives! Just look at them!" and she looked and smiled at their bespattered legs, lolling tongues, and happy eyes.

"Oh, I am sure of that," she replied; "for they are three town dogs! However, I must send the poor fellows away, all the same. I want to be with Jim altogether, and without his knowing it. You see, he will never allow me to walk with him; and he always fancies he is being watched, and looks behind him every now and then. All the same, I mean to follow him."

Wynyard listened in silence. Mrs. Ramsay was, in his opinion, little short of a saint; for years and years she had devoted her own individual life to this unhappy madman. It was for him she slaved to increase their small income, trading in plants and cuttings, and keeping other people's dogs. With the money she earned she made Ivy House homelike and comfortable. The captain's food, drink, tobacco, and surroundings were of a class that the exterior of the place did not seem to warrant, and were accepted by him as a matter of course. Nothing could induce him to believe that their income was less than a thousand a year; he had no recollection of his money losses. But this long-drawn-out effort and strain was beginning to tell on his wife. There were many white strands in her thick black hair, many lines in her face; she had grown thin and haggard, her beautiful Irish eyes were sunken, and wore an expression of tragic anxiety. She alone knew what she dreaded, and at last she put her fears into words—not to old friends like the Parson, or Susan Parrett, but to this recent acquaintance, this young Wynyard, who knew so much already.

"Tell me, Owen, don't you think that Jim looks rather strange of late?" she asked him, in a low voice.

"No—much as usual."

"He sleeps so badly, and has no appetite, and seems horribly depressed. Oh, I feel miserable about him!" and she buried her face in her thin hands.

"I wish I could do something, Mrs. Ramsay. Would you like me to stop here at night—you know you've only to say the word," he urged, in a boyish tone that was irresistible.

"Oh no, no, no; but it's awfully good of you to offer. It's not at night, but when he is out by himself that is so trying. I do follow as much as I dare. You see," now lowering her voice, "once this mental breakdown of his took the form of suicide"—and here her voice sank to a whisper—"he tried to hang himself in Claringbold's barn; but I caught him just in time, and it never got out. That was years ago; and afterwards he made a wonderful recovery. Now, it seems to me more like a decay of will-power and memory, with occasional outbreaks of violence—I can manage him then—but it's the dying of the mind!" and she gave a little sob.

"If I may speak plainly, Mrs. Ramsay, I really think you should get an experienced man to look after him at once. I know nothing of mental disease, but I'm sure it's not right for you to be alone here with him, and just two maids and old Mary."

"You mean for me to get a keeper? No; I couldn't do it; and think of what people would suppose."

Poor innocent lady! Did she imagine for a moment that all Ottinge did not know for a fact that her husband was insane?

"You might let them suppose he had come to help with the dogs," he suggested, after a moment's hesitation.

"Of course—of course—what a splendid idea!"

"And you will send for him to-morrow, won't you? Or would you like me to wire or write to-night? I know some one in London who would see about this."

(Leila would have been considerably astonished if her brother's first commission from Ottinge was to dispatch a keeper for a male lunatic!)

"I must consult Dr. Boas. Thank you very much. I won't do anything in a hurry."

"Won't you? Why not? I think you should see Dr. Boas at once."

"Well, then, I will to-morrow. Jim complains of his head—he often does, but now he says the pain is like a saw, and he can't stand it. Then he imagines he is back in the Service, and expecting to be warned for parade or a court martial, and talks very strangely. Dr. Boas has gone away to a funeral, and won't be back till to-night, and then I must confess Jim doesn't like him; he likes no one but you, and some of the dogs—and *me*, of course," she added, with a sickly smile.

"Shall I come in this evening?"

"Oh, do; you *are* a kind fellow! Even if he never speaks now, sure I know he loves to see you sitting there. Ah, here he is, and I must go and coax him to eat some dinner!"

To his visitor's surprise, Captain Ramsay was unusually animated and talkative that night, and mentioned many little details about his father, and recalled certain daredevil deeds, acts of generosity, and even nascent love-affairs.

"I say, Owen, you remember the pretty girl up at Simla—the dark-eyed one you were so mad about—and how you swore you'd run away with her, and marry her in spite of her father, the General, and the whole family? Oh, of course I know—what a duffer I am! You eloped, tore down the hill by special dâk, and were married at Saharanpore. Where is she now?"

Wynyard made no reply. Captain Ramsay's wandering memory had evidently evoked a vision of his dark-eyed and remarkably pretty mother. She had run away with the handsome Hussar officer, and had, in consequence, been cast off by her relations.

"Dead?" inquired the other after a pause.

Wynyard nodded.

"Ah, well, we shall all be dead one day—some sooner—and some later," and he fell into one of his sudden silences.

"I think he is better!" whispered his wife to Wynyard, as they parted at the hall door. "Didn't he seem almost himself this evening? And he took great notice of Topsy and Darkie, and made their dinner himself."

Two days later, as the chauffeur was leaving Mrs. Hogben's cottage after his midday meal, preparatory to getting ready the car, Mrs. Ramsay suddenly appeared at her gate and beckoned to him frantically. She looked white and frightened.

"Jim went off this morning," she began, "and hasn't been home since. He never did this before. Oh, I *ought* to have taken your advice," and she wrung her hands. "I've been searching for him since eight o'clock."

"Did he speak to any one before he left the house?" inquired Wynyard.

"No. Fanny saw him going out in a terrible hurry; he had on a pair of white gloves, and said he would be late for parade."

"Poor fellow!"

"And the stupid girl never said one word to me till she brought me my hot water at eight o'clock."

"I'm just off with the car, taking Miss Susan to a croquet tournament, or I'd go and have a look round. What about the policeman?"

"The policeman! Why, he cannot walk! He weighs sixteen stone."

"Well, anyway, if you don't mind, I'll send Tom Hogben and Jones; they know the country, and will keep a shut mouth. I'll just tell them now," and he hurried away.

Although Miss Susan had no money wherewith to buy diamonds, sables, and motor cars, she contrived to extract a great deal of pleasure out of her elderly spinster life. She enjoyed mild little tea-parties, followed by bridge at sixpence a hundred—and received her partner's scoldings with disarming humility. Her one passion was croquet. "Miss S. Parrett" was a notable player—her name appeared in print in connection with local tournaments; her arm was steady, her aim was deadly, and, not only this, she played the game with her head as well as with her hands.

On the present occasion Miss Susan had lured her reluctant niece to a meeting at Upstreet—a village about ten miles from Ottinge; in fact, she made such a point of Aurea's company, of Aurea's support—whether in success or failure—that the girl felt compelled to go—and, at any rate, she took a sincere pride in Susan's modest triumphs. The tournament was prolonged till seven o'clock; Miss Susan was detained, being in the Finals. Dusk was closing on the world when the two ladies, with two prizes (salad bowl and a silver cigarette-case), took their departure. The prize-winner, in exuberant spirits, uttering effusive expressions of enjoyment and thanks, had talked herself into the car, and there were so many after-thoughts and messages that even the chauffeur became impatient with his dear Miss Susan; he was desperately anxious to get home and hear the result of the search for Captain Ramsay.

It was an unusually close evening—there was thunder in the air—and the interior of the motor was stuffy even with the windows down on both sides—and how they rattled! The old machine trundled along at its best speed, as if inspired by the fear of Miss Parrett awaiting its arrival, watch in hand. Its driver had another and more well-grounded dread in his mind.

The ladies within discussed the recent party, the play, the prizes, and the guests.

"The Wendovers were there; did you see them?" said Miss Susan— "Mrs. Wendover and Gertrude. I thought they both looked very ill."

"Yes, and I believe it was from hunger, Susan," was her niece's surprising reply. "I never saw such a tea as they had—surreptitiously. It's shameful to watch, I know, but I was not playing, and happened to be sitting near, and could not help myself. I felt so frightfully sorry for them—I was inclined to cry!"

"My dear girl, surely you are not in earnest?"

"I only wish I wasn't. Gertrude had a whole plate of sandwiches, besides cakes; she took them quietly, when no one was looking, and devoured them ravenously, and her mother pocketed several buns and lumps of sugar."

"But why? I don't understand."

"Because probably they have nothing to eat at home! Mrs. Lucas, the parson's wife, told me in confidence that they are almost penniless; the little money they had has been lost in some bank that tempted people with high interest and then went smash. The Wendovers cling to the old cottage—it's their own—but they have no servant; they do their own washing and, very early in the morning, their own doorstep! Everything is spick and span still. After dark they steal out and collect firewood and apples, and even field turnips, and yet they hold up their heads and 'pretend.' I heard Mrs. Wade pressing them to have cake and tea—and they declined."

"Have they no friends or relations?"

"I don't know. Mrs. Lucas said she did not like to ask for their confidence. She always has them to supper on Sundays, and sends them eggs; but she is poor enough herself with eight children. She thinks the Wendovers will break down now that the winter is coming, and yet they won't allow any one to guess that they are destitute."

"Dear, dear, dear, how shocking! What *is* to be done, Aurea?"

"I've just had my allowance, and I'll post them a five-pound note to-morrow anonymously, and I'll get something later on from dad."

"Yes, yes, yes, and I must see what I can do too. Poverty is cruel—a terrible thing—what a trial of one's character!"

"It is indeed, and so are riches sometimes. They seem to change people's dispositions—if they come in for a fortune."

"That's true; but I do hope, dear child, you are not thinking of your poor Aunt Bella?"

"Aunt Bella was much nicer when she lived in the Red Cottage, dined at one o'clock, and put a penny in the plate."

"Oh, now, Aurea, I can't let you say that; she is very proud of you, and a dear, kind sister to me. Why, only last week she gave me a lovely lace parasol, and when she writes to me it is always 'My own darling Susan.'"

Aurea was silent. She was thinking of darling Susan's many deprivations, humiliations, and hardships.

"We all have our foibles, have we not, Aurea, my child?"

"Oh, I know that, Susan, and I— —"

Whatever Aurea was going to add was cut short by her aunt's piercing scream. From some thick bushes on the left bank, a tall figure had shot out; there was a lightning rush, a shout from the chauffeur, who jammed on the brake, then a violent swerve, an upheaval, and a sickening, crunching sensation.

A man had deliberately flung himself in front of the car, which had gone over him, then stopped abruptly, shuddering throughout its rickety frame.

The driver sprang off and dragged from beneath the wheels a limp and motionless body. Yes, his vague fears had been justified.

"It's Captain Ramsay!" he called to Aurea, who had already hurled herself into the road. "I'm afraid he is done for. Stay where you are."

As he spoke, he raised a limp and bleeding figure in his arms, which he carried to the hedgerow; next, he took off his coat and laid him upon it, and ran and lit a motor lamp. All his actions were surprisingly prompt and vigorous.

"Now, will you come over here, miss?" he called to Susan authoritatively, but she was almost beside him. In a crisis, simple, talkative Susan was another person, and could rise to the occasion. "And you, Miss Morven, try and find some water—we passed a stream just now; bring it in anything—your hat or—yes, the salad bowl! I'm afraid it's a bad business," he continued, "and his head is all cut—and his wrist—it's an artery. Miss Susan, fetch a stick quickly, quickly, and I'll make a tourniquet."

The chauffeur seemed to have taken complete command of the situation; he ordered the ladies hither and thither, he bandaged up Captain Ramsay's head with Aurea's white scarf—which he tore into strips—whilst Aurea stood by, eager to help, but trembling like an aspen. She had never heard a man moan, or witnessed such a scene.

"I think I've fixed him up just for the moment," said Owen, rising, "and now I'll fetch the doctor. You two ladies won't mind stopping, will you?"

"Certainly not! What do you think we are made of?" rejoined Miss Susan. "Here,"—now sinking down—"place his head in my lap, and just go as hard as ever you can!"

"He is in a very bad way, I'm afraid, and I really don't like leaving you, but there's no help for it." Then, after sticking a flaring lamp on the ground beside them, he climbed into his place and sped away.

In less than half an hour he had returned, accompanied by Dr. Boas; they found the poor sufferer still alive and moaning, his head supported by Miss Susan, and his lips bathed by her niece.

"I half expected this," said the doctor, as he knelt beside Captain Ramsay. "Internal injuries," he announced, after a rapid examination, "and fatal."

"The stretcher and the parish nurse will be here presently," said Owen; and, hearing a familiar voice, Captain Ramsay slowly opened his eyes and asked—

"Oh, it's cold. Where am I? Where's Katie?"

As he recognised Owen bending over him, he murmured—

"Wynyard, Wynyard—hold on—I'm coming!"

"You see he is off his head," said Miss Susan, "poor fellow; he did not know what he was doing."

Then, as the chauffeur relieved her of the dying man's weight, he regained consciousness, and, again opening his eyes, he whispered *"Wynyard!"* and passed away in the arms of Wynyard's son.

CHAPTER XXI
BY THE SUNDIAL

A long time had elapsed since a tragedy or an inquest had taken place in Ottinge; the last had occurred twenty years previously, when Joe Watkins (a village name), being jealous, had thrown his wife down a well, and, despite her prayers, entreaties, and screams, had left her to drown, for which crime he had paid the extreme penalty of the law in Brodfield Gaol.

A suicide was something entirely foreign to the character of the community, and the topic was exhaustively debated in the Drum. Joe Thunder gave it as *his* opinion that the remains of Captain Ramsay—speaking from recollection—would be buried with a stake at a cross-roads—probably at Crampton, being nearest. The village was stirred out of its normal lethargy and, secretly, rather proud of being the scene of a sensation, and newspaper paragraphs.

The Parson and Miss Morven spent the night succeeding Captain Ramsay's death at Ivy House, and were anxious to carry his widow off to the Rectory; but she preferred to remain in her own home until after the funeral, and then leave Ottinge. All Mrs. Ramsay's little world, gentle and simple, had shown her their kindness and sympathy: the Rector looked after business matters, Miss Susan had undertaken correspondence (she enjoyed letter-writing), Wynyard took charge of the dogs, whilst Aurea gave personal attendance and warm affection.

The inquest was conducted as quietly and as speedily as possible, thanks to the good offices of Dr. Boas; the verdict returned was "suicide whilst of unsound mind," and the jury offered their sincere condolences with the widow. At the funeral Ottinge was proud to note a lord and two honourables appearing as mourners, and the remains of Captain Ramsay received Christian interment in the churchyard; there was no word of cross-roads—much less a stake!

Afterwards, Mrs. Ramsay's brothers, who were guests at the Rectory, took their departure, and it was generally known that their sister would follow them to Ireland within a week. Her obstinate persistence in for years clinging to a man who by rights should be in an asylum had alienated her friends; but now that he was no more, there reigned a great peace. The boarder dogs had been abruptly dispersed, and Wynyard, who obtained special leave, personally conducted several parties over the fields to Catsfield station, and wound up matters out of doors. Aurea did the same within—but they rarely met. She was surprised to discover the footing on which her aunts' chauffeur stood at Ivy House. Till now she knew little of their acquaintance; it was a before-breakfast and after-dark affair.

It was also Wynyard's task to collect and sort and pack the Captain's belongings, by his widow's particular desire.

"I like to have you about," she said. "Is it not wonderful how well we have got to know one another, and how much we have in common, since I opened the hall door to you, a stranger, that wet morning last April? Jim was devoted to you, and you were so good to him—sitting here, evening after evening, talking and listening and playing picquet with that poor fellow. Oh, Owen, if you had known him as your father and I knew him, you would understand why I, forsaking all my own people, clung to him till the *end*!"

"Yes, you did that!" he answered, with emphasis.

"Only think of the tragedy of his life," she resumed, in a broken voice, "the last fifteen years, all through a branch knocking off his sun topee and his determination to get first spear. Oh, what a little thing to mean so much! The way of life."

Wynyard, the handy man, packed up cases containing old Indian relics, such as faded photographs, horns, bear skins, khaki uniforms, Sam Brown belts, packets of tiger claws, and all sorts of rubbish dear to Mrs. Ramsay. Among the collection was a photograph album, aged at least thirty years, and considerably the worse for Indian rains and Ottinge damp.

"I think this must be your father," said Mrs. Ramsay, pointing to the old-fashioned carte-de-visite of a handsome man in Hussar uniform, "and this is your mother opposite," indicating a pretty, dark-eyed girl holding up a puppy. "You see, she was fond of dogs, like you and me! Do you care to have them?" drawing them out as she spoke.

"Yes, thank you most awfully, I should. It's funny that I should come upon my people and hear so much of them in Ottinge of all the world! I don't remember either of them, for my mother died when I was two years old, and my father was killed at polo—it killed her too—and then my sister and I were sent home."

"So you have a sister?"

"I have very much a sister," and he laughed; "she has all the family brains—and her own as well."

"I will not allow that, Mr. Wynyard; it was marvellous how, with a few hints from me, you threw yourself into a life before you were born. Isn't it strange that I am the only one in Ottinge who knows your real name?"

"Except Miss Morven," he corrected. "You know he recognised me, and said 'Wynyard.'"

"Yes, but no doubt she believes he was wandering. You don't wish your surname to be known here, do you?"

"No, my christian name does as well."

"I must confess I wonder you remain! You are so young, and life here is deadly dull for such as you, with all the years and energies before you," and she looked at him interrogatively. It was dusk; she was sitting in the deep drawing-room window, her slim figure silhouetted against the fading light. Wynyard had been nailing down some cases, and came and stood, hammer in hand, in the middle of the room. She knew perfectly well why he remained in the sleepy village; it was because Aurea Morven had glorified Ottinge.

"I believe I know your secret," she remarked suddenly. He made no reply. Mrs. Ramsay was no doubt thinking of Aurea, whilst he was dwelling on the bargain with his uncle. Should he tell her? They had of late been drawn so much to one another—she already knew half his story, and had just given him the photographs of his father and mother—her husband and his father had been like brothers—yes—he would!

And there in the semi-dusk, leaning his hands on the back of a chair, in as few words as possible, he related his tale, and how he had made a solemn compact for two years, which compact he was bound to keep to the letter and the bitter end.

"And it's a good deal more bitter than I expected," he concluded.

Listening with tightly folded hands, the slim figure in black accorded him her entire sympathy. Now she was in possession of all his confidence, and such was his unhappy plight, he was desperately in love with a girl, and could neither speak nor show a sign—nor make his real position known. What an amazing state of affairs! Did Aurea recognise in Wynyard a silent worshipper? And was it not true that love and smoke cannot be concealed?

"You will keep this to yourself, I know," he said. "I'm not *sure* that I'm within my right in telling you, but somehow I had to."

"You may be certain I shall never breathe it till you give me permission," she answered, drawing a long breath; "but what an extraordinary man your uncle must be!"

"Yes, he is eccentric; but I believe he is right—this sort of apprenticeship will do me a jolly lot of good. I know more of the people now I'm one of them. Many a thing I've learnt here, that I'd never have had a glimpse of, and I must tell you fair and square that I gave Uncle Dick a lot of bother in the way of my debts."

"Hereditary extravagance—your father—a younger son—drove a four-in-hand, you know. Ah, here comes Aurea," as the little gate swung. "I half promised to go over there this evening."

"Then good-bye, I'm off; I'll finish the packing to-morrow," and he escaped through the back garden.

It was abundantly evident that of late Miss Morven avoided him, and he had not spoken to her since the tragic occasion when they both hung over a dying man on the high road to Upstreet.

More than six months had gone by since he had come to Ottinge; sometimes it seemed an endless time, at others as but yesterday. One thing was clear and stationary in his mind—his living among working people had opened the eyes of a future landowner, given him a better estimate of his responsibilities, and a sympathy and understanding that nothing could obliterate.

At last Ivy House was closed; the blinds were drawn down, the key hung in Mrs. Hogben's bedroom, and the memory of the recent catastrophe had become a little dim. It was three weeks since the Captain had killed himself, and other events had begun to press upon public attention. Since the tragedy Aurea had absolutely refused to drive in the motor, to her Aunt Bella's great annoyance; she was painfully anxious to have it in daily use, for she feared that being the cause of a man's death might depreciate the car's value! And when the girl announced she would never get into it again, she was furious, and her face assumed a dull red shade as she asked—

"Do you mean to tell me that, if there's an accident to a carriage, or if a cart runs over somebody, that cart is never to be used? How could people get on?" she demanded. "I never heard of such affected nonsense. And now I suppose you will go and give my nice car a bad name? As if it could help the madman throwing himself under it!"

"I'll say nothing about it, Aunt Bella, you know that perfectly well; but if you had been in the motor yourself and felt the *crunch*, I don't think you would have cared ever to drive in it again."

"Rubbish—you are hysterical! You should get Dr. Boas to give you a tonic and go away somewhere for a change; only you are too much away from your father as it is—every one says so. It was remarked to me only the other day."

"It is funny, Aunt Bella, how many people make nasty remarks about me to you. Do you suppose that they think you like hearing them?" and she laughed, and before Miss Parrett could find her breath or an answer had left her.

It was a fact that Miss Parrett cultivated a cordon of idle, elderly women, who came to tea or lunch or to spend the day, who were aware that Miss Parrett had "a good deal in her power to bestow" (not only in the form of fruit and vegetables), and who knew that, even more than talking of herself and her wonderful successes in her youth, her many broken-hearted lovers, she liked to discuss her pretty, popular niece and to listen to their hostile criticisms. Miss Parrett was openly jealous of this girl's ascendancy in Ottinge, where *she* was the great lady. After all, Aurea was only a sort of half-niece, and she could leave her money where she liked. This notification was promptly repeated, and received with unqualified and respectful approval, by the two Miss Dabbs and Mrs. Forbes Cattermole and her freckled daughters. On these occasions, when Aurea was the topic, and her appearance, manners, and customs were figuratively placed under the microscope, and then exhaustively debated, the entrance of Miss Susan was invariably followed by an abrupt and awkward silence.

It was a lovely afternoon—Saturday—the third day of September, and the chauffeur was working in the Manor garden close by the sundial, repairing some of the rose pergolas with nails and wire. Suddenly, to his delight, he beheld Miss Morven coming through the yew arch nearest to the house—a slim white figure in a dark green frame—with her hat over her arm, and accompanied by Joss, who, in exuberant joy, was leaping his own height from the ground.

As the young lady sauntered slowly up the broad walk, she stopped every now and then to pick flowers from the luxuriant borders on either hand. As these were white, she was evidently gathering them for the church. He watched, surreptitiously, her wonderfully supple figure, her lithe grace, as she stooped and stretched hither and thither. Aurea had grown thin, her lovely colour had certainly faded, no doubt she had not yet recovered from the shock of Captain Ramsay's horribly sudden death.

By and by his vicinity was discovered to her by Joss, who had been dashing about among the cabbages in chase of an historic pheasant, and now accorded him a rapturous acknowledgment. He had just finished his task, and stepped out into the walk; as the young lady approached he touched his cap, and she halted for a moment and said, with obvious hesitation—

"A lovely day, isn't it?"

"Yes, miss;" and then he ventured to add, "You never come out in the car now?"

"No," she answered, "never again; it's a juggernaut!"

"I would not say that!" he protested. "What happened could not have been helped; of course, it's an old machine and out of date"—(he was thinking of the 60 h.p. Napier at Westmere)—"and requires a lot of humouring to get her to run at all, and if put to too high a pressure might go to pieces—still——"

But here Miss Morven interrupted with a hasty gesture, and, laying her flowers upon the sundial, turned to face him fully, and said—

"I'm rather surprised"—she paused for a moment, and then resumed— "that when you saw what a dull sort of place this was, and what a wretched old car you had to drive, you stayed on. You really have no proper job; my aunt's motoring is absurd. I cannot imagine why you remain here."

"Can you not, miss?" he answered, in a low voice, his gaze fixed on the sundial and its motto, "Time Trieth All." Suddenly raising his eyes, he met hers steadily—for one unguarded moment the truth was in his face!—and there was a thrill of passion in his voice as he added, "Then, in that case, I am afraid it would be impossible for me to tell you."

For as long as one could count ten, there was an expressive silence, only broken by the crashing of cabbage leaves, the notes of wood pigeons, the boom of a passing bee.

Miss Morven remained motionless, but the trembling of her lip indicated the tension of her self-control, and a wave of sudden colour invaded her cheeks, and raced up into her wavy dark hair. This tell-tale blush betrayed that she knew as well as the chauffeur, his sole reason for remaining in Ottinge.

Then without a word she lifted the flowers, and, holding herself unusually erect, the slim white figure proceeded down the walk that led towards the old bowling-green.

Wynyard, as he stood watching her, asked himself, Was she also passing out of his life? In another moment a yew hedge had hid her from his eyes.

"I believe I've done it now!" he muttered. "I could not help it; she knows, and is ready to kill me for my presumption! She will tell her aunts, and I shall get the sack."

He picked up a small blossom that Aurea had dropped on the sundial, opened his watch, and carefully placed the little flower along with the little photograph. When people are in love, what irrational follies tempt them!

CHAPTER XXII
AUREA'S REFLECTIONS

But Aurea had no intention of "telling her aunts"; on the contrary, she crossed the old bowling-green in order to avoid the Manor, and returned home across the meadows that led by Claringbold's Farm. In the dim hall of the Rectory she encountered Norris—who, of an afternoon, often haunted that vicinity—and said, as she handed her the flowers—

"Will you please fill the church vases? I've rather a headache from the sun."

The girl really did feel considerably dazed and bewildered, and passed into the drawing-room, where she ruthlessly dislodged Mac from her own particular pet chair. Mac vacated the seat with an air of injured deliberation, found another, and sighed as heavily as if he were a human being.

The time had come for thinking things out, and his mistress, having seated herself, prepared to hold a court of inquiry on Aurea Morven. One would suppose that she really had had a sunstroke like poor Captain Ramsay! What mad impulse had urged her to question the chauffeur? At the moment, she seemed to be listening to another personality speaking by her lips. She felt a fluttering in her throat as she told herself that this inscrutable young man was certainly in love with her. Behold, she summoned her evidence! The photograph in the watch, the village concert, when, after a rousing camp song, he had given, as an encore, "I'll sing thee songs of Araby"; she believed that the words were addressed to herself, that the singer was pouring out his soul to *her*. Possibly other girls shared her conviction, and had taken it to their tender and palpitating hearts. When the last note had died away in a ringing silence, Ottinge recognised a gentleman's song and a gentleman's voice; after a pause of astonishment, there came a storm of belated clapping and applause, and one or two timid female voices were heard to cry out "Encore!" Some of the rustic audience grinned, and declared that the words were no good, and damned nonsense, but the tune was pretty enough; it was whistled in the street within the week.

Aurea summed up the photograph, the song, and the recent interview by the sundial; the recollection of Owen's voice, the look in his extremely expressive grey eyes, set her heart beating. At the same time she blamed herself for her amazing indiscretion. She, who had lately avoided this gentleman chauffeur at choir practice, at the Manor, and in the village—she, who knew that he treasured her photo, to actually accost him in the garden, and demand what he meant by remaining in Ottinge!

She felt her face burning, and no wonder! Well, at any rate the scene had given her a shock—it had roused her to the knowledge of her own feelings. It was with difficulty her maidenly reticence could put the thing into thought, but it simply came to this—she had arrived, at last, at the clear realisation that the daughter of the Rector of Ottinge was in love with her aunts' chauffeur! She whispered it to herself and Mackenzie! How did it sound? How would it sound when talked abroad, all over the parish and the county? What would people say? When she thought of her Aunt Bella, she actually laughed aloud, and Mackenzie, whom she had disturbed, raised his head and gave a low growl.

The chauffeur disturbed her—even now her pulses were racing; she had never felt like this when in the company of Bertie Woolcock—no, nor any of Aunt Morven's young eligibles—but this man affected her differently. Was it because she knew that he cared for her? Was it because he was handsome, reserved, and self-reliant? Was it because there was a mystery about him? No; it was simply because he was himself; his voice was still speaking to her inward ear—"It would be impossible for me to tell you!" Nevertheless, his eyes had been eloquent, and, since the truth must be confessed, her heart was in a wild whirl of happiness.

But why was he here in retreat? Surely not because he had done anything disgraceful? Mrs. Ramsay liked him, and said he had been such a comfort to her husband and herself; her father liked him, so did Susan, so did the village; the dogs adored him—all but Mackenzie, an exception who proved the rule!

Yes, she would give her heart to the chauffeur—as a matter of fact it was not a case of giving; it was already bestowed—and keep the knowledge to herself. No one should ever know—above all, *he* should not know. "Time Tries All." His affairs might improve; some day he might be able to throw off his chauffeur's disguise and be himself; meanwhile, she determined to avoid him, and never again enter the Manor garden when there was a chance of meeting him; as to the green motor, she had, as she assured him, done with it for ever.

CHAPTER XXIII
AN HOUR OF LIBERTY

The white flowers had been gathered on Saturday in the Manor garden, and it was now Monday. Miss Parrett had adventured a drive to Westmere, returning home by four o'clock, and the car being washed and put away betimes, the chauffeur found himself at liberty. The glowing and golden September evening was enticing, and, whistling for Joss, he set out for a good long stretch before supper. On this occasion, man and dog deserted the low country and the water-meadows, and climbed the hills which sheltered the village. Their road lay by a grassy cart-track, which ran sometimes between high hedges, sometimes along a headland, with here and there a hoary old gate—it was chiefly used in harvest-time (indeed, wisps of fresh hay and straw were still clinging to the bushes), and was the short-cut to Shrapton-le-Steeple, a hamlet which lay eight miles south of Ottinge. The track emerged upon a bare plateau, from whence was a fine view of the surrounding country, and here was also a sharp freshness in the air, which the man inhaled with unmistakable enjoyment. Here, too, in the banks, were inviting burrows, and these afforded the dog an absorbing interest, as he drew their savour into his nostrils with long-drawn sniffs of ecstatic satisfaction.

After a tramp of between three and four miles, Wynyard threw himself down on a tempting patch of grass, drew out his case, and lit one of Martin Kesters' excellent cigars. His eyes roamed meditatively over the broad landscape below, stretching away into the dim distance—the spreading uplands splashed with orange gorse, dotted with sheep and cattle, with here and there a rust-coloured farmhouse, whose pale blue smoke lazily ascended into the cool clear air. Wynyard enjoyed the scene and the sensation of absolute freedom; at least he was out of livery—he glanced at his shabby tweed coat—beyond the reach of orders, and master of himself! Not much to boast of! To think that this job was the only one he could take on when driven into a corner by circumstances and Uncle Dick! He had no head, that was his trouble, although he could keep it at a pinch—and wasn't this what was called a paradox? If he were only clever with his tongue and his pen, like Leila, and had her talent for languages and for organisation, her genius for saying and doing the right thing!

As he unconsciously picked bits of grass, his thoughts returned to Aurea and their recent meeting in the Manor garden. Her confusion and her vivid blush held for him a most stupendous significance. Memory and imagination had magnified the occasion, until it seemed to be the one important event in his whole life!

If, by any chance, Aurea cared for him, and saw in him something more than her aunts' civil man-servant, why should he not present himself in his true character? The gruff replies in imitation of Tom Hogben were surely an unnecessary handicap? Anyway, he had let himself go on the night of the accident, hustling and ordering on the spur of the moment, sending Miss Morven for water, Miss Susan for wood—though no doubt they were both too much upset to have noticed anything besides the tragedy.

Possibly a change of manner would make a difference, and Aurea was so bright, and so wonderfully clear-sighted, she might divine something of his situation, and wait. "Wait!" repeated incredulous common sense, "wait eighteen months till he had cast off his shackles!" On the other hand, Bertie Woolcock loomed large. Undoubtedly he would not wait, nor would Aurea's own relations. The Rector himself was a good, unworldly old scribbler, but the people that mattered, such as Miss Parrett and General and Mrs. Morven, they would never allow their niece to refuse many thousands a year and Woolcock, in order to keep faith with a mysterious and penniless chauffeur. And Bertie undoubtedly meant business; he was continually appearing at the Rectory or the Manor, charged with paltry messages and unnecessary notes—any excuse or none served him! He even attended evening church, where he openly and shamelessly worshipped the Rector's daughter, and not the Rector's God.

As Wynyard contemplated Woolcock's position and the desperate obstacles that lay in his own path, he picked many blades of grass. Naturally he disliked his rival; he remembered him when he was in the upper fourth at Eton, a big, loutish fellow—not of course in Pop—and an awful duffer at games; who never did anything for himself, that others could be bullied into doing for him. "Woolly" was now a stout, sleek, well-groomed man of thirty, with a heavy red face, a lethargic manner, and—in the company of respectable women—a great talent for silence.

Supposing that Aurea was talked over? Westmere was a temptation. No; he could not face such a hideous possibility—yet he was penniless and gagged. Woolly, a rich man and free; he, a prisoner to a promise and in a false position—a position which compelled him to touch his cap, not only to his lady-love, but to his rival! and the latter salutation made him feel murderous.

Woolly had tons of money; he was so rich that possibly he had never seen a penny! His attentions to Aurea, his rides, his churchgoing, his marked civilities to Miss Parrett, paraded themselves before Wynyard's mental sight—and the old Polly bird was all for the match! Why, that very afternoon, as she was leaving Westmere, she had held a long, mysterious "last word" conversation with Mrs. Waring before she bundled into the car, and squeaked out "Home—and go slowly!" Meanwhile, Woolcock's fluffy-haired sister stood on the steps with her hands on her hips, a newly lit cigarette in her mouth, the very embodiment of triumphant satisfaction!

Undoubtedly a solemn treaty had been signed and sealed. He had no powerful allies, how could he interfere? His mind groped round the puzzle in confusion and despair. If his own forefathers had not been such crazy, spendthrift fools, he would not have found himself in this maddening situation. To think that his great-grandfather had lost thousands of pounds and hundreds of acres, racing snails on the dining-room mahogany, against another lunatic! However, the original place still remained in the family, also the most important heirlooms, and these were *pucka* (good old Indian word!) and not those of other people.

If he could only hold on to the end, and put in his time fairly and squarely, he might yet see Aurea at Wynyard—though at present his prospects were blank; all he had to his name was his weekly wages, and these wages, figuratively, bore him into the presence of Miss Parrett. What an old bully she was! how she brow-beat and hectored her unfortunate sister, and what a jabbering impostor! talking incessantly of all she did, and was going to do, but leaving everything in the way of work to Miss Susan and her niece—whilst *she* trotted round spying and scolding.

As Wynyard reclined against the bank smoking, absorbed in his reflections—and Joss was equally engrossed in an adjacent ditch—a far-away sound broke faintly on their ears. In a few seconds this had resolved itself into the regular "thud, thud, thud," of a galloping horse, and here he came into sight—a chestnut in a lather, with streaming reins, and exultant tail, carrying an empty side saddle.

Wynyard instantly recognised Aurea's weedy thoroughbred, and, flinging away his cigar, ran forward, but the animal, bound for his stable, was not thus to be captured and detained; with a snort of defiance, he made a violent swerve, and tore on, hotly pursued by Joss.

CHAPTER XXIV
ON YAMPTON HILL

It was not the horse, but the horse's rider that was of consequence. Where was she? What had happened? Spurred by an agony of apprehension, Wynyard ran in the direction from which the runaway had appeared. In five minutes' time a speck, and then a figure came into sight, and this presently resolved itself into Miss Morven—apparently unhurt. She, too, had been running; her habit was splashed, she carried her hat in her hand, her beautiful hair was becomingly loosened, and she had a brilliant colour.

As Wynyard slowed down to a walk, she called to him—

"Have you seen my horse?"

"Yes; he must be in Ottinge by this time," was the comforting rejoinder.

"Why didn't you stop him?"

"It would have wasted a lot of time, and I wanted to see what had happened to you.—I was afraid you'd had a spill."

This was not the ever silent and respectful chauffeur to whom Miss Morven had been hitherto accustomed; but no less a person than Lieutenant Wynyard, late of the Red Hussars, who, in a cheery voice, addressed her as an equal—as no doubt he was. So be it. She instantly decided to abandon herself to the situation. Possibly he would now confide something about himself, and how and why he came to be in her aunts' service. So, after a momentary hesitation, she replied—

"Oh no, I only got off to open a gate, and Rufus broke away. I suppose I shall have to walk home!"

To this Wynyard secretly and joyfully agreed, but merely said—

"I see you are alone."

"Yes; father and I rode over to Shrapton-le-Steeple; he wanted to see Mr. Harnett, a literary friend, and Mr. Harnett had so much to show and to say that he persuaded father to stay and dine, as there is a moon, and I came home by the short-cut. I must be three miles from Ottinge?" and she halted and deliberately looked about her.

"Yes," he replied; "a good three miles."

(Oh, a very good three miles, during which he would have Aurea's undivided company—what a piece of luck!)

For some little time the couple proceeded in silence—a sensitive silence. During the interval since their last meeting, they had accomplished a vast amount of very special thinking—many disturbing, dominating, and dangerous thoughts had entered the young lady's brain, and she said to herself—

"I must keep perfectly composed, and if ever he intends to speak freely, now—now is the time! To think of us two alone on Yampton Hills, three miles away from home!"

Somehow those three miles held a thrilling prospect. Wynyard, for his part, was longing to utter what was in his mind; here was his one grand opportunity; and yet for several hundred yards a strange silence hung between them, though the man was burning to speak and the girl was longing to listen; meanwhile moments, precious as life itself, were ebbing fast! At last the conversation began to trickle; the topics were the choir, the boy scouts, old Thunder's pig, and Mrs. Hogben's face-ache—a spent cartridge in the path introduced sport and shooting.

"I wonder why men are so keen on killing things?" said Aurea.

"I believe we inherit it from our ancestors, who had to kill wild creatures or starve. I must say I like shooting."

"Oh, do you!"—a blank pause—"the only sport I can imagine any pleasure in, is hunting."

"Do you hunt?"

"No; I only wish I did; but Aunt Bella thinks it so improper for a woman to follow the hounds, and father could not escort me."

"But parsons do hunt."

"They did; a vicar of Ottinge actually kept hounds. Father says he only left a dozen dusty books in the library, but a hundred dozen of sound wine in the cellar."

"Yes, those were the good old days!"

"I'm not so sure that they were superior to our own times. What do you say?"

"That I hope you will always have a good time, Miss Morven."

Miss Morven coloured and bit her lip, but resumed—

"If I only might hunt, I would be bound to have a good time."

"Is your horse a clever jumper?"

"No; he either blunders on his head, or sits down."

"Doesn't sound very promising!" and they both laughed. "Anyway, it's a rotten, bad country," said Wynyard, with a contemptuous wave of his hand; "the uplands are full of rabbit holes, and as for the lowlands—you'd want a boat! You should see Leicestershire—big fields and sound turf."

"Yes; but I'm afraid I can't hunt in Leicestershire from Ottinge," she answered, with a smile; "and I have some hopes of sport this winter. Mrs. Waring, who is tremendously keen, wants me to go out with her."

"On a pillion?"

"No; her brother has a capital horse, not up to his weight, that would just carry me. He is so anxious that I should try it; it jumps beautifully."

"And what does Miss Parrett say?"

"I think Mrs. Waring may talk her over, and Mr. Woolcock promises to look after me."

This information roused Wynyard's ire, his face hardened, and his tone was dry as he said—

"Woolcock is too heavy to hunt, except pounding along the road. He must weigh seventeen stone!"

"Very likely; but he is going to do a cure before the season opens."

"Why not a couple of hours with the garden roller, and save the donkey?"

Miss Morven took no notice of this impudent suggestion—merely flicked her habit with her hunting crop, and he continued—

"Westmere is a fine old place."

"Yes, isn't it? The hall and galleries are real Tudor, and the park is lovely."

"How would you like to live there?"

"I?" and as she turned to him her air was lofty. "What a—a—an extraordinary question!"

"Yes," he replied, with hasty penitence; "please forgive me, it was more than extraordinary, it was impertinent."

"By the way (it was, after all, the girl who broke the ice), I must ask you to excuse me for my inquisitive question the other day in the garden."

"You wanted to know why I hung on at Ottinge, with little or nothing to do?" and he paused. "I think you do know, Miss Morven, in fact, I'm sure you know. I'd be only too glad to speak out, but my hands and tongue are tied. I've given a promise I'm bound to keep, and between you and my absolute confidence, there stands at present an enormous obstacle."

"Oh!"

"I ought to tell you that I'm not what I seem."

"Of course," with a touch of impatience, "you are a gentleman by birth; I've always known that."

"Nor am I here in my own name—only my christian name; but I've never done anything to disgrace it, I give you my word of honour." As he came to a halt and faced her, and the setting sun shone into his truthful eyes and touched his crisp brown locks, the glow of the evening air seemed to give added force to his personality. "I've played the fool—the silly ass—and I've got to pay. How I wish I might talk to you openly, and tell you all about myself!"

"I wish you might," repeated the girl, and her voice shook; an emotional tension had crept into the situation—her pulses beat wildly, and her mind was in a tumult.

"You cannot imagine what it is to be in my fix," he continued, speaking with low, passionate intensity; "for months and months to love some one with all my soul, and never be able to open my lips."

"It must be trying," she answered, now moving on, with her eyes on the ground.

"And when I'm free, I may be too late!" he said gloomily.

"You may," she assented; "for how could some one guess?"

"That's it! That is what is the awful part of the whole thing; but, look here, Miss Morven, let me state a case. Supposing you knew a fellow in such a hole, and felt that you cared for him, and could trust him and stick to him, as it were, blindly for a time; supposing he were your social equal, and had a clean record, and that you knew he worshipped your very shadow— would"—and here he looked straight into her face—"*you* wait?" To this question, impetuously delivered, there followed a silence.

"This is a sort of problem, isn't it?" she faltered at last, "like the Hard Cases in Vanity Fair?"

"No, by Jove, part of it is God's truth! but I'm only talking like an idiot. Of course no girl that ever was born could do it."

"I'm not so sure," she murmured, with her eyes on the ground, her heart beating in hurried thumps.

"Miss Morven—Aurea," he went on, now moved out of all discretion, and casting self-control to the winds, "you are the only girl I've ever cared for in all my life. I fell in love with you the first moment I ever saw you, when you danced with Mackenzie in the Manor drawing-room. This meeting to-day has been the one good turn luck has done me in three years—and I seize upon it perhaps unlawfully; perhaps it's not just cricket, my talking to you in this way, but it's my only chance, so I snatch it, for I may never see you alone again—and all is fair in love and war."

At this moment he caught sight of a stout figure, far below, labouring up the winding lane; it was Miss Morven's maid, Norris. He recognised her bright blue gown. Oh, the precious moments were numbered, and it was now—or never!

"What do you say?" he demanded, coming to a standstill.

"But what can I say?" she rejoined, lifting her startled eyes to his. "I don't know anything about you. You cannot even tell me your name." (Naturally she did not mention that it was already known to her.) "It's all rather bewildering, isn't it?"

"Yes, it's simply crazy," he admitted; "here am I, your aunts' chauffeur, receiving weekly wages, living like a working man, telling you, with the most audacious and astounding impertinence, that I've been in love with you for months. You know that I'm of your own class, but who I am, or where I come from, I refuse to disclose. No wonder you feel dazed." They were now within sight of the village and of Norris. "Look here, Miss Morven," he continued, and his voice was a little hoarse, "I see your maid coming, and my priceless, precious time is running out. Let me ask you one question; supposing I were not Owen, the chauffeur, but had fair prospects, good friends, and say a thousand a year to start with—would you—marry me?"

Aurea knew perfectly well that she would marry him if he had only a few hundreds a year, no prospects, and no friends; but she took refuge in that nice, useful, and evasive word "Perhaps."

"Perhaps"—he stooped and kissed her gloved hand—"perhaps—will keep me going! Even if I don't see you, I shall *live* on that one little word for the next eighteen months. I don't suppose I shall have another opportunity of speaking to you."

Here he was interrupted by Norris, who suddenly appeared round a bend in the lane, puffing like a grampus, her hat on the back of her head, and her face crimson from exertion.

"Oh, Miss Aurea!" she screamed, as she halted and held her fat sides, "such a cruel fright as you give me—and the three men gone by the road looking to find your corpse! and I ran this way, after your horse come home all loose and wild. Are you hurt?"

"No; he only broke away when I was opening a gate, and I had to walk," replied the young lady with wonderful composure.

Norris threw a sharp glance at the chauffeur.

"And couldn't *he* have helped you? What was he about?"

"I'm afraid, like yourself, I was looking for Miss Morven," he replied.

Norris turned from him with a sniff of disparagement, and, addressing herself to her mistress, said—

"And where's the Rector?"

"He is dining with Mr. Harnett."

"Tut, tut, tut! And he will stay half the night talking books, and there are a brace of grouse for dinner—kept to the hour—and all he will get at Harnett's will be green vegetables, like a goat—he's a sexagenarian!"

At this Aurea laughed and the chauffeur smiled; he was now walking alongside of Miss Aurea, as much at his ease as if he were a gentleman! Norris turned on him abruptly, and said—

"Look here, young man, you'd better be getting on—it's your supper-time, and Mother Hogben won't keep it hot for you."

"It's very good of you to think of my supper," he replied, with a touch of hauteur; "but I'm not in any hurry."

He spoke to her as her superior; his was the voice and air of the ruling and upper class, and Norris' dislike to the insolent young ne'er-do-well suddenly flared into active hatred. Meanwhile, he walked with them to the very end of the lane, and opened the side gate for Miss Morven and herself; and as he held it, he took off his cap to Miss Aurea and said—

"Good-night—miss."

As mistress and maid crossed the lawn, the latter burst out—

"I can't abide that young fellow, with his fine manners and his taking off his cap like a lord! Miss Aurea dear, I'm thinking the Rector would not be too well pleased to see you in the lanes a-walking out like any village girl along of your aunts' chauffeur."

"Norris, how dare you speak to me in such a way!" cried Aurea passionately. And yet, why be furious? She *had* been "a-walking out" precisely like any other country girl.

"Well, well, well, dearie, don't be angry. I'm only giving you a hint for your good, and I know you are a real lady, as proud as proud, and as high-minded as a queen or an angel. Still and all, I'm mighty glad that none of our *talkers* happened to come across you!"

CHAPTER XXV
LADY KESTERS AT THE DRUM

Jane Norris, who had been Aurea's nurse, was now her maid and housekeeper, a most efficient individual in both capacities. Jane was a woman of fifty, with a round, fat face, a complacent double chin, a comfortable figure, and a quantity of ginger-coloured hair—of which she was unreasonably vain. Jane had also a pair of prominent brown eyes (which gave the impression of watchfulness), a sharp tongue, a very sincere affection for her child, and an insatiable appetite for gossip. She was left in sole charge of the Rector and Rectory when Aurea was absent, and considered herself a person of paramount importance in the community, not only on account of her position at the Rectory, but also for being the happy possessor of a real fur coat, a gold watch, and, last, but by no means least, considerable savings. Her circle was naturally contracted and select; her intimates, the village dressmaker, Miss Poult—who had many clients in the neighbourhood—Mrs. Frickett, of the Drum; and Mrs. Gill, the schoolmistress. (Mrs. Hogben, who took in washing, needless to say, was not in her set.) Miss Norris had a *flair* for uncloaking scandals, and was a veritable Captain Cook in the way of making marvellous and unsuspected discoveries. She had always been particularly anxious to explore the chauffeur's past and to learn what she called the "geography" of this young man. Hitherto the young man had defeated her efforts, and baffled her most insidious inquiries. He did not drink or talk or give himself away; he did not carry on with girls, or encourage them. Oh, it was an old head on young shoulders, and there was something about him that was not fair and square—and *she* was bound to know it!

Miss Norris had been occasionally disturbed by a vague apprehension (resembling some persistent and irritating insect) that her mistress was interested in this good-looking stranger, but she thrust the idea angrily aside. Miss Aurea was not like those bold, chattering minxes who were always throwing themselves in his way! She was really ashamed of herself, and her wicked mind. Of course, Miss Aurea would make a grand match, and marry young Woolcock—who was just crazy about her, as all the world knew—and *she* would go with her as maid to Westmere Park. But the vision of her young lady and the chauffeur talking to her so earnestly in the hill lane had excited her fears, and she resolved to give Miss Aurea something to think of, and put her from speaking to the upsetting, impudent fellow—who got more notice and made more talk in Ottinge than the Rector himself!

Aurea, who had been accustomed to Norris ever since the days of socks and strapped shoes, regarded her as a friend, and even suffered her to gossip (mildly) as she dressed her hair, for she said to herself—

"The poor thing has no one else to talk to all day long"—Simple Aurea!—"being set in authority over the other servants, and must have some safety-valve."

The night after her walk with Wynyard, Aurea slept but little; she was thinking, and wondering, and happy. As she dressed, she was unusually abstracted, and when Norris began her *coiffure*, she did not as usual read the Psalms for the day, but sat with crossed hands in a trance of meditation, whilst her maid brushed her soft and lustrous locks. After twice clearing her throat with energetic significance, Norris began—

"So Mrs. Ramsay is letting the house for six months, I hear?"

"Yes," was the languid reply.

"To a sort of county inspector; the chauffeur fellow showed him in— *he* has a finger in every one's pie."

"I don't know what you mean, Norris."

"Well, anyway, he did a lot for Mrs. Ramsay," she answered, with significance. "He was in and out at all hours—some think he is good-looking—and ladies like him."

"What ladies?"

"Well, now, Miss Aurea, you know I don't intend any harm, but the talk is that your aunt, Miss Susan, makes too great a pet of him. Why, half his day he's helping her in the garden or potting plants in the greenhouse; and she lends him books, and talks and makes a fuss of him, just as if he were in her own station."

Norris' speech was so rapid, such a cataract of words, that her young mistress had not been able to interrupt; at last she broke in—

"How wicked of people!" endeavouring to wrench her hair away. "Poor Aunt Susan—so good, unselfish, and kind—not even spared! Oh, it's too abominable! I'm ashamed of you, Norrie; how can you listen to such things?"

"Indeed, Miss Aurea, I said just what you said, and that Miss Susan was too old; but they say there is no fool like an old one—and some folk *will* gossip. And there was Mrs. Lambert, who married a boy that was at school with her own son. You know there's not much to talk of here—now the Ramsays are gone. As for the young man, as I told you to-night, *I* never held a good opinion of him; he's too secret and too off-hand to please *me*. He goes out of a night for exercise, so he says, walking the country till daybreak; but that's just a blind. Who is he with?—tell me that?"

Aurea remembered, with a sudden stinging pang, how she and her father had overtaken him one evening escorting Dilly Topham. Dilly had been crying, and she was holding his hand!

"Why, I saw him myself in the theatre at Brodfield," resumed Norris, "and he had a young woman with him—so he had."

"And why not?" bravely demanded Aurea, but her lips were white.

"The two were in a box, and he sat back—but *I* knew him—and afterwards they walked together to the Coach and Horses Hotel, the best in Brodfield. She was tall and slim, and wore a long coat and black lace scarf over her head—I call it very bold in the public street."

"One of his friends," explained Aurea, with a stoical indifference her heart belied; and to cut short any further disclosures, she released herself from her handmaiden's clutches and knelt down to say her prayers.

By a disagreeable and curious coincidence, Miss Morven received that same evening ample confirmation of Norris' arraignment!

Lady Kesters had decided to pay her brother another visit, and wrote to announce that, as she and Martin were within fifty miles, she would fly down to see him for a few hours.

> "I'll come to Brodfield by train and motor over. Don't breathe a word to the Parretts. I can put up at the Drum and meet you there. I've ever so much to say and hear; your letters are miserable, and I've not seen you for more than two months. Martin is off to America in October—he has to look after some business—and I am going with him, as I want to see the country, but I shudder to think of the crossing. Uncle Dick is at Carlsbad. If you come over to the churchyard about six to-morrow, I shall be there. I'll hire a car for the day and get back to Brodfield for the night, and rush to Rothes next morning with the milk; if you will make an appointment, I can meet you, and go for a stroll and a talk."

A smart Napier and a motor-veiled lady were not now a startling novelty in Ottinge—it was the highway to many places; but the 40 h.p. motor and lady who put up at the Drum was a refreshing novelty—and a novelty invested in mystery.

The Drum jutted out obtrusively; the front faced down the road towards the Manor, and one side was parallel to the street, and whoever entered or left was well in evidence. Lady Kesters asked for dinner and a sitting-room, as if such were a matter of course! The sole sitting-room was just across the passage from the bar and overlooked the street. It was oak-panelled, very low, the walls were decorated with cheap prints and faded photographs of cricket groups, there was a round table, three or four chairs, and an overpowering atmosphere of stale beer.

"Oh, let me see—I'll have some tea and roast chicken," announced the traveller.

"Chicken, ma'am?" repeated Mrs. Frickett, and her tone was dubious. "I don't know as I can run to that. The hens is roosting now."

"Oh, well,"—impatiently—"bacon and eggs. I'll go and take a turn about the village."

With her veil drawn over her face, Lady Kesters walked out, went slowly up to the church, and critically inspected the Parsonage. Then, just inside the churchyard, she discovered her brother sitting on a tombstone. As he sprang to meet her, she exclaimed—

"Are you smiling at Grief?"

"Hullo, Sis, this is most awfully good of you! How are you? Very fit?"

"Yes. Do come out of this horribly dismal rendezvous, and let us go down one of the lanes, and talk."

"Aren't you tired?"

"No, only hungry. I've ordered a meal at the Drum. I'm tired of sitting in a train or motor, and glad of a walk. Well, Owen, so far so good—six months are gone—hurrah!"

"Yes, thank goodness, but it's been a pretty stiff job."

"An uphill business, and terribly dull! Again I repeat, would you like to move? You could so easily better yourself."

"No, I stop on till the car breaks up."

Lady Kesters raised her eyebrows.

"Well, I can only hope that blest epoch will be *soon*! I met Miss Susan, you know, and the crafty old thing was fishing to find out who you are? She has her suspicions, but I gave her no assistance. The niece was with her— Miss Aurea——" She paused expressively, then went on, "Owen—she's a remarkably pretty girl."

He nodded.

"Yes, I understand your reason for remaining in Ottinge; it is beautiful— simplicity itself." She looked at her brother attentively. "Are you making love to her?"

"I—her aunts' chauffeur?"

"Nonsense! *Are* you in love with her?" she persisted. "Come, tell the truth, my dear boy. Why should you not take *me* into your confidence? Are you?"

"Well—I am."

"And she?"

"Don't I tell you that I'm only her aunts' chauffeur, and my tongue is tied? All the same, Sis—it's beastly hard lines."

"Then, Owen, you really ought to go away; you'll soon forget her and Ottinge. I'll find you another opening at once."

"No, I won't stir yet," he answered doggedly.

"You are wrong, and on your head be it! I wish you could come out to America with us; but foreign countries are barred."

"Why are you and Martin off there?" artfully changing the subject.

"Partly business—chiefly, indeed. He has not been well, and I can't allow him to go alone; but, anyway, I'm looking forward to the trip. Tell me, how are you off for money?"

"All right; I fare sumptuously on a pound a week and washing extra."

"I suppose you live on bacon? That's to be *my* dinner."

"Bacon—eggs—fowl—steak. Mrs. Hogben is a mother to me, and a real good sort."

"I must say I think you look rather thin, Owen."

"I'm glad of it; I'm as fit as a fiddle, and made sixty runs last week for Ottinge. They little dream that I was in the Eton Eleven! Hullo! here are some people coming. I say—what a bore!"

No less than two couples now approached arm in arm; as they passed, they stared hard, and even halted to look back.

"What *will* they think, Owen?" and she laughed gaily.

"I don't care a blow what they think!" he answered recklessly; "but all the same you'd better return to the Drum alone."

"Well, mind you come in this evening—I start at nine; you can pretend my chauffeur is your pal—pretend anything!"

"Oh, I'm good enough at *pretending*; it's now my second nature! Joking apart, you ought to be going back to the inn, and getting something to eat."

.

CHAPTER XXVI
THE OBSTACLE

At seven o'clock Wynyard went boldly to the Drum and inquired for the lady who was stopping there.

Mrs. Frickett stared at him with a stony expression in her dull grey eyes. She had heard of his airs and his impudence from Norris.

"Will she see you?" she asked, and her tone was aggressively insolent.

"Oh yes," was the ready answer; "it's business."

"Oh, if it's business——" and she gave an incredulous sniff and, flinging open the parlour door, ushered him into the presence of his sister.

Lady Kesters had removed her cap and motor coat, and was seated at the table in a careless attitude, leaning her head on her hand and smoking a cigarette. The door was exactly opposite to the taproom, and the assembled crowd enjoyed a rare and unexpected spectacle. A woman smoking—ay, and looking as if she were well used to it and enjoying herself—a lady, too—there was a string of pearls round her throat, and the hand that supported her dark head was ablaze with diamonds. Ottinge had heard and read that females were taking to tobacco, and here was the actual demonstration before their gloating eyes. A fine, handsome young madam, too, with a car in the yard—ay, and a friend to visit her! They craned over to catch a glimpse of the figure ushered in by Mrs. Frickett. The man's back and shoulders had a familiar look. Why, if it wasn't Owen, Miss Parrett's chauffeur! The immediate result of this astounding discovery was a deadly and expressive silence.

Since Wynyard had parted with his sister he had made up his mind to tell her all about Aurea. He longed to share his secret with some one, and who could be better than Leila? She would give him her sympathy and—what was more—a helping hand; if any one could unravel a hopeless tangle, it was she. After a little commonplace talk, in a few abrupt sentences he commenced to state his case.

"Ah!" she exclaimed as he paused, and she dabbed the end of her cigarette on the old oak table, "so it's all coming out now! You show your good sense, Owen, in confiding in *me*—two heads are better than one. I've seen the young lady; she is distractingly pretty—and I think I approve."

"Think!" The words were a text upon which her brother delivered to his astounded listener an address of such emotional eloquence, that she sat and stared in bewildered silence.

As he spoke, he strode about the room, carried away by his adorable subject—Aurea's beauty, her cleverness, her unselfishness, her simple and single-hearted disposition, her good influence in Ottinge, her delicious voice, and her entrancing smile. Oh, it was a wonderful relief to share with another the raptures so long bottled up in his own breast!

In the middle of his discourse, the door, which was flung open to admit "two lemonades,"—Owen had warned his sister against the deadly Drum coffee,—revealed to a profoundly interested tap, young Owen, the shover, "a-walkin' and a-talkin' and a-carryin' on like old Billy, and in such a takin' as never was seen."

"She's his sweetheart, 'tis sure!" suggested one sightseer.

"Nay, more likely his missus," argued another; "she was a-laughin' at him!"

As the door closed Leila threw her cigarette into the grate with a quick, decided gesture, and, leaning both elbows on the table, said, as she looked up at her brother—

"It's an extraordinary entanglement, my dear boy. You are in love—for the first and only time in your life. Of course I can believe as much of that as I like!"

"You can!" His voice was sharp and combative.

"In love with an angel. I may tell you that she really is a fellow-creature! You think she likes you, but for one solid year and a half you may not impart to her who you are, or where you come from, or even your name—I mean your surname. You are at liberty to inform her that you are 'Owen St. John Willoughby FitzGibbon'—a nice long string!—but must never breathe the magic word 'Wynyard.'"

"No, you know I can't," he answered irritably.

"You are her aunts' servant now, though you will be, if you live, Sir Owen Wynyard of Wynyard; but you may not give her the faintest hint, as you must stick to your bargain with Uncle Dick and he to his with you. Now, let me consider," and she held up a finger: "if you speak, and reveal your identity, and become engaged, you lose a fortune."

"Yes," he agreed, a trifle dryly.

"If you don't speak, you run a great chance of losing the young lady! Mr. Woolcock is on the spot, and as willing as Barkis. Westmere is close by—an ever-enticing temptation—and he has the goodwill of the girl's relations."

"Yes, that's a true bill; it's wonderful how you grasp things."

"What grounds have you for supposing the girl would wait for eighteen months in absolute ignorance of who you were? Have you ever spoken to her, as her equal?"

"Yes, once," and he described their walk two days previously. "I stated a similar case; I made the most of my time, and asked her what *she* would do under such circumstances."

"My dear Owen," —and she looked at him with an expression of wonder in her eyes— "I am simply staggered at your presumption!"

"Yes, so was I; but, you see, it was my only chance, and I snatched it."

"And what did she answer. That it was evident you were an uncertified lunatic!"

"No; she said 'Perhaps.'"

"'Je m'en vais, chercher un grand peut-être,' as some one said on his death-bed."

"Don't talk French—or of death-beds, Sis."

"No, I won't. I see that your divinity is a clever, modern young woman, who refuses to commit herself. Look here, Owen, I won't tease you any more; this situation is such that it even baffles the activity of *my* clever and contriving mind! I'm afraid I can do nothing at present; but when we return from America, I shall make a point of cultivating General and Mrs. Morven, on account of the girl. I'll cultivate the girl for your sake, and ask her to stay in Mount Street. Possibly she may open her heart to me, and tell me everything! I have a wonderful knack of extracting similar confidences even from my housemaids! I shall listen sympathetically, advise sagaciously, and urge her to stick to you!"

"Yes, I know that once you take a thing in hand, Sis, it goes like an express train; but you will be away for six months—six months is a long time."

"Time!"—springing to her feet—"and talking of time, I must be off. Ring the bell, my dear boy, and order the car at once."

Miss Morven had been dining at the Manor. She had endured a long, leaden evening playing draughts with her Aunt Bella; she played so carelessly that Bella had repeatedly huffed her, and eventually won with six kings to the good! After their niece's departure, the sisters were for once unanimous in their opinion: they had never seen Aurea looking so well, as that night.

"What a rose-blush complexion, what clear, glowing eyes!" said Susan, with enthusiasm.

"Yes," agreed Miss Parrett, who was putting away the draught-board, "she's got *my* skin, and her mother's eyes. I've often been asked if I were painted!" she announced, with serene complacency.

Susan felt inclined to say, "And *were* you?" but her courage failed her. Bella could never see a joke! She had no recollection of Bella's beauty— Bella's complexion, as long as she could remember it, had been the colour of mutton fat—but Bella was twenty-five years her senior—and no doubt her bloom had withered early.

"The girl looks to me—as if—as if——"

"Bertie Woolcock had proposed!" supplemented Bella. "Yes, I shouldn't wonder."

"No—not that."

"Then what?" snapped her sister. "As if—and you stop; it's a dreadful habit not to be able to finish a sentence—it shows a weak intellect."

"Well, since you must have it, Bella—as if she were in love."

"So she is—with young Woolcock."

"Nonsense," repeated Susan, with unusual decision.

"Susan, don't you dare to say 'nonsense' when *I* say a thing is so; you forget yourself. Aurea will be married to Herbert Woolcock before Christmas—that is pretty well settled. And now you may lock up the silver; I am going to bed."

As Miss Morven was proceeding homewards, and, as usual, unattended (in spite of her Aunt Bella's repeated remonstrances), she passed the Drum, and noticed a motor in waiting, and also a light in a conspicuous part of the premises—the little, bulging, front sitting-room. Here two figures were sharply outlined on the yellow blind. As Aurea looked, she saw a man and woman standing face to face; the man put his hands on the woman's shoulders and stooped and kissed her. She recognised his profile in that instant—it was the profile of Owen Wynyard!

Although brother and sister had taken leave of one another, when they reached the car Wynyard looked up at the sky and said—

"It's a splendid night; I believe I'll go on with you to Brodfield, and walk back."

The motor overtook Miss Morven as she reached the Rectory gate; here she stood for a moment in the shadow of the beech trees, and as the car and its occupants swung into the full light of the last lamp (oil) in Ottinge, she had a view of the back of the woman's head—a woman talking eagerly to her companion, who faced her in an easy attitude, cigar in hand. The man was her aunts' chauffeur. As the car glided by, he laughed an involuntary, appreciative, and familiar laugh that spoke of years of intimacy—a laugh that pierced the heart of its unseen listener with the force and agony of a two-edged sword.

For a moment the girl felt stunned; then she began to experience the shock of wounded pride, of insulted love, of intolerable humiliation.

So the dark-haired lady was "the Obstacle!" That impassioned declaration on Yampton Hill had been—what? Mr. Wynyard was merely experimenting on her credulity; he wished to discover how far he might go, how much she would believe? A gay Hussar, who had got into such trouble that he was compelled to hide his whereabouts and name, until he could return to the world after a decent interval of obscurity and repentance! Meanwhile, he played the mysterious adorer, and amused himself with "a country heart," *pour passer le temps.*

And yet—and yet—when she recalled his steadfast eyes, the tremulous ardour of his bearing in the garden, and, on the hillside, he had looked in desperate earnest.

"Yes," jeered another voice, "and in deadly earnest in the Drum window!"

And she? She had actually believed that he was hopelessly in love; and she, who had been ready to stand by him against all her kindred, who had blushed and trembled before his eyes and voice, had kissed her own glove where his lips had pressed it! As these memories raced through her brain an awful sensation of sinking down into the solid earth possessed her. Aurea groped blindly for the gate and rested her head upon it. It seemed to her as if, under the shade of those beeches, a something not of this world, some terrible and relentless force, had fought and wrested from her, her unacknowledged hopes, and her happy youth.

Half an hour later she toiled up the drive with dragging, unsteady steps. Prayers were over when she entered the library—a white ghost of herself, and, with a mumbled apology, she went over and bade her father good-night, and touched his cheek with lips that were dry and feverish. He, simple, blind man, absorbed in proofs, barely lifted his head, and said—

"Good-night, my child, sleep well!"

And his child, evading Norris with a gesture of dismissal, hurried to the seclusion of her own apartment, and locked the door.

Three days later, Miss Morven left home somewhat unexpectedly; but it was conceded even by her Aunt Bella that the shock of Captain Ramsay's death had upset the girl. She wanted a change, and a lively place and lively society would divert her mind.

Wynyard had not once seen her since their never-to-be-forgotten walk, and the news of her departure came as a shock—although his outward composure was admirable—when he was informed that Miss Morven had left home, to be followed by her father. The Rector would return in three weeks, but Ottinge was not likely to see his daughter for a considerable time. Miss Davis had taken over the surplices, Miss Jones the girls' sewing-class, and Miss Norris the altar flowers.

Wynyard put artful and carefully guarded inquiries, respecting her niece, to his friend, Miss Susan, who was never reticent, and talked as long as she found a sympathetic and intelligent listener.

"Well, indeed, Owen, I must confess Miss Morven's going was a great surprise," she volunteered, in a burst of confidence, as she swiftly snipped off dead leaves. "I'd no idea of it till she came to me on Wednesday, and asked me to help her pack, and take over some of her parish accounts. She looked pale and not a bit like herself; though she said she was all right, I didn't believe her. It struck me she had had some sort of shock, she looked as if she hadn't slept, but she wouldn't see the doctor, and was quite vexed at the idea. Dr. Boas told me it was really the reaction of the dreadful tragedy that she and I witnessed. So I'm glad she's gone, though I miss her terribly!"

And what was her loss to his? Wynyard had believed he was on the point of establishing a firm if inarticulate understanding—at least he had shown his colours, and she had said "Perhaps." This morsel of comfort was all that remained to him; and oh, the many, many things that he could and should have said during that memorable walk! These unspoken sentences tormented him with cruel persistency. Had he wasted the opportunity of a lifetime?

CHAPTER XXVII
SCANDAL ABOUT MISS SUSAN

Before Aurea had departed—and her departure was, as we know, in the nature of a flight—she had paid the necessary visit of ceremony to her Aunt Bella, who imagined herself to be busy making plum jam, but was really obstructing the operations and straining the forbearance of the new cook to a dangerous limit. The old lady trotted into the drawing-room with sticky outstretched fingers, and announced—

"Susan is out laying the croquet ground—the old bowling-green; you may go and find her."

"If you don't mind sending for her, Aunt Bella."

"Oh, I know you like giving your orders! Then ring the bell. Well, and so you are off to-morrow?"

"Yes, father will come up later; he has a good deal of work in hand, and he wants to go over to Hillminster once or twice."

"I know; I'm lending him my car on Friday."

"Aunt Bella, I do wish you'd sell it!" said Aurea, speaking on an irrepressible impulse; "do get rid of it."

"Rid of it! you silly, excitable girl, certainly not. I'm more likely to get rid of the chauffeur; he does not know his place, and he does other people's jobs, too, in my time. He exercised Katie's dogs, and attended the Hanns' sick pony, and, when the carrier lost his horse, I believe he doctored it and probably killed it—and they sent round for subscriptions for another, *I* gave ten shillings—handsome, I call it!—and what do you think I saw in the list afterwards? 'J. O., One Guinea.' My own servant giving double—such unheard of impertinence! But Susan has spoiled him; I blame *her*. She talks to him as if he were an equal; I declare, if she were a girl, I'd be in a fine fright."

Aurea maintained a pale silence.

"Yes; and Mrs. Riggs and others have remarked to me that they really thought it was dangerous to have such a good-looking young man about the place, though *I* don't think him good-looking—a conceited, dressed-up puppy. Oh, here's Susan. Susan,"—raising her voice—"you see, Aurea sends for *you* now!"

"And welcome! Now, my dear child, come along; I want to show you my—I mean—the new croquet ground; it's going to be splendid! Won't you come out and have a look at it?"

"No, thank you, Susan. It will be something to see when I come back. Let me get your hat, and we will stroll up together to the Rectory."

"Oh, very well, my dear; but I'd like you to see the croquet lawn. Owen has made it. He really is worth half a dozen of Tom Hogben—and it's as level as a billiard-table."

But nothing would induce Aurea to change her mind.

Miss Susan accompanied her brother-in-law over to Hillminster, where he was due at a Diocesan meeting; it was thirty miles off, and he had suggested the train, but Miss Susan assured him, with eloquence, that "it was ten times better to motor, and to go through nice, out-of-the-way parts of the country, and see dear old villages and churches, instead of kicking your heels in odd little waiting-rooms, trying to catch one's cross-country slow coach, and catching a cold instead." It happened that Mr. Morven had arranged to spend the night with friends in the Cathedral Close, but Susan Parrett was bound to be home before sunset; only on these conditions was she suffered to undertake this unusually long expedition with the precious car.

"Yes, Bella, I'll be back without fail," she declared; "though I'd like to stay for the three o'clock service in the Cathedral," and she gazed at her tyrant appealingly.

"Not to be thought of," was the inflexible reply; "you will be here at six.—Remember the motor must be washed and put away, and the evenings are already shortening."

The run was made without any mishap, and accomplished under three hours. It happened to be market day in Hillminster, the main street was crowded with vehicles, and Miss Susan could not but admire the neat and ready manner in which their driver steered amongst carts, wagons, gigs, and carriages, with practised dexterity.

Presently they drove into the yard of the Rose Inn, and there alighted. Mr. Morven and his sister-in-law were lunching with the Dean in the Close, and Miss Susan notified to Owen, ere she left him, that she proposed to start at half-past two sharp, adding—

"For, if we are late, Miss Parrett is so nervous, you know."

The drive home began propitiously; but after a while, and in the mean way so peculiar to motors, the car, when they were about ten miles out of Hillminster, and a long distance from any little village or even farmhouse, began to exhibit signs of fatigue. For some time Wynyard coaxed and petted her; he got out of the machine several times and crawled underneath, and they staggered along for yet another mile, when there was a dead halt of over an hour. Here Miss Susan sat on the bank, talking with the fluency of a perennial fountain, and offering encouragement and advice.

Once more they set out, and, before they had gone far, met a boy on a bicycle, and asked him the way to the nearest forge?

With surprising volubility and civility, this boy told them to go ahead till they came to a certain finger-post, not to mind the finger-post, but to turn down a lane, and in a quarter of a mile they would come to the finest forge in the country! The misguided pair duly arrived at the finger-post, turned to the left as directed, and descended a steep lane—so narrow that the motor brushed the branches on either side, and Miss Susan wondered what would become of them if they met a cart? They crept on and on till they found themselves in some woods, with long grass drives or rides diverging on either side—undoubtedly they were now on the borders of some large property! The lane continued to get worse and worse—in fact, it became like the stony bed of a river, and the motor, which had long been crawling like some sick insect, finally collapsed, and, so to speak, gave up the ghost! The axle had broken; there it lay upon its side with an air of aggravating helplessness! and it was after six o'clock by Miss Susan's watch!

"Now," she inquired, with wide-open eyes, "what is to be done?"

"We must go and look for some farmhouse; I'm afraid you will have to pass the night there, Miss Susan, unless they can raise a trap of some sort!"

"Oh, but I'm bound to get home," she protested, "if I have to walk the whole way. How far should you say we were from Ottinge?"

"Well, I'm not very sure—I don't know this part of the country—but I should think about fifteen miles. You might manage to send a telegram to Miss Parrett,—in fact, I wouldn't mind walking there myself, but of course I must stick by the car."

"See!" she exclaimed, "there are chimneys in the hollow—red chimneys—among those trees." And she was right.

As they descended the hill, in a cosy nook at the foot they discovered, hiding itself after the manner of old houses, an ancient dwelling with imposing chimney-stacks, and immense black out-buildings. Here Miss Susan volubly told her story to a respectable elderly woman, who, judging by her pail and hands, had evidently just been feeding the calves.

"I don't know as how I can help you much," she said; "this is Lord Lambourne's property as you've got into somehow. Whatever brought you down off the high road, ma'am?"

"We were told to come this way by a boy on a bicycle. We asked him to direct us to a forge."

"The young limb was just a-making game of you, he was! There ain't a forge nearer than five miles, and my master took the horses in there this afternoon; he's not back yet."

"I suppose," said Miss Susan, "that you have no way of sending me in to Ottinge—no cart or pony you could hire me?"

"I'm afraid not, ma'am. Where be Ottinge?"

Here was ignorance, or was it envy?

"Then I don't know what I'm to do," said Miss Susan helplessly. "My sister will be terribly anxious, and I'm sure the motor won't be fit to travel for quite a long time. What do you think, Owen?"

"I think that the motor is about done!" he answered, with emphatic decision. "To-morrow morning I must get a couple of horses somewhere, and cart her home. I wonder if this good woman could put you up for the night? This lady and I," he explained, "went to Hillminster from Ottinge to-day, and were on our way home when the motor broke down; and I don't think there's any chance of our getting to Ottinge to-night."

"Oh yes, I can put the two of you up," she said, addressing Miss Susan, "both you and your son."

Miss Susan became crimson.

"I am Miss Parrett of Ottinge," she announced, with tremulous dignity; "that is to say, Miss Susan Parrett."

"I'm sure I beg your pardon, Miss Parrett; I can find you a bed for the night. This is a rare big house—it were once a Manor—and we have several empty bedrooms—our family being large, and some of the boys out in the world. Mayhap you'd like something to eat?"

"I should—very much," replied Miss Susan, whose face had cooled, "tea or milk or anything!"

At this moment a respectable-looking, elderly man rode up, leading another horse.

"Hullo, Hetty," he said to his wife, "I see you ha' company, and there's a sort of motor thing all smashed up, a-lyin' there in the Blue Gate Lane."

"It's my motor," explained Miss Susan, "and we have walked down here just to see what you and your wife could do for us."

"Our best, you may be sure, ma'am," rejoined the farmer, and descended heavily from his horse, then led the pair towards the stables, where he was followed by Wynyard, who gave him a hand with them and borrowed their services for the morrow.

A meal was served in the very tidy little sitting-room, where Miss Susan found that places had been laid for Owen and herself; it was evident that the farmer's wife considered him—if not her son—her equal! To this arrangement she assented, and, in spite of his apologies, Miss Susan and her chauffeur for once had supper together without any mutual embarrassment.

Afterwards, he went out to a neighbouring farm to see if he could hire a pony-trap for the following day, and although Miss Susan was painfully nervous about her sister, she was secretly delighted with a sense of freedom and adventure, and slept soundly in the middle of a high feather-bed—in a big four-poster—into which it was necessary to ascend by steps.

Owing to vexatious delays in securing a trap, driver, and harness, it was tea-time the next afternoon when Miss Susan drove sedately up to the hall door at the Manor.

Miss Parrett was prostrate, and in the hands of the doctor! The telegram, dispatched at an early hour from the nearest office to Moppington, was—on a principle that occasionally prevails in out-of-the-way places—delivered hours after Miss Susan had set the minds of her little world at rest! There had been an exciting rumour in the village—emanating from the Drum— that "Miss Susan had eloped with the good-looking shover," at any rate no one could deny that they had gone to Hillminster the day before, had probably been married at the registry office, and subsequently fled! The Drum was crowded with impassioned talkers, Mrs. Hogben was besieged, and the whole of Ottinge was pervaded by a general air of pleasurable anticipation. One fact was certain, that, up till three o'clock of this, the following afternoon, neither of the runaways had returned! However, just as it had gone four, here was Miss Susan—bringing to some a distinct feeling of disappointment—seated erect in a little basket carriage, drawn by an immense cart-horse, driven at a foot pace by a boy; and a couple of hours later she was followed by the motor, this time on a lorry, and, undoubtedly, also, on what is called "its last legs."

When everything had been exhaustively explained to Miss Parrett, she, having solemnly inspected the remains of her beautiful green car and heard what its repairs were likely to cost, heard also the price which she would be offered for it—fifteen pounds—broke into a furious passion and declared, with much vehemence and in her shrillest pipe, that never, never more would she again own a motor!

And, since the motor had ceased to be required, there was no further use for a chauffeur, and once more Owen Wynyard was looking for a situation.

CHAPTER XXVIII
A NEW SITUATION

The venerable green motor, whose value by an expert had been so brutally assessed, was not considered worth repair, yet Miss Bella Parrett could not endure to part with a possession which had cost five hundred pounds, for fifteen sovereigns; so it was thrust into a coach-house, shut in the dark with cobwebs and rats, and abandoned to its fate.

Miss Susan, who enjoyed motoring and liked the chauffeur, was exceedingly anxious that Bella should purchase another car, but of course she was powerless, being next to penniless herself; indeed, at the outside, her income amounted to one hundred a year—less income tax. The mere word *motor* seemed now to operate upon her wealthy sister as a red rag to a bull; for the loss of five hundred pounds rankled in her heart like a poisoned arrow.

The old lady had decided for a brougham, a middle-aged driver, and a steady horse. (It may here be added that the animal, which was coal-black and had a flowing tail, came out of the stables of an undertaker, and was as sedate and slow as any funeral procession could desire.)

As for Wynyard, his fate was sealed! A chauffeur without a car is as a swan upon a turnpike road. He had had visions of proposing himself as coachman—for he did not wish to leave the village, and the vicinity of Aurea Morven—but Miss Parrett had other plans. In her opinion Owen, the chauffeur, was too good-looking to remain about the place—on account of the maids—and indeed her sister Susan treated him with most shocking familiarity, and spoke to him almost as if he were her equal. Her quick little eyes had also noticed in church that, during her brother-in-law's most eloquent sermon, the chauffeur's attention was concentrated upon her niece Aurea; and so, without any preamble, she called him into the library and handed him his pay, a month in advance, promised a first-rate reference, and waved him from her presence.

And Wynyard's occupation was gone! There would be no more expeditions in the ramshackle old motor, no more potting of geraniums for Miss Susan, no more clipping of hedges, or singing in the choir. He must depart.

Departures, to be effective, should be abrupt; possibly Wynyard was unconscious of this, but the following day he left for London; his yellow tin box went over in a cart to Catsfield, whilst he walked to the station across the fields by the same road as he had come. His absence caused an unexpected blank in the little community; the Hogbens regretted him sorely, he was such a cheery inmate, and gave no trouble. His absence was deplored at the Drum; the village dogs looked for him in vain; his voice was missed in the choir; other people missed him who shall be nameless; and Joss howled for a week.

Wynyard had written to his sister to inform her that, owing to the breakdown of the dilapidated old car, he was once more out of a job, and found, in reply, that she was on the eve of sailing for America. He went round to see her in Mount Street, two days before she started.

"You are looking remarkably fit, Owen," she said, "and the Parretts can't say too much for you; indeed, in Susan's letter I observe a tone of actual distress! Six months of the time have passed. I suppose you have saved a little money?"

"I have twenty pounds in the bank, and a couple of sovereigns to go on with. Of course I must look out for another billet at once."

"And on this occasion you will take with you a really well-earned character. You have no debts and no matrimonial entanglements—eh? What about Miss Morven?"

"I've never laid eyes on her since I saw you."

"How is that?"

"She's been in London."

"And now *you* are here—ah!"

"I didn't follow her, as you seem to suppose. I wasn't likely to get another billet in Ottinge, and anyway, I was a bit tired of having Miss Parrett's heel on my neck."

"Tired of 'ordering yourself humbly and lowly to all your betters,' poor boy! But to return to the young lady; are you still thinking of her?"

Was he not always thinking of her? But he merely nodded.

"You haven't written?"

"No; I'm not such a sweep as all that!"

"But, Owen, didn't you wring a sort of half promise from the unfortunate girl? I know it was only 'perhaps,' but *château qui parle—femme qui écoute.*"

"I think it will be all right."

"And that her 'perhaps' is as good as another's solemn vow! I must say you show extraordinary confidence in yourself and in her, and yet you scarcely know one another."

"No, not in the usual dancing, dining-out, race-going style; I give in to that, or, indeed, in the ordinary way at all. She only saw me driving or washing the motor, or doing a bit of gardening."

"And you think you were so admirable in these occupations that you captured her heart! Owen, I'm seeing you in quite a new light, and I think you are deceiving yourself. I expect the young woman has forgotten you by this time. London has—attractions."

"Time will tell; anyhow, she's refused the great Bertie Woolcock."

"No!" incredulously, "who told you? When did you hear it?"

"It was all over Ottinge a week ago, and I heard it at the Drum. I was also given to understand that Miss Parrett was fit to be tied!"

"If she had an inkling of her late chauffeur's pretensions, a strait waistcoat would hardly meet the occasion. How I wish we could take you with us to America; but it's not in the bond. Martin has a great deal of capital invested out there; he is not very strong, and after we have put all his business through, we are going to spend the winter in Florida. We shall not be back before April, and then I will keep my promise. I am so sorry, dear old boy, that I shall be out of the country while you are 'dreeing your weird' and not able to help you; but of course Uncle Dick's great object is for you to learn absolute independence. I will give you my permanent address and a code-book, and if anything happens for good or bad, you must cable. We have let this house for six months—to friends. We may as well have it aired, and have the good rent! Every one lets now—even dukes and duchesses! I wonder what your next billet will be? You had better advertise."

"What shall I say?" he asked.

"Let me think." After a moment she rose and went to her writing-table, scribbled for a few moments, and brought him the following: 'As chauffeur, smart young man, experienced, aged 26, steady, well recommended, wants situation. Apply— — Office of this paper.' "Just send this to the *Car*, the *Morning Post*, the *Field*, *Country Life*; it will cost you altogether about twenty-five shillings, and I'll pay for it."

"No, no, Sis," he protested, "that's not in the bond. And, as it is, you are keeping up my club subscription."

"Pooh!" she exclaimed, "what's that? I hope this time you will get into a nice rich family who have a good car, and that you will be able to have a little more variety than in your last place, and no young ladies. You will be sure and write to me every week?"

At this moment the door opened and Sir Martin Kesters entered, and paused in the doorway.

"Hullo, Owen, glad to see you," holding out his hand; "so you are back?"

"Only temporarily—for a day or two."

"You've done six months, and the worst is over."

"Well, I hope so; but one never can tell."

"Upon my word, I don't know how you stood it. Leila described the place. I'm not a gay young fellow of six-and-twenty, and a week would have seen me out of it; but six months— —" and he gazed at him in blank astonishment.

"Oh, well," apologetically, "I've learnt all sorts of things. I'm quite a fair gardener, and can clip a hedge too; I know how to physic dogs, and fasten up the back of a blouse."

"*Owen!*" exclaimed his sister, "*I* am present!"

"It was only Mrs. Hogben; she had no woman in the house, and Tom's hands were generally dirty, and she said she looked upon me as her other son. She is a rare good old soul, and I'd do more for her than that."

"You must feel as if you'd been underground, and come up for a breather," said his brother-in-law.

"My breather must be short; but I'm not going to take any situation with ladies."

"Why so proud and particular? They won't all be Miss Parretts!"

"Oh, you women are so irregular, unpunctual, and undecided—yes, and nervous. Even Miss Susan clawed me by the arm when we took a sharp turn."

"I hope the next year will fly," said Sir Martin; "I tried my hand on your uncle, you know—did Leila tell you? I have got him to make it eighteen months hard labour—and eighteen months it is."

"No! I say—that is splendid news! How awfully good of you!"

"I fancy he's a little bit indulgent now; he finds that you can stick it, and have brought such a magnificent character."

"Profound regrets," supplemented Leila, "if not tears. Ah, here is dinner! I don't suppose you've *dined* since you were here in April; come along, Owen, we are quite alone, and let us drink your health."

Two days later Wynyard saw his sister and her husband off from Euston by the White Star Express, and felt that his holiday—his breathing time, was over. He must get into harness at once. His one hope, as he wandered about the streets, was that he might catch sight of Aurea. By all accounts, she was staying in Eaton Place; more than once he walked over there, and strolled up and down on the opposite side, and gazed at No. 303 as if he would see through the walls. But it was no use—telepathy sometimes fails; Aurea never appeared, and, had she done so—though he was not aware of the sad fact—she would not have vouchsafed the smallest notice of her aunts' former employé.

The daily post brought several replies to Owen's advertisements. When he had looked through and sorted them, he found that, after all, the most tempting was from a woman—a certain Mrs. Cavendish Foote, whose address was Rockingham Mansions, S.W.

The lady announced that she required a really smart, experienced chauffeur for town—she had a new Renault car; he would have to live out, and she offered him four guineas a week, and to find himself in clothes and minor repairs. She wrote from Manchester. He replied, forwarding his references, and she engaged him by telegram, saying she would be back in London the following day, when he was to enter her service, and call to interview her.

It seemed to him that this was good enough! He would rather like a job in town for a change—the more particularly as Aurea and her father were staying with General Morven in Eaton Place, and now and then he might obtain a glimpse of her! He glanced through the other letters before finally making up his mind; one was from a nobleman in the north of Scotland, who lived thirty miles from a railway station. He thought of the bitter Scotch winters, and how he would be cut off from all society but that of the servants' hall; no, that was no good. Another was from a lady who was going on tour to the south of France and Italy. The terms she offered were low, and she preferred as chauffeur, a married man. There were several others, but on the whole the situation in London seemed to be the best. He debated as to whether he should put on his chauffeur clothes or not, but decided against it, and, hailing a taxi-cab, found himself at Rockingham Mansions in ten minutes.

These were a fine set of flats, with carpeted stairs, imposing hall, and gorgeously liveried attendants. He asked to be shown to Mrs. Cavendish Foote's address. It was No. 20 on the third floor. The door was opened by a smart maid with a very small cap, an immensely frizzled head, and sallow cheeks.

"To see Mrs. Cavendish Foote on business?" she repeated, and ushered him into the tiny hall, which was decorated with a curious assortment of pictures, stuffed heads, arms, and looking-glasses.

"Oh, bring him in here," commanded a shrill treble voice, and Wynyard found himself entering a large sitting-room, where he was saluted by an overwhelming perfume of scent, and the angry barking of a tiny black Pom. with a pink bow in his hair.

The apartment had been recently decorated; the prevailing colours were white and pink—white walls, into which large mirrors had been introduced—pink curtains, pink carpets, pink and white chintz. Two or three half-dead bouquets stood in vases, an opera cloak and a feather boa encumbered one chair, a motor coat another, several papers and letters were strewn upon the floor, and on a long lounge under the windows, a lady— white and pink to match her room—lay extended at full length, her shapely legs crossed, and a cigarette in her mouth. She wore a loose pink *negligé*— the wide sleeves exhibiting her arms bare to the shoulder.

"Hullo!" she exclaimed, when she caught sight of Wynyard, as he emerged from behind the screen.

"Mrs. Cavendish Foote, I presume?" he inquired.

"Right-o!" she answered, suddenly assuming a sitting posture; "and who may *you* be?"

"I've come about the situation as chauffeur."

"The chauffeur!" she screamed. "Good Lord! why, I'm blessed if you ain't a toff!"

"Is that a drawback?" he asked gravely.

"Well, no—I suppose, rather an advantage! I thought you were my manager, or I wouldn't have let you in," and she pulled down her sleeves, and threw the stump of her cigarette into the fireplace. "You see, though I'm Mrs. Cavendish Foote, my professional name is Tottie Toye. I dare say, you have seen me on the boards?"

"Yes, I have had the pleasure," he answered politely.

"Oh my!" she ejaculated. "Well, anyhow, you've got pretty manners. Can you drive?"

"Yes."

"I mean in London traffic. I don't want to get smashed up, you know; if I break a leg, where am I? How long were you in your last place?"

"Six months."

"And your reason for leaving?"

"They gave up keeping a motor."

"*Idiots!*" she exclaimed. "I couldn't live without mine! Your job will be to take me to the shop, and fetch me back at night, and to run me about London in the daytime, and out into the country on Sundays—home on Monday night. Do you think you can manage all that?"

"I think so."

"The car is in the garage close to this. I dare say you would like to take her out for a run and try her? I shall want you this evening at seven o'clock."

"Very well," he agreed.

"I suppose you're one of these gentlemen that have come down in the world, and, of course, a chauffeur has a ripping good time. I like your looks. By the way, what's your name?"

"Owen."

"And I suspect you are at this game, because you are *owing* money—eh?" and she burst into a shriek of laughter at her own joke. "Well, life has its ups and downs! If it was all just flat, I should be bored stiff. I've had some queer old turns myself."

At this moment the door opened, and a stout, prosperous-looking gentleman made his appearance—red-faced, blue-chinned, wonderfully got up, with shining hair, and shining boots.

"Hullo, Tottie!" he exclaimed; "who have we got here?" glancing suspiciously at Owen. "A new Johnny—eh—you *naughty* girl?"

"No, no, dear old man," she protested; "and do you know, that you are twenty minutes late? so I have given him your precious time. This"—waving her hand at Owen—"is Mr. Cloake, my manager. Mr. Cloake, let me present you to my new chauffeur."

CHAPTER XXIX
TOTTIE TOYE

Miss Tottie Toye's Renault was a beauty, and, after the old rickety green car, it afforded Wynyard a real pleasure to handle it. He took it for a trial turn to Bushey, in order to get accustomed to its mechanism—for every motor has its peculiar little ways and its own little tempers—and punctually at seven o'clock he was at Rockingham Mansions, awaiting his employer, the dancer.

Presently, heralded by her high, shrill voice, she appeared, accompanied by a melancholy young man, and bringing with her such a reek of scent, that it almost deadened the petrol. Tottie was wrapped in a magnificent pink velvet cloak trimmed with ermine, and, as she stepped into the car, turned to her companion and said—

"Teddy boy, just look at my beautiful new chauffeur! Isn't he like a young duke?"

Teddy grunted some inaudible reply, slammed the door of the car with unnecessary violence, and they were off. The London streets at this hour were swarming with motor busses, cars, cabs, and carriages—people going to dinners or the play. It was rather different to the empty roads in the neighbourhood of Ottinge, but Wynyard managed to thread his way to the theatre dexterously and speedily, and, when the lady jumped out of the car at the stage door, she clapped him on the back and said—

"You'll do all right! Come round for me again at eleven—and don't be getting into any mischief."

He touched his cap and moved away. Precisely at eleven o'clock he was waiting, and after some delay Tottie reappeared, in a condition of the highest excitement, screaming with laughter and carrying a gigantic bouquet. She was accompanied by a very *prononcée* lady and three young men. With a good deal of noisy talking and chaffing they all packed themselves into the car, sitting on one another's knees, and fared to the Savoy, where they had supper. Here again he waited outside until twelve o'clock and closing time; and as he sat, a motionless figure, a great deal of London life drifted by him: the rolling "Limousine," emblem of luxury—broken-down, hopeless-looking men—members of the dreadful army of the unemployed—flaming women with the scarlet sign of sin in high relief. What a diabolical existence!

At twelve his party reappeared—noisier and more hilarious than ever. It struck him that Tottie's lady friend and two of the young men had had quite as much supper as was good for them. Once more they crammed into the car, the party returned to the flat to play bridge, and he at last was released!

So this was now his life! late hours, excursions into the country on Sundays, trips to Brighton, to Folkestone, to Margate; he had no leisure, for, when Tottie was not making use of the car, the good-natured little creature—unlike Bella Parrett—lent it to her friends, and her friends made unreasonable use of it. They were all of the same class as herself: exuberant youths, who imagined that they were seeing life; prettily painted, beautifully dressed young women, whom the men called by their christian names; certain elderly gentlemen; and now and then a portly dame, who was spoken of as "Ma."

On one occasion, in Bond Street, Tottie and some of her vivacious companions were shopping—a showy party, with loud voices and louder clothes, scrambling into the motor at the door of a shop—when who should pass by but Sir Richard Wynyard! He glared at them, then glanced at the chauffeur. *What!* his own nephew in the middle of such a rowdy crew! Owen touched his cap to him, but he vouchsafed no notice, and, with a glassy stare, stalked on.

Another time, as Wynyard was waiting outside a theatre, Aurea Morven and her uncle were coming out. She looked so pretty—lovely, indeed—in a white cloak with a knot of silver ribbon in her dark hair. Fortunately, she did not recognise him, for at the moment Tottie dashed out of the stage door in a violent hurry, followed by two women and a man, and called authoritatively—

"Go ahead, Owen, old boy! The 'Troc.' as hard as you can tear!"

Wynyard had been in the present situation for six weeks, and, although the pay was good and punctual, he found the life wearing. He never knew what it was to have a day off—or any time to himself; other employés had Sundays—Sunday to him was the heaviest day in the whole week. Tottie, besides her professional engagements, appeared to live in an irregular round of luncheons, suppers, bridge, and balls—of a certain class. She was madly extravagant, and seemed to take a peculiar delight in throwing away her money. The sallow-cheeked parlour-maid, who had a fancy for Wynyard, and generally contrived to have a word with him when she came downstairs with cloaks or shoes—informed him in confidence that "the missus was a-goin' it!"

"But what can you expect?" she asked, with her nose in the air. "Her mother kept a tripe shop; she ain't no class! Of course the money's good as long as it's there; but I don't fancy these sort of fast situations. Give *me* gentry."

"But Mrs. Foote's all right," protested Wynyard; "it's her friends that are such a queer lot—and, I'm afraid, they cheat her."

"You bet they do! And as to her being all right—I should say she was all wrong, if you ask *me*. She's no more Mrs. Cavendish Foote than I am; she was divorced three years ago. Cavendish Foote—he was a young fool on the Stock Exchange; she broke him, and now he's gone to America."

An exceedingly unpleasant idea had lately been born in Owen's mind; it was this—that his employer had taken a fancy to *him*. She leant with unnecessary weight on his arm when she stepped in and out of the motor; summoned him to her sitting-room on various pretexts to give him notes; offered cigarettes, talked to him confidentially, and begged him "to look upon her as a friend."

"I like you, Owen, I swear I do, and I'd do a lot for you, so I would too— and don't you make any mistake about that!"

Wynyard found this state of affairs extremely embarrassing—especially when they went for trips into the country alone, and, wrapped up in furs, she would come and sit beside him, and tell him of all her successes; stop at inns, order lunch, and invite him to share the meal, and drink champagne! But this he steadily declined. The cooler and more reserved he was, naturally the more *empressé* she became; and one of her pals, in his hearing, had loudly chaffed her on being "*mashed on her chauffeur.*"

Once or twice, she found some one to mind the car, and gave him a ticket for the theatre, in order that he might witness her performance. Tottie really was marvellous; it was no wonder that she was earning two hundred pounds a week! Her dancing, her agility, her vivacity, and her impudence, enraptured each nightly audience. There was something in her gaiety and her unstudied animation that reminded him of Aurea Morven; yet to think of the two in the same moment was neither more or less than profanation—the one was a sort of irresponsible imp, whilst the other resembled a beautiful and benevolent fairy.

It was early in December, Tottie had run over to Paris with Mr. Cloake and suitable pals, and Wynyard had got his neck out of the collar for a few days. In fact, he had insisted on a holiday, and treated himself to a dinner at his club. Here he met some old friends—that is to say, young men of his own age, who had been at Eton, or in the Service with him. He always looked well turned out, and none of them ever thought of asking "What are you doing now?" except a schoolfellow, who said—

"I say, old man, we don't often see *you* here! What's your job? I know the uncle has cut up rusty, and that you are on your own. Fellows say that you are down in some big steel works at Sheffield, and they have seen you out with the hounds."

"No, they're wrong—that's a bad shot. I don't mind telling you, old pal, that I'm a *chauffeur*."

His friend stared, and then burst out into a roar of laughter.

"Yes, I'm the chauffeur of the well-known Tottie Toye."

This information seemed to leave the other not only solemn, but speechless—which being the case, Wynyard went on to impart to him in confidence all the particulars of his uncle's manifesto, and how he was endeavouring to keep himself in independence, without as much as a penny stamp from one of his relatives.

"I've done eight months," he said, "and I've saved thirty pounds. I seem to see the Winning Post."

"By George!" exclaimed his friend, "I don't know how you can stick it. Fancy being mixed up with Tottie and her crowd!"

"Oh, for that matter, I've nothing to say to them. 'Needs must when the devil drives,' and the pay is good."

"I believe Tottie has a mania for spending money. She has been twice married; her extravagance is crazy, and her generosity boundless—of course, she is robbed all round. Now she has got into the hands of a fellow called Cloake—and unless I'm mistaken the end is near. Get out of it as soon as you can, Wynyard, my friend."

"I believe I shall. I can't say it's a job I fancy."

"Look here, I've an idea. There's a friend of mine—Masham—an enormously rich chap, a bachelor, mad keen about motoring—racing, you know. He was in the Paris to Berlin race—and has been over to Long Island—and on the slightest provocation would be off to Timbuctoo! He's looking for a man, not so much to drive—but, of course, he must be a chauffeur—as to go about with him—a gentleman. I should say it was the very billet for you—*if* he doesn't kill you! It's not every one's job; he is so confoundedly rash, and is always ready to take risks."

"I don't mind that," said Wynyard; "'nothing venture—nothing have.'"

"He wants a smart chap—a well-bred 'un—with no nerves. Shall I undertake the delicate negotiation? I expect you'd suit him down to the ground!"

CHAPTER XXX
MASHAM—THE MOTORIST

"I'll go over and have a jaw with him; you stay here till I come back," said Wynyard's friend, rising as he spoke.

Ten minutes later, he appeared accompanied by a clean-shaven, bullet-headed little man—with a brick-coloured complexion, sleek black hair, a pair of small, piercing grey eyes, and the shoulders of a Hercules.

"Wynyard, let me introduce you to Masham, the celebrated motorist. Masham, this is my old chum Wynyard; we were in the same house at Eton. He is in want of a job—you are in want of a chauffeur—and here you are!" Then, with a wave of his hand, he added, "Now, I'll leave you to worry it out between you. You will find me in the card-room," and he took his departure.

"Well," said Masham, throwing himself back in an arm-chair, and stretching out his legs, "our mutual friend has been telling me all about you, and how you are an Army chap, awfully sportin', and have no nerves to speak of."

"Yes, I shouldn't call myself—er—nervous," said Wynyard, lighting a cigarette.

"I suppose Eustace has told you that I'm motor mad? Motoring is my fad. I expect I've put in more miles than any man of my age in England. On these long journeys I like to have a pal who can drive a bit, is a gentleman, and has got his head screwed on the right way. By the bye, are you a married man?"

"No."

"Good! That's all right. Well, the ordinary chauffeur palls a bit after a time, and you can't well have him to dine with you—and—er—in fact—he's not your *own* sort! On the other hand, there are one's relatives and chums; but some of these—and I've sampled a good few—know nothing of the mechanism of a car—racer and runabout, it's all one to *them*—and they bar going with me. I put them in a first-class blue funk when my speed is eighty miles an hour, and hats and things fly out of the car. Of course, it's not always possible; but sometimes in the very early mornings on those long flat roads in France I let her out! I tell you, it's an experience. However, the last time when I got her up to ninety kilometres, at the first halt, my chauffeur got off and left me! I'm not a bad sort to deal with, as old Eustace can tell you; you just let me alone, and you'll be all right. You live with me—same quarters, same table—and your billet will be that of chauffeur-companion—*compagnon de voyage*—with an eye to the car and to take the wheel now and then. If you can talk French it will be an advantage; but I don't suppose you picked up much French at Eton?"

"I picked it up when I was a small boy. I had a French nurse," replied Wynyard, "and I can get along all right."

"Good! My idea is to motor down to Biarritz, then across to Marseilles, and afterwards, with a look in at Monte, take part in some international racing. Who were you with last, or who are you with now?"

"Just at present I'm chauffeur to Tottie Toye."

"My great aunt!"

"Well, you see, when she engaged me from an advertisement, she represented herself as Mrs. Cavendish Foote—the terms were liberal, and I agreed."

"Yes, and when you saw her?" His little eyes twinkled.

"I must confess I was rather taken aback; theatrical folk are not much in my line—irregular hours and sudden odd jobs—sometimes I've been out with the car till three in the morning. However, it was a question of money, and I took it."

"May I ask what she pays you?"

"Four guineas a week."

"I'll go one better than that. I'll give you three hundred a year—twenty-five pounds a month, and all found; but, mark you, you had better insure your life, for I've had some uncommonly narrow squeaks."

"I'll take the risk," said Wynyard. "Would you mind telling me what is *your* idea of a narrow squeak?"

"Well, once crossing a railway line an express missed me by twenty seconds; another was when the car ran backwards down a pass in the Tyrol, and over the bridge at the bottom; that time the chauffeur was killed.

I'm keeping his family, of course—and henceforth I bar married men! I broke three ribs and a leg; however, we won't dwell on these unpleasant memories. Do you think you will be ready to start in a week? The car is down at Coventry. I'll fetch her up day after to-morrow."

"I shall be ready; but I have one stipulation to make."

"All right—let's have it."

"As a chauffeur my name is Owen—not Wynyard."

"Same thing to me. Uncle objects, eh?"

"I suppose Miss Toye will accept a week's notice?"

"Of course she will," declared Masham. "We will have a day or two at Brookwood, to see how the car travels, and then cross the Channel. Have a drink?"

"Thank you, a small whisky and large soda."

Mr. Masham ordered for himself a large whisky and a very small soda; indeed, the soda water in his glass was a negligible quantity.

"I don't drink much—but I take it strong," he remarked as he gulped it down, "and I never smoke—bad for the nerves;" and then he began to discourse of motors and the class and style he believed in. He believed in single-cylinder machines, a short wheel base, wide handle-bars, and a large petrol tank. He did not believe in the aeroplane craze, and, indeed, became both hot and excited when Wynyard introduced the subject.

"Madness! Wild goose business! Can come to nothing—look at the accidents! Stick to Mother Earth, I say! I'm an earth man—a motor man. The sea for fish, the sky for birds, earth for humans. I bar both air and sea."

After a few minor arrangements, Wynyard took leave of Mr. Masham, went in search of his friend, and informed him that all was fixed up; he had accepted the post of companion-chauffeur to the celebrated Harry Masham, and was about to tender his resignation to the equally celebrated Tottie Toye.

During Lady Kesters' stay in the United States, she had kept up a brisk correspondence with her brother, and written long and enthusiastic descriptions of her impressions of New York, Washington, and Boston; for his part, he had sent her somewhat scanty news. The following, is one of his longest letters:—

"Dear Leila,—I am still with Miss T. Toye, and giving (I hope) satisfaction and saving hand over fist. I can't say, however, that the berth is congenial. I am kept pretty busy, taking Tottie to the theatre, fetching her home, motoring her about town to shops and restaurants, and dashing into the country for weekends. In Town, I wear my goggles as much as possible. I tell her my eyes are weak—I dare say she doesn't believe me! I'm not proud, but I don't want my old friends to spot me as Tottie's chauffeur. The other day I was in Bond Street in the afternoon, with a car full of a noisy painted crew, and they attracted the attention of no less a person than *Uncle Dick*. He stared at them, and then at me. I thought he was going to have an apoplectic seizure, and I'm sure he thinks I've gone to the devil! Perhaps you'd let him know that I've got to live, and Tottie pays well, and her money is as good as another's. All the same, I am not sure that I can stand her much longer; she and her particular lot are a bit too rowdy. The other night a fellow dared her to kiss me as she got out of the motor, and, by Jove! she *did*. I was not at all grateful. I was nearly stifled, and I've not got the better of her scented embrace yet. She talks of buying another car—price fifteen hundred pounds—simply because Vixie Beaufort has a better one than hers, and she's not going to be beat. She has a funny way of asking all sorts of people to supper, and is surprised when the crowd turns up; and sometimes she forgets her party altogether, and sups out, then the boot is on the other foot! She plays bridge of a sort, and loses her money (and her temper), and throws the cards at her partner. The frizzy parlour-maid is my informant; she comes down with cloaks and furs, and generally contrives to have a word with me. She says the place is getting too hot, and if I will leave, *she* will! Think of that! I'm glad to hear such good news of Martin. I expect you will both be home by April, and by that time I should not wonder if I were in another situation. Ryder Street will always find—Your affectionate brother,

"O. W."

To this he received a long reply from Florida. Martin was better, shares were booming, and The Palm Branch was the most delicious spot on earth. No wonder that Florida boasted the largest hotel in the world; the climate, the tropical flowers and fruit, the bicycling and bathing, and the immense variety of visitors were all a delightful novelty.

She went on to say—

> "I do wish you were with us; there are such charming girls to be met and known—bright, well-bred, intellectual, and fascinating. I am in love with several of them myself. I hope we shall be back in Mount Street at the end of April; meanwhile we are sunning ourselves here. Take my advice, and give the vivacious Tottie notice, and try for nice country place with some wealthy old squire who is not *exigeant* with respect to work, and would only require to be motored to the Sessions or to church; in such a place, you can lie perdue instead of flaring about town with Tottie and Co. I would be perfectly happy if you were here, dear old boy; the only drawback to my enjoyment is the fear that you are hard worked, and hard up! Bear this in mind, 'Time and tide run through the longest day;' in ten months you will be settled at Wynyard, and your *own* master."

As it happened, there was no occasion for Wynyard to formally tender his resignation to Miss Toye. The morning after his interview with Mr. Masham, when he arrived at the garage where the car was kept, another chauffeur came up to him with a sympathetic grin upon his face.

"Hullo, Jack—your car is took! There's an execution in your missus' flat, and the men came round 'ere first thing. Very nippy, wasn't it?"

"I don't know what you are talking about," rejoined Wynyard. He walked over to the place where the car was always garaged, and it was empty; everything was gone—even to the oil cans!

"There, now, you see it's a true bill," said the other man, who had followed him. "Tottie Toye is broke; there was a great burst-up at the theatre, and she has cut it."

This was true. Wynyard now remembered that the last time he had driven Tottie from the hall there had been something of a scene at the stage door—loud talking, an eager crowd, and Mr. Cloake, very red and excited, had supported Tottie into the motor, apparently in hysterics and tears. He went round to the flat, and discovered that men were already in possession, busily making an inventory of its contents. Tottie had effected her escape with all her jewels, her best clothes, and her dog, and was reported to be at San Sebastian.

It seemed to Wynyard that something was bound to happen to whoever employed him—one time it was a breakdown, now the bailiffs.

Before he and his new employer went abroad, they spent several days at Brookwood, and here the new chauffeur was first introduced to the machine—a long, bare, business-looking car, built for speed, not comfort, and painted a dull slate colour.

"She's as ugly as she can stick!" admitted her owner; "but she runs sweetly and is a magnificent machine; has won three big races, a grand goer, and ab-so-lutely reliable!"

Flying round the track at Brookwood she certainly bore out her reputation for speed; but as to whether she was absolutely reliable, remained to be proved.

CHAPTER XXXI
TAKING RISKS

Early in January Wynyard found himself on the Continent, roaming hither and thither as dictated by the caprice of his employer. First they went to Paris, then, leaving behind them the intricacies of the traffic, departed from that gay city by the Port de Choisy for Mellun, Sens, and Dijon. From Dijon (the Charing Cross of motors) they sped across to Biarritz, over the Pyrenees to Madrid, then back to the Riviera, *via* Carcassonne and Toulouse.

It was Masham's custom to start at daybreak; the car was on the wing as soon as the birds. They swept along the great straight highways, by quiet sleeping farms, through low-hanging mists, and now and then past an old white-faced château, staring sternly from amidst its woods—or again, a gaudy red villa smothered in lime trees. Masham had not overstated the case when he declared that he "took risks." Once or twice, when they hummed along wide, empty roads, as the wind roared past their ears, and the engine vibration was such that every nerve was ajar, it appeared to the chauffeur that he was trusting his life to a madman! *Speed*, his employer's passion, seemed to grow insatiable with time—his appetite for eating up, with furious haste, miles and miles and miles, and ever hurrying onwards to the unattainable horizon, increased with indulgence. The intoxication of motion appeared to lift him completely out of himself—and to change his personality.

Wynyard had once quoted to his friend, "Needs must when the devil drives!" Now at times he could readily believe that the old gentleman himself was holding the steering-wheel!

Sometimes, as they tore through villages, they left a track of whirling feathers—the remains of a flock of geese or poultry; and Masham boasted, to his chauffeur's disgust, that once, between Pau and Biarritz, he and his machine had been the death of five dogs. On more than one occasion, when his excitement was frenzied, and he undoubtedly saw *red*, Wynyard had endeavoured to wrest the steering-wheel from his employer. They had several narrow escapes, and many of their skids were neither more nor less than hair-raising. Wynyard's face, which was tanned and weather-beaten, displayed several new lines, and sometimes wore a very grim expression, as the car whirled round a sharp corner with a single and defiant hoot! But these risks were his price; it was all in the day's work, for three hundred a year.

It seemed strange that he was unable to find a commonplace situation, which offered the happy medium; either he drove an old doddering car at infrequent intervals, or he was bound to this grey racer, like Ixion to his wheel.

Excepting on the occasions when Masham was specially reckless, the situation was all right. They lived at the best hotels, and he sat at the same table with his employer—whose talk was ever and always of the car, or other people's cars—of petrol, garages, tyres, and racing. He was a man of one idea.

His companion-chauffeur was a good deal staggered by the large quantity of cognac absorbed by his patron; but it never appeared to affect his nerves, and merely rendered him unsociable and morose. His one, all-devouring ambition was to win a race for the highest speed, and to be known as the most daring and successful motorist in Europe! When they stopped at hotels he herded with his kind—after the manner of golfers and racing people—comparing cars, speeds, weights, and prices, talking knowingly of "mushroom valves" and the "new sliding sleeve engine." On such occasions, instead of being, as usual, somewhat stolid and glum, he became extraordinarily animated and eloquent!

Masham was a man of good family, his own master, and the non-resident owner of a fine property in the north of England, which, in order to indulge his passion for speed, he neglected shamefully.

Arrived at Nice, he put up at one of the fashionable hotels, running over daily to Monte Carlo, which, in the month of March, was crammed. On these expeditions, he was accompanied by his companion, and the car was garaged, whilst its owner took what he called "a turn in the rooms." He played for high stakes, generally put down a *mille* note, and was uncannily lucky. This good fortune he attributed to the little silver figure of a certain saint, which he clutched in one hand, whilst he staked with the other; this saint was his mascot. He never remained long in the Casino, being too impatient and restless; and when he had made a round of his favourite tables, would sally forth in search of refreshment, or to saunter about the square and the exquisite gardens. His companion did not gamble—strong as were inherited instincts, and hot as was the gambling fever which ran in his blood;—he had no money to lose, and the prize he wished to win was Aurea Morven.

Naturally, Masham came across many acquaintances in such a cosmopolitan rendezvous as "Monte." Wynyard also encountered several familiar faces, and, one afternoon, as he was passing through a great crowd at the "Café de Paris," a light hand was laid on his arm, and, looking down, he was astonished to meet the upturned blue eyes of Mrs. Ramsay—Mrs. Ramsay in black, but no longer in weeds; Mrs. Ramsay another woman, and ten years younger; Mrs. Ramsay self-confident, prosperous, and handsome.

"Why, it's *Owen!*" she exclaimed. "Who would have thought of seeing you here?"

He smiled affirmatively, and glanced at her companions round the tea-table. Ottinge was strongly represented: here were the Rector and Miss Aurea, also General and Mrs. Morven, and a smart young man in attendance on the younger lady.

"Hullo, Owen!" exclaimed Mr. Morven, rising and shaking hands; "this *is* an unexpected meeting!" and he stared with puzzled interest at the erect figure, high-bred face, unimpeachable grey suit, and Homburg hat.

"I'm not over here to gamble," he continued. "We are at Mentone, and I've come to have a look at this pretty, wicked place."

"It's pretty wicked by all accounts!" replied Wynyard, speaking now, as Mr. Morven noted, in the tone of equal to equal.

"Aurea," he said, turning to his daughter, "don't you see Owen?"

Miss Morven—who had entirely regained her beauty, and was charmingly dressed—glanced up from underneath her immense rose-wreathed hat, and coolly surveyed her former lover. She was, if possible, prettier than ever, he said to himself, as he doffed his hat in acknowledgment of her curt nod; but her eyes, as they met his, resembled two dark pools— frozen. For some unknown and unguessed-at reason, Aurea was no longer friendly to him—much less anything nearer—and the discovery seemed to plant a dagger in his throat. He found it desperately difficult to utter a word, much less to carry on a brisk conversation with the Rector and Mrs. Ramsay. General and Mrs. Morven were, he concluded, the important elderly couple who sat at the other side of the table, and the young man, who was engrossing Miss Morven's sole attention, was some idle ass, who wore his hair parted in the middle, and three rings on his left hand. He hated him then and there!

Meanwhile, Miss Morven encouraged him, and kept up a conversation in low, confidential tones. Her hat concealed her face, and Wynyard realised, for the first time in his life, how rude a hat could be! This black hat, garlanded with pink flowers, was but too eloquently expressive of the fact, that its wearer desired to ignore the existence—much less the presence—of her aunts' late employé.

However, the Rector and Mrs. Ramsay were most anxiously disposed to make amends for Miss Morven's detachment.

"What do you think of the gardens?" inquired the former, indicating the flower-beds that lay between them and the Casino—a blaze of velvet violas. "Quite in your line, eh?"

Wynyard muttered an inarticulate assent—all his thoughts were concentrated on Aurea.

"I'm glad to see you are getting on," resumed the Rector cheerily; "prospects improving, eh?"

"I'm afraid not," answered the chauffeur; his mind full of this gentleman's only daughter, and the haughty little face which was so studiously concealed.

"What are you doing now, eh?"

"I'm with Masham, a man who has a racing motor, as useful companion."

"Oh, by Jove, I know him!" broke in the General. "Masham's the wildest driver in England, or, indeed, Europe—a racing lunatic—wish you safely out of his company! Is he here?"

"Yes, in the rooms; and I'm just loafing about till he is ready to go back to Nice."

"You have never asked about poor dear little Ottinge," interposed Mrs. Ramsay, with an injured air,—Mrs. Ramsay who had hitherto been a silent and much interested spectator of Wynyard and Aurea. What *was* the matter with the girl?

"And how is Ottinge?" he inquired, turning to the Rector.

"Oh, pretty well, thank you. Young Hogben is married to Dilly Topham. I must say I never thought *that* would come off, but it has; and they seem fairly happy. Old Mrs. Topham, however, gave no dowry; she cannot bear to part with a penny, but she sent a present of three jars of mouldy jam, and a broken-down lamp."

"Miss Parrett has been dangerously ill," supplemented Mrs. Ramsay, "but is better. Old Thunder has bought a donkey and a bath-chair; and oh, sad news indeed!—how *am* I to tell you?—Mackenzie is no more."

"I can bear up," he answered, with a short laugh. This was ungrateful, for was it not Mackenzie who had introduced him to Aurea?

"He was kicked by a horse, and was killed on the spot," said the Rector; "I think, Mrs. Ramsay, you show a very unneighbourly spirit."

"But I never considered myself the neighbour of Mackenzie!" she argued, "just the opposite—and he was not an estimable character. A good man should not own a bad dog."

"Oh, well, give a dog a bad name——"

"And Mackenzie deserved it," she interrupted; "he was the village bully. If he met a smaller dog, it was death for the small dog; if one of his own size, he passed on. You know, or you may not know, that, at teas at the Rectory, he sat on the laps of timid ladies, devoured their offerings, and intimidated them with growls—they dared not displace him." Then, turning her head, "Aurea, we are talking of Mackenzie and his enormities."

"Oh, are you?" she rejoined, with civil indifference.

"Yes," resumed Mrs. Ramsay; "and is not it well known that he attacked a solitary visitor in the Rectory drawing-room—whose furs affronted him—and tore her muff to shreds with ferocious satisfaction? I believe her screams could be heard at the Drum, and she had to be restored with brandy and burnt feathers."

"You would delight Dr. Johnson, my dear lady," said the Parson; "he loved a good hater."

"Oh, if you only knew how he treated and maltreated my poor paying guests,"—and she looked at Wynyard—"*you* remember the beagle, and how you doctored him; only for you he would have died."

"Yes; but the beagle survives—Mackenzie is no more. *De mortuis nil nisi bonum.*"

To hear this chauffeur with a ready Latin quotation in his mouth! What was the world coming to? thought Mrs. Morven, who had finished her tea, and was now playing the part of a dignified audience.

"We are all at the Hôtel des Montaignes, Mentone," continued Mrs. Ramsay; "I want you to come over and see me, will you?"

"I should be delighted, but my time is not my own—perhaps I can get off on Sunday. May I write?"

"Do; and I shall expect to hear that you are coming to lunch."

"Here is Masham," he announced, as the muscular, brick-faced gentleman pushed and elbowed his way towards them.

"Hullo, Owen, ready to start, eh? We must get a move on."—"Oh," to the General, "glad to see you—splendid weather out here, eh?"

At this moment a party of compatriots arrived, and figuratively swallowed up General and Mrs. Morven, the Rector, Mrs. Ramsay, and even the celebrated Mr. Masham. Here was Wynyard's opportunity, and, as usual, he seized upon it without ceremony. It was impossible that Aurea (who was rarely out of his thoughts), whose little word, "perhaps," had buoyed him up on many stormy waters, meant what her looks and attitude implied. Resolutely he came up to her, ignoring the glassy stare of her companion, and said—

"Miss Morven—has forgotten me—*perhaps*?"

Miss Morven looked up at him with an expression of delicate disdain. Could this self-possessed young lady, in a wonderful hat and Parisian frock, be the self-same girl who had stood beside him on Yampton Hill, with loosened hair and spattered habit?

After a reflective pause, she murmured—

"No, I've not forgotten my aunts'—er—chauffeur; but I do not think we were ever—*acquainted*."

Wynyard had wonderful self-command, but mentally he reeled; he felt as if some one had suddenly dealt him a terrible blow between the eyes. Outwardly he turned a sudden, pallid white, and drew back, as Miss Morven rose, picked up her parasol, and said to her companion—

"*Now*, if you like, I will go down to the Condamine and see the motor boats."

And, almost at the same moment, Mr. Masham claimed his companion and hurried him away to the garage.

"I say," said the General to his brother (he usually prefaced his remarks with "I say"), "who was the young stranger who seemed to know Ottinge? 'Pon my word, he deserves a medal for the discovery. Wait, I seem to know his face! Yes, I've got it. Wynyard of the Red Hussars—he went the pace—uncle cut up rough—he's in my club."

"No, for once you are a bit out! You will be amused to hear that that good-looking, well-set-up young man was Bella's chauffeur."

"Nonsense!"

"It's a sober fact. I liked him," continued the Rector; "he has good manners—manners make the man—I had him in the choir, and he's a first-class cricketer. I always, between you and me, believed him to be a gentleman who was expiating some—er—mistake. I declare, Susan was actually fond of him, and he turned the heads, unintentionally—I'll say that for him—of every girl in the village."

"Well, I'm blowed! He is the very image of Dick Wynyard's heir—next to the baronetcy and property. Old Dick never speaks of him now, and I've not seen him about for nearly two years. Mrs. Ramsay, what do you say to a village romance, and a chauffeur being as like a young swell as two peas?"

"Oh," replied the lady, deliberately moulding on her gloves, "truth is stranger than fiction; I've known some funny things in my life. I always liked Owen, and I am glad to see he is getting up in the world."

"Up!" repeated the General; "if he is companion to Masham, he is much more likely to leave the world altogether—and that at an early date! Well, Edgar, Aurea has gone off with young Beauclerc and his people to the boats. Shall we go to La Turbie as arranged, and have the honour of escorting the two ladies?"

And then, with one consent, they rose with a loud noise of scraping chairs, and passed into the square in single file.

CHAPTER XXXII
AN EXPLANATION

Mrs. Ramsay's trip to the Sunny South was accounted for by the fact that she had recently come into possession of a comfortable fortune, left to her by her godfather "in recognition and admiration," said the will, "of the noble way in which Kathleen Ramsay had carried out her marriage vow—for better or worse."

The widow had gladly accepted an invitation, and joined the Morven party. She was extremely fond of Aurea, the girl's sunny nature and light-heartedness was a grateful tonic for her own sad frame of mind; but she now felt deeply indignant with her friend for her treatment of Mr. Wynyard, and could not have believed her capable of such snobbishness, had she not witnessed it with her own eyes. She had noticed his hurried address, Aurea's quick reply, and then his face. *What* had the girl said, to thus turn him into stone? Personally, she liked Owen immensely! was deeply in his debt, and ready to forward his happiness and his interests to the best of her ability. Kathleen Ramsay, a woman of warm feelings and responsive susceptibilities, would have been delighted to promote a love-match between Owen Wynyard and Aurea Morven.

Aurea's unexpected attitude had filled her with amazement and rage; she could hardly restrain herself, but managed to hold her peace—and that with pain and grief—for four whole days; at the end of the time, she received a letter from Aurea's lover, which caused her restraint to break all bonds:—

"Dear Mrs. Ramsay,—I find it will be impossible for me to go over and see you, as we are leaving for Milan to-morrow. I should have liked to have had a long talk with you—you and I have few secrets from one another—but, as the Rector and Miss Morven are in your hotel, I could not have faced them again, and given Miss Morven the trouble of cutting me for a second time. You suspected me, I know, and I may tell you that it was Aurea Morven who kept me in Ottinge for six months; that, chiefly for her sake, I took on a detestable job in Town, and engaged to risk my neck with this crazy motorist; for every week that I was earning my bread and keeping my promise, was bringing me, I believed, nearer to *her*. To the best of my knowledge I have never given her any reason to think ill of me; on the contrary, I have striven tremendously hard to make myself more worthy of her, and the other day, when I met her accidentally, I thought it was a wonderful piece of good luck for me; instead of which, it was the blackest day I've ever known. She refused to remember or recognise me. I have only six months more to work off—sometimes I think I'll chuck the whole thing and enlist; I would, only for my sister. What's the good of trying? I'm afraid this is a beastly sort of letter, but...."

Some words were scratched out, but read, very carefully, and held up to the light, they were faintly decipherable.

"I sometimes feel as if I were going mad—I don't care now if we have some bad accident. I only hope it will kill me.— Yours sincerely,

"Owen Wynyard."

It was the Honourable Mrs. Ramsay, daughter of the late, and sister of the present, Viscount Ballingarry—and not Katie—who, that evening, entered Aurea's bedroom immediately after a knock. She discovered her young victim in a charming white *negligé* and a rose silk petticoat, engaged in brushing her magnificent hair. There was war in the visitor's face as she seated herself, and, after a moment's expressive silence, fired her first gun.

"Aurea, I want you to tell me why you were so amazingly, so cruelly, rude to Owen, your aunts' chauffeur?"

Miss Aurea, after a glance at her friend, coolly replied—

"Why should *I* be called upon to do the polite to my aunts' *ci-devant* employé?"

"Aurea! This is not you—there must be some crooked turn in you, or there's some other detestable girl in your body!"

"It is Aurea Morven, I assure you," and she drew herself together with a quick movement; "and I do not wish to hear anything of Owen, the chauffeur. *I* know more about him than you suppose."

"You don't know a quarter as much as I do!" retorted Mrs. Ramsay with decision, and her eyes gleamed.

"I know that he was on a ranch in South America, that he was a waiter on the *Anaconda*——"

"Oh yes, go on."

"That he was probably in the Army, that he is in disgrace with his family, and came to hide himself in Ottinge till the storm, whatever it was, blew over! and that a tall dark lady came to meet him at Brodfield, and even at the Drum."

"How do you know?" inquired Mrs. Ramsay.

"I saw her—I saw him kissing a woman at the Drum as I passed; all Ottinge might have done the same! Their shadows were on the blind. I saw him and the woman drive away; they passed me in a motor, he, leaning back delightfully at his ease, and she bending over him as if she adored him! And this is not second-hand news, for I witnessed it myself."

"Why should you be so furious, Aurea? Aurea, *I* know why!" and her tone was vibrating and sarcastic.

The girl turned upon her with flashing eyes; but, before she could speak, Mrs. Ramsay said—

"You say your news is first-hand—so is mine; I promised to keep Mr. Wynyard's secret."

"Oh yes, I knew his name was Wynyard," interrupted Aurea.

"Of course—my poor old man uttered it with his last breath. He was fond of Owen; he mistook him for his friend and schoolfellow—Owen's father—and Owen allowed him to think so. I pledged myself to silence, but even *he* would permit me to break it now. The lady who came to see Owen, and who has so excited your wrath, was"—speaking very deliberately—"his sister, Lady Kesters."

Aurea's tortoiseshell brush fell to the floor with a resounding clang. Then, in a very few words, Mrs. Ramsay—impulsive, eloquent, and Irish— laid the whole story of Sir Richard's bargain before the girl, who stood listening as if in a dream.

"Mr. Wynyard was so good to my poor husband, and, indeed, to me, I'll never, never forget it. And, you see, Jimmy knew his father and mother, whom he could not remember, and one night in the dusk, just before I left, he told me his whole story. Of course I had always known he was the son of Captain Wynyard, and that he himself had been in the Red Hussars, but I did *not* know why he was earning his bread as your aunts' chauffeur! He never said a word of you, but I understood—I realised the attraction that kept him, a young man of the world, in out-of-the-way Ottinge. He opened his heart to me that August night, and now, Aurea, you have broken it."

"I?"

"Don't pretend," she cried passionately, and she looked at her almost threateningly; "don't add to your sins. *You* know as well as I do how you treated him—certainly not as a lady should do; why, if I were to meet one of the Brodfield fly-drivers here I'd give him a civil greeting. You were outrageously rude—you overdid it. My only comfort is that, to be so jealous, you must have been extremely fond of him."

Aurea coloured—she could blush furiously—and her complexion was very pink indeed, as seen through long strands of hair.

Then she sat down rather suddenly, and said—

"What's done is done—and never can be undone!" and buried her face in her hands.

Whereupon the Honourable Mrs. Ramsay, having said her say, and "rubbed it in" remorselessly, quietly effected her departure.

CHAPTER XXXIII
SITUATION THE FOURTH

It was evident that some kind of armistice or *pourparlers* had been arranged between Mrs. Ramsay and her misguided young companion, for, when the General, the Rector, and Mrs. Morven returned to England, home, and duty, these ladies still remained abroad, and went together to a small and picturesque village in the very heart of the Alpes-Maritimes. Aurea longed for some such quiet retreat, where she could hide herself, and recover from a blow which had still left its quivering traces. Love and happiness were possibly within her reach, and she had, in all ignorance, cast them aside; her widowed chaperone understood and sympathised, and, though it was she who had inflicted the wound, she was absolved.

In the inn of a little mountain village the friends spent three weeks far from the giddy crowds, aloof from luxury, and the world. Here were thick cups, thin candles, good coffee, and sour bread. What long walks and talks they enjoyed, and how fully the girl opened her innocent heart to the experienced, world-worn matron! Letters were rare, and newspapers ignored; in Aurea's mental condition, what were to her the fate of plays, of Cabinets, yea, of nations? She was never likely to hear tidings of *him* through the Press; but here Aurea was wrong. The unexpected—as is so frequently the case—declared itself. One afternoon the two ladies walked to a town at some distance, and as they waited for a well-deserved *café complét*, Mrs. Ramsay idly glanced over an old and fly-blown copy of the continental *Daily Mail*, and the following paragraph caught her eye and seemed to stab her in the face:—

"The neighbourhood of Villo, near Turin, has been shocked by a terrible accident, which took place yesterday. Mr. H. Masham, the well-known racing motorist, returning victorious from a competition, in order to avoid a wagon, dashed into a hillside at full speed. The motor turned over completely; he and the chauffeur were pinned underneath. Mr. Masham was dead when extricated, and there are no hopes of the recovery of his companion."

Mrs. Ramsay made a desperate attempt to hide the paper, but it was impossible to hide her own white face, and Aurea insisted on reading the paragraph. When she had grasped its contents, she turned to her friend for a moment with great, agonised, unseeing eyes, and for the first time in her life of twenty-one years Aurea Morven fainted.

That same hour Mrs. Ramsay despatched a reply-paid telegram to the Italian Hospital, asking for immediate tidings of Mr. Owen, and the answer received was—

"Owen left yesterday—address unknown."

Well, at any rate, he was still in the land of the living, and from this important fact Miss Morven must extract such comfort as she deserved.

The truth was, that the chauffeur's injuries were not so severe as had been supposed—a few cuts and bruises, a slight concussion, and a broken collar-bone. His fine constitution had speedily carried him out of the doctor's hands, and when Wynyard returned to London, it was to find that his sister and her husband had arrived as a part of the great tide that flows annually from the West. Lady Kesters had heard of her brother's accident in New York, and spent a small fortune in cables, and now they met again, after a separation of six months, with mutual satisfaction; but, in spite of her insistence, Wynyard firmly resisted his sister's invitation to take up his quarters in Mount Street.

"No, no," he answered, "that is not in the bond; I'll get through on my own. I've only four months to work off. I can run in and out till I find another place."

"What about money, my dear boy? Your stay in that Italian hospital must have been expensive."

"I was heavily insured against accidents; after my first week with Masham—when I realised his style of driving, I took out a policy for fifteen hundred pounds!"

"I wonder you dare get into a motor," she said. "I don't see how you can possibly have any nerve left."

"Oh, I'm not such a wreck as all that; and, considering everything, I got off uncommonly well. I'm sure poor Masham was insane. He certainly looked it at times. It's my experience that there are quite a good-sized crowd of lunatics about at large; I've knocked up against one or two lately. Masham always prophesied he would be killed in a motor accident—and seemed rather to glory in the prospect."

"You do tumble into the queerest situations—old maids, dancers, madman! I must confess I cannot understand why you remained with him, carrying your life in your hands?"

"In Masham's hands, you mean!" corrected her brother; "he seldom allowed me to drive."

"And if you had been killed, where, pray, did I come in—or Aurea Morven?"

Owen Wynyard's next situation as chauffeur was with a certain Mrs. Buckingham Brune, a wealthy matron who had a fine place in the north of England. Miss Weedon, her daughter by a first marriage, was a notable heiress, and her mother was determined that she should make an alliance befitting her great fortune and fame. Her father, Sir Jacob Weedon, the son of a peasant, had risen to wealth and honour solely through his own active brain and dogged industry. He had not the smallest desire to conceal his origin, and often alluded to the days when he was "a poor, half-fed body"; and his coal-pick actually hung as a glorious trophy over the chimneypiece in his smoking-room. But his wife was of a different type; she smothered (when possible) his reminiscences, and desired, since his death, to soar to other worlds—on the wings of Ermentrude's fortune; but Betsy Ermentrude, a simple maiden in her prime, inherited her father's character and ideas, and had no craving for super-society or to wear the coronet of a peeress. Her mother had married a second time, a good-looking young man, many years her junior; he was a lazy member of an impoverished family, who had no objection to a luxurious home, hunters, motors, pocket-money, and the best of shooting. It was considered (among his intimates) that Toby Brune had dropped into a "nice soft thing." They were not, however, thinking of Mrs. Brune, who was notoriously as hard as nails, but of Toby's enviable surroundings.

Miss Weedon made no rash assertions, never took exception to her mother's gay guests, but quietly made up her mind that, as her parent had pleased herself, she would do likewise, and shape her own life. Betsy was a slight, sandy-haired girl with appealing blue eyes, a determined mouth, and a radiant smile. Her figure was willowy and graceful; in short, she was unnecessarily pretty for an heiress.

This was the entourage in which the chauffeur now found himself, his sole stipulation being to "live out." He had no desire to mix with the great staff of servants, and found comfortable quarters at one of the gate lodges. The family owned no less than three fine cars; the one Wynyard drove was a Panhard—the exclusive possession of Miss Weedon and her friends. Mrs. Brune toured the country in a magnificent Mercédès. She was a stout, black-haired lady, with a short neck and a full meridian. To make her look young and slender was the hopeless task of milliner and maid. Their employer had, however, contrived to squeeze herself into the best society, was a clever, pushing woman, who had early acquired the art of "Who to know, and who not to know." Her cook was a notable French chef, and smart guests, who stayed at the Court, invariably carried away with them the happy tidings that "they had been done remarkably well, and indirect everything was topping!"

Mrs. Buckingham Brune, for her husband's benefit, rented a fine moor in Scotland, and here the family were luxuriously established for August and September. Owen, by special permission, lived with one of the keepers, and was chiefly employed to fetch guests to and from the station, or to motor the ladies to the neighbouring sights.

Occasionally Miss Weedon adventured forth alone, and, at a discreet distance from the lodge, picked up a certain young man—who, as it happened, was an acquaintance of the chauffeur's. Miss Weedon's love-affairs were not precisely his business, but they had his sympathy and, if desired, his sanction. Supposing Teddy Wantage were anxious to marry the heiress and they liked one another, supposing he were man enough to carry her off—who was to stand in their way? Not he! He detested Mrs. Buckingham Brune, her preposterous pretensions, and shameless tuft-hunting, and was fully prepared to help old lame-dog Teddy over an awkward matrimonial stile.

CHAPTER XXXIV
SIR RICHARD AS CHAPERON

Sir Richard Wynyard was passing through Edinburgh on his way to London; he had been shooting up in Perthshire, and found, as he drove up to Waverley Station, that he had missed his train by two minutes—this, and the fact that he felt some acute twinges of gout, combined to make him a little short in his manner. As he had an hour's wait, he pushed up to the book-stall, gruffly demanded an English paper, and tossed a copper in payment. The copper missed its goal, fell with a clang on the flags, and a young man, who was also buying papers—a chauffeur chap,—turned about, and Sir Richard found that he was face to face with his nephew—also that he was extremely glad of the meeting. The baronet was beginning to feel a bit lonely in life; now that old age was reaching for him, he experienced the lack of some personal belongings, of comfort and hope in the future, and a sense of exclusion and loneliness invaded him, especially in those hours when he lay awake 'twixt dark and dawn. His nearest of kin, Leila and Owen, had been out of touch with him for many months—Leila away in the United States, and Owen working his life or death sentence.

He had been terribly frightened at the time of Mr. Masham's accident, had sorely repented of his bargain with his heir, and repeatedly said to himself, "There was no doubt that motoring was an infernally risky business."

"Hullo, Owen!" he exclaimed, "what are you doing here?"

"I'm driving a car. My people have just gone off by the express."

"Um—quite fit now?" looking him over from head to foot.

"Yes, thanks; I'm all right."

"And what's your job?"

"I'm chauffeur to Mrs. Buckingham Brune, of Ashbourne Court. She's up here on a moor just now."

"Buckingham Brune—yes—yes—I know—enormously rich; daughter, a great heiress—let's see—a quarter of a million—Miss Weedon?"

"She was Miss Weedon till an hour ago; now she's Mrs. Wantage! I brought her in from the lodge this morning, attended the wedding, and saw the runaway couple off ten minutes ago."

"Bless my soul!" Sir Richard gave a little stagger. "What! eh? You don't mean it! I say, what a fellow you are for being in the thick of rows and bothers!"

"Oh, no bother to *me*," replied his nephew carelessly; "I'm only a chauffeur, not a chaperon; but I must say I'm awfully glad Wantage brought it off!"

"And what a haul—half a million!"

"Yes; but, upon my honour, I don't believe he was thinking of the money. She's an uncommonly nice girl."

Sir Richard's face expressed scornful incredulity.

"Pity you didn't go in for her yourself, eh!" Then, after a meditative pause, "I expect there will be a holy row! What will her mother say?"

"That remains to be heard! She wanted her daughter to marry that drunken little sweep, Vippen—he's staying there now."

"Lord Vippen?"

He nodded.

"And it's my painful duty to face the music, and deliver the fatal letter."

Sir Richard gave a long whistle.

"Yes; it's a job I don't half fancy. Well, I must be getting a move on—the car is just outside." Then, holding out his hand, "I'm awfully glad to have seen you, Uncle Dick, and looking so fit."

"I say, Owen," suddenly taking him by the arm and leading him aside, "*I've* had enough of this."

His nephew stared at him interrogatively.

"Let's cry quits—time's up—all but a few weeks! You have done uncommonly well, and I was an old idiot."

"No, I don't think so, sir. I believe it was quite a sound idea; but, since you've given me the word, I must confess I'm not sorry it's finished."

"And I'll tell you what, my boy—you gave me a jolly good fright the time Masham was killed."

"Nothing to my own fright when the car turned over; but, I say, I must be off to Hillstan—it's thirty miles away—and do my errand. Where shall I find you when I come back? I'm fairly safe to get the kick out, and I expect I'll have to walk to our nearest drivelling little station."

"Look here, Owen, I'll hire a car. I'll telephone now, and go with you, and this other can fetch us back—we'll have a good talk."

Owen was secretly amused, though his face was impassive. Here was Uncle Dick, extraordinarily eager for his company, actually chartering a motor, and grudging him out of his sight for a couple of hours! He never dreamt of the old man's hungry heart—how, at times, life seemed empty and hopeless—and he had nothing to look forward to but the grave.

The narrow escape of his nephew had brought home to him that he was really fond of the scapegrace now confronting him; even in a holland coat and chauffeur's cap, what a handsome, well-set-up young fellow! And there was something different in this Owen: a look of decision, manliness, and independence in his face; a strain of confidence in his speech; even if he were not the future Sir Owen Wynyard, this individual was undeniably capable of "hoeing his own row."

He felt proud of this nephew, who seemed to be years older than the Owen of the Red Hussars or Owen of the ranch—here was a full-grown man! As a boy, Owen had never been afraid to look him squarely in the face, but now his nephew's eyes seemed to dominate him altogether. Was it the younger generation knocking at the door?

"Mind you, if we meet Mrs. Brune, and you are in her car, she will run you in for a Joy rider!" said his nephew, with a grin.

"Well, perhaps you'd better go alone. I was only thinking of backing you up when she tackles you."

"Awfully good of you. I'll get you to back me up in earnest in another direction."

"As long as it's not a bill!" and Sir Richard actually laughed.

"No, no; I've lots of money for a chauffeur—here's the car, a 45 h.p. Panhard—isn't she a beauty?" he said, as they arrived at the station entrance. "I'll get it over as soon as I can, and bring my traps to the Station Hotel."

"Yes, I dine at eight sharp—good luck to you!" and he waved his hand to his nephew, and then stood watching him as he steered through the traffic with admirable judgment, and presently sped out of sight.

Then Sir Richard collected his luggage, engaged rooms at the hotel, ordered a special reconciliation dinner, and wired to Lady Kesters, "Have seen Owen—all is square. Expect us to-morrow."

At eight o'clock uncle and nephew, in glossy shirts and evening-dress, sat down *tête-à-tête*, to enjoy their oysters.

"And what about Mrs. Buckingham Brune?" inquired Sir Richard.

"She took it better than I expected. At first I thought she was going to strike me, and I was in for a bad time; but when she heard that Wantage was no pauper, and that his maternal uncle was a duke, she calmed down, and I expect after a little time they will be all right. She actually got the *Peerage* and looked him up on the spot—my word did not count! However, we parted friends; and she sent me over in the car and offered me a splendid reference."

"Oh, so you got round her! And what are your own plans, my boy?"

"The agency—and Wynyard—and——"

"Oh, that's of course," he interrupted; "but I mean now—to-morrow?"

"To-morrow I'd like to run up to Lossiemouth."

"For golf—yes; but why not Berwick? It's much handier!"

"Well, you see, Uncle Dick, I'm not specially interested in any one in Berwick; but there's a girl up north that interests me more than any one in the world."

"*Ah!*" hastily emptying his champagne glass, and putting it down with a jerk.

"Now I'm no longer in service, and have some prospects, I want to find out if she will marry me!"

"So it's got as far as that, has it?"

"No, it has not even started. Last time we met, she would not speak to me."

"And what are you going on, then?"

"A mere chance. I believe there was a—a—misunderstanding, so a friend told me; anyway, she's the only girl I could ever care for."

Sir Richard became more and more interested. Could it be possible that Owen had inherited such loyal devotion from himself?

"Who is she?" he asked.

"She is Miss Morven, daughter of the Rector at Ottinge and the Parretts' niece. She sometimes came out in the motor, and I used to see her in the garden."

"And how did you make love to her—language of flowers, hey?"

"No; I never was anything but the chauffeur. I see by the *Scotsman* she is up at Lossiemouth with her uncle, General Morven."

"What—old Charlie Morven! Why, I know him. I'll go up there with you and see you through—and take him out of your way."

"Do—it will be awfully decent of you; but Miss Morven may not have anything to do with *me*!"

"What! not marry my nephew with Wynyard at his back and a fine fat fortune! Nonsense, nonsense! Here, waiter, just fetch me a *Bradshaw*." Then to his companion, "I'll wire for rooms to-night, and we will make a start for Lossiemouth first thing to-morrow morning."

CHAPTER XXXV
REINSTATED

It was dinner time in one of the larger hotels at Lossiemouth—a soft September evening, the windows stood wide, admitting the warm salt air, and above the clattering of plates and voices, one occasionally caught the murmuring of the North Atlantic, the creak of an oar, or the scream of a seagull. At a table in one corner a party of three were seated—a party that were, as a rule, accorded an unusual and flattering amount of attention—a white-moustached soldier, a dignified, elderly lady (whose grey hair was undoubtedly dressed by a maid), and a remarkably pretty, dark-eyed girl. They were in mourning, but nothing so deep as to suggest an overwhelming calamity; the young lady wore white, the elder black crêpe-de-chine, the man black studs and a black tie, and their names in the hotel register were "Major-General, Mrs., and Miss Morven, London."

Miss Parrett was no more; a sudden attack of "her bronchitis"—she always spoke as if it were an exclusive possession—had hurried her out of existence. She had, however, executed her will, and after elaborate directions respecting her funeral, her monument, and her hatchment, it was found that she had bequeathed all she possessed to her sister Susan, with the exception of her automobile, which was left to her dear friend, Mrs. Maria Wiggens; and whether this memento was instigated by generosity or malice, is a debated question until the present hour. There were no legacies to charities, or even the smallest souvenir for her special little clique. The contents of the testament were a sore disappointment to some, but few grudged Miss Susan independence and fortune, for she knew how to make excellent use of both. Isabella Parrett was no more, and Susan, her sister, reigned in her stead.

The Morven family, who were not real heart-and-soul golfers, were beginning to weary of the one perpetual subject that surrounded them from morning till night. The difficulties of the fifth tee, vivid descriptions of the various approaches, bunkers, and greens, had palled somewhat—even on the General. He secretly languished for the society of some one who had been in the Service, and a chance of discussing the late manœuvres as described in the daily Press. New arrivals were always a matter of interest, and here came two—ushered by the head waiter. There was a certain stir and a good deal of staring as a little elderly gentleman, with very square shoulders, and a young man—possibly his son—approached.

"I say!" ejaculated General Morven, laying down his spoon, "if here isn't old Dicky Wynyard!" and he rose from his seat and made signals. "Yes—and his nephew."

Aurea looked up with startled eyes, and became suddenly white. There was Owen approaching in the wake of his uncle; he wore an air of complete self-possession, the usual dinner-coat, and had undoubtedly cast off the rôle of chauffeur.

"I say, this *is* good luck!" exclaimed the General, extending a genial hand. "Fancy meeting you up here, Sir Richard! I did not know you ever came North! Hullo, Wynyard, glad to see you. I've not come across you in the club for ages."

"Yes; I've been recommended to Lossiemouth to get the real, unadulterated air straight from the North Pole and to have a little golf, and I've brought this young fellow along with me," Sir Richard answered, lying boldly and with ease; his nephew was positively staggered by such fluent proficiency.

"I think you know my wife," said the General. "Yes; let me introduce you to my niece, Miss Morven."

Sir Richard bowed, and said—

"And allow me to present my nephew, Mr. Wynyard—Mrs. Morven," and, accompanying his introduction with a sharp glance, "Miss Morven."

"Mr. Wynyard and I have already met," she announced, in a faint voice.

"That's all right, then," said her uncle heartily. "Now we all know one another," and he rubbed his hands. "Sir Richard, will you sit at our table? There is lots of room for five."

"Thanks, we shall be delighted."

"How did you discover Lossiemouth?" inquired Mrs. Morven when the newcomers were seated.

"Well, the fact is, I never heard of it till lately, and then a friend strongly advised me to try it—he said it was just the place to suit me." He glanced complacently at his nephew, as much as to claim approval. "I'm uncommonly glad to meet you, General; we can have some rounds together. What's your handicap?"

As the two older men talked, Mrs. Morven proceeded to cultivate the younger, and Aurea for once felt herself out in the cold and—what was more serious—indescribably ill at ease. She dropped her fork, helped herself twice to salt, and crumbled her uncle's bread.

It was evident that Owen, or, rather, Mr. Wynyard, had made his peace and was reinstated in his proper niche in society. Why had he come to Lossiemouth? Why was Sir Richard looking at her so keenly with his little searching eyes? Why was Owen making himself so extremely agreeable to her aunt?—listening, with reverent sympathy, to a harrowing description of her neuralgia, and a still more harrowing account of the death of her beautiful prize blue Persian—run over by a motor in Eaton Place.

"Think of it! A motor—a motor going over a cat!"

"I'm afraid motors are no respecter of persons or cats. As to dogs, they are killed by the dozen."

Mrs. Morven shuddered, sipped her claret, and turned the subject to books and fiction.

"I hope you have brought something fresh? Our stock is nearly exhausted."

"I'm afraid not, only a couple of magazines; I was reading a thriller in the train. The worst of it is, that just as you become passionately interested and something tremendous is going to happen, you are choked off by a full-page advertisement of pills or boot polish. I like my fiction undiluted; don't you?"

Aurea was amazed at this flow of conversation from the monosyllabic Owen. Evidently Owen was one individual, and Mr. Wynyard another. She was even more impressed by the quiet confidence of his manner. Had he noted her embarrassment and nervousness? Suddenly he turned to her, and said—

"And how is Ottinge, Miss Morven?"

The question was so unexpected that for an instant she could not find her voice; there seemed to be an obstruction in her throat, but she managed to reply—

"It is much as usual."

"What! no change in twelve months!" he exclaimed, in a key of surprise. "Oh, but, of course, the world flows very deliberately in that sleepy old village. And how is Mrs. Ramsay?"

"Very well; she generally has a houseful of nephews and nieces, very Irish and lively."

"And the Hogbens—are they flourishing?"

"Yes, old Mrs. Topham is dead; she left a great deal of money in unexpected places. Tom and Dilly are comparatively rich, and have moved into Claringsbold."

"So Miss Susan will have to look out for another gardener?"

"Yes; but she keeps three and a boy. She has a beautiful Panhard landaulet."

"I say—you don't mean it!"

"And she is talking of putting up a conservatory, and has begun to build a cottage hospital."

"I won't recognise the place. Is the Drum still standing? Have you a rink and a theatre?"

Aurea smiled.

"And how is my dear old pal, Joss?"

"Getting a little stout for want of exercise."

"I'd no idea you knew Ottinge so well," put in Mrs. Morven. "What a memory you have!"

"For some things, my memory is like a rat-trap, and for others my mind is a blank."

"I suppose you stayed at Westmere for the shooting?" broke in the General.

"No; but"—and he glanced at Aurea—"I've often been there. What has become of Bertie Woolcock?"

"Oh, by Jove! didn't you hear? He went off to India to shoot big game, and got caught himself! A very pretty, smart American girl he met on board ship—no money—so on this occasion Uncle Sam has scored as regards the dollars."

By this time dinner had been brought to a close with large cups of milky coffee, and the Morven party rose and drifted into the hall. It was

Aurea's custom to sit out on the verandah with her uncle as he smoked; her aunt betook herself and her neuralgia into the drawing-room and there sat knitting amidst an agreeable circle of matrons—chiefly Scotch. To-night, she half expected Aurea to accompany her, and the young lady herself was undecided. The two elder men were lingering in the hall, lighting up, and had already commenced an animated discussion.—Owen had not yet produced his cigar case.—She was on the point of following her chaperon, much as she disliked sitting indoors this exquisite September night, when he said—

"Will you come for a stroll with me?"

She nodded assent, and turned to reach for her wrap with a fast beating heart. The door had already closed on Mrs. Morven's stately form, and the young couple walked out through the porch, with a matter of course air, and crossed the road towards the golf links and the beach. Sir Richard followed them with his keen little eyes, but General Morven was far too much engrossed in a Service grievance to see beyond his nose.

CHAPTER XXXVI
BY MOONLIGHT

As it was a lovely evening, many other couples were on the links or the shore, lured abroad by the beauty of the scene, the clear radiance of the northern sky, and the brilliance of a harvest moon. A soft, almost languorous little breeze, stirred the long coarse grass among the dunes—perhaps it had stolen across the bay from those dark mountains of Rossshire, carrying tender messages from the purple heather? To-night, the great burners in the lighthouse had a sinecure, for it was as bright as day. From a villa overlooking the sea, a violin and piano flooded the air with sounds that seemed to evoke the very spirit of romance—a passionate triumph of the greatest gift in life.

As Aurea and her companion descended to the shore, they had scarcely exchanged a word beyond Wynyard's "Mind that stone," and "Let us get away from the crowd, right down to the sea."

Aurea felt inwardly agitated, but determined to do her utmost to exercise self-control. She knew instinctively that the most critical hour in her life was about to strike. In a somewhat unsteady voice she broke the silence—a woman sometimes does speak first.

"You are the very last person in the world I expected to see."

He turned and faced her.

"Why?"

"For several reasons."

"Can you guess the reason why I came up to Lossiemouth, and why I have asked you to come out with me? I am a free man since yesterday; the yoke is off, the gag is out of my mouth, and I want to repeat what I told you on Yampton Hill—that I love you."

There was a long pause, broken by the soft whispering of the ebbing waves.

"I wonder you do!" said the girl at last; her voice broke as she added, "after Monte Carlo."

"Well, yes; I admit that that was pretty bad, and quite bowled me over; but Mrs. Ramsay explained—she has been a good friend to me."

"I did not know you had a sister," continued Aurea, with a sort of sob.

"You knew nothing about me, and now you shall hear everything;" and in a few hurried sentences he told her of India, Canterbury, and the bill, his debts, of the City office, and the ranch.

"You see, Uncle Dick's patience was fairly worn out, and, honestly, I don't wonder. I was always coming back on his hands; so he gave me the two years' sentence to earn my own bread, and be independent. I'm an awful duffer in many ways, and I talked it over with Leila—my sister, you know. I had to make a start at once, for one thing, and I'd no chance of any good billet—everything now is examinations, or capital. I suggested enlisting or breaking horses, but she put forward the chauffeur scheme; it was rather a crazy idea, wasn't it?"

"I don't know. You were a capital driver—even Bertie Woolcock allowed that!"

"Well, anyway, Leila foisted me on your aunts—it was pretty cool, I'll admit—and just at first—I—well—I felt I couldn't stand it. I'd had a fairly rough time in the Argentine—it wasn't that—but— —"

"I know," she broke in, "it was Aunt Bella."

"I was not used to old ladies, and she was so—er—peculiar; I believe, to the last, she thought I sold or drank the petrol. Well, I'd made up my mind to clear out, and then—I saw you, and I decided to hold on—yes, like grim death. It was a lucky day for me when you came to the Manor—otherwise, I'd have gone away, and no doubt drifted about, and become a regular slacker; but you held me fast. I settled down, I made the best of the job, and took everything as it came in the day's work—for your sake."

Aurea nodded.

"I got to like the Ottinge folk, and to know them and their rustic ways, and, living as a working man, it was a splendid chance for me to learn many things I was as ignorant of, as that stone. I used to sit in the tap and listen to the talk, and got to see things from a different perspective. And I'd some good times, too, at choir practice, and penny readings, and the night of the servants' ball at Westmere, when I had one delicious waltz with you—do you remember?"

"I do, indeed, and how Bertie Woolcock snatched me away, and said ladies should never dance with men-servants, and I replied, that his mother had opened the ball with the butler!"

"You had him there; and then came my London situation, and the time with Masham, and now it's all over. I met Uncle Dick yesterday by chance, and he has been a brick. We had a rare good old talk last night, and I told him the history of the last eighteen months. I'm to manage the property, go into the Yeomanry, live at Wynyard—it's a big rambling old house—and he thinks I ought to marry; what do *you* say?"

Aurea was silent.

"My sister declares that in all her life she never heard of anything so outrageously audacious and impertinent, as my imploring you to accept me blindfold; and, as it is—you know so little of me. Why, we never sat at table together till to-night. I've always been below the salt!"

As he ceased speaking and awaited her reply, Aurea plucked up her courage and said: "But I do know you—I know you are kind and patient, and good-tempered, and to be trusted."

"And you do care for me?"

"Yes—I—always did—though I fought against it; and most of the time I knew your name was Wynyard, and that you'd been in the Service."

"But how on earth did you find it out?"

"By chance, from a Hussar in Brodfield; as he passed I heard him say to his companion, 'That's Lieutenant Wynyard,' but I kept the information to myself."

"And now there are no longer any secrets between us—you and I belong to one another, don't we?"

As Aurea, with a slight but significant gesture, assented, he drew her close to him, she yielded, and he stooped and kissed her.

Someone in the villa above was playing Tschaikowsky's "Chant sans paroles," and its tender and exquisite harmonies seemed an appropriate accompaniment to the scene upon the shore.

It was ten o'clock, and Mrs. Morven, who was knitting and counting, frowning and thinking, suddenly overheard a long-legged lassie, with a tawny mane, say to her mother, in a tone of repressed excitement—

"Mother—only think! You know the pretty girl—the one we all admire—I saw her on the beach just now, a good bit away, and she was crying I'm sure—and the young gentleman who came at dinner time *kissed* her!"

Mrs. Morven rolled up her stocking, arose with deliberate dignity, and sailed forth into the hall, where she found her husband and Sir Richard talking to one another, with great animation, on the subject of rubber shares.

"Where," she inquired, with a dramatic gesture, "is Aurea? and," casting a keen glance at Sir Richard, "where is Mr. Wynyard?"

The General could put two and two together as well as most men. Yes, it would do—nice young fellow—old family—baronetcy—and lots of money; and, nodding at his companion with undisguised significance, he said, as he rose—

"I say, Sir Richard, I suppose you and I will have to make a search-party and bring our young people home!" (Our young people!)

Perhaps it is unnecessary to add that the same young people were by no means grateful for their disinterested exertions. That night, at a very late hour, Aurea confided to her aunt that she was engaged to Owen Wynyard. Mrs. Morven, who had accompanied her niece to her bedroom, stood by the table, knitting in hand—an embodiment of the judicial British matron.

"Engaged! What nonsense, my dear girl! Why, you don't know him! Where have you met him?"

"Oh yes, I do; I knew him at Ottinge. He was Aunt Bella's chauffeur for six months."

Mrs. Morven took two hurried steps to a chair, sat down upon it, and gasped.

"Your aunts' chauffeur!" she exclaimed at last. New and bright ideas suddenly dawned upon her mental horizon. She never remembered to have heard her niece mention the chauffeur—though more than once she had spoken disparagingly of the green car. This silence, she now realised, had held a most deadly significance. Yes, she saw it all—the good-looking chauffeur had been at the bottom of *everything*: of Aurea's indifference to young men, her indifference to amusement—was he the reason that last winter her niece's brilliant young beauty had become tarnished? She looked up at her to-night; Aurea was supremely lovely.

"I see I have stunned you, Aunt Maggie."

"And he was at Monte Carlo. Yes; I now remember him perfectly. I thought the face was familiar; but why a chauffeur?"

"For the reason I refer you to his humpy little old uncle; but it's all right now."

"Of course he is Leila Hesters' brother, and Sir Richard's heir—Wynyard of Wynyard. Yes; I remember hearing that the young man was very wild and extravagant, raced and gambled. However, he is remarkably good-looking, and has charming manners; no doubt he has sown his wild oats—I don't envy him being in your Aunt Parrett's service for six months!" (These ladies had detested one another.) "*That* was enough punishment for anything! I suppose he really was employed—not make-believe?"

"Make-believe! Employed! I should just think so—washing the car, gardening, clipping hedges, cleaning windows——"

"Good heavens!" throwing up her delicate hands; "what possessed him to stay?"

Aurea laughed and coloured, and then said—

"Well, Aunt Maggie—I—I suppose *I* had something to say to it."

"He must be extraordinarily devoted! Why, he must adore you, my dear! I'm sure your uncle would never have cleaned windows and washed cars for *me*! Ha! ha! well, Aurea, I confess I like your—er—chauffeur."

"But he's not a chauffeur now, and will soon have a motor of his own. He is his uncle's agent; we are to live at Wynyard, and have a splendid allowance. Owen means to do a lot for the tenants, and I'm to take over the village girls—oh, we have had such a talk!"

"A talk! Yes, no doubt. What will your father and Susan say?"

"They will be enchanted; they are both fond of Owen; indeed, for one whole day, the village was thrilled with the idea that Susan and Owen had *eloped*!" and she related the story with so much of her old spirit, that her aunt lay back in her chair and laughed till she wept.

"I believe I shall like young Wynyard," she repeated, as she dried her eyes, "and you know your uncle and I look on you, Aurea, as our own child, so the General will have a word in the settlements; and when you marry, you shall have my emerald necklace. Good-night, dearest. I must go off and talk this over with my old man. I declare I feel so excited, that I'm sure I shall not sleep a wink."

And what of Aurea, to whom Destiny had brought a rapturous fate within the last two hours? She pulled up the blind, opened wide the window, and, leaning her arms on the sill, gazed upon the scene—the gently heaving ocean, the vast, limitless firmament, the silver moonlight—and wondered, was any girl in all the wide world as happy as herself?